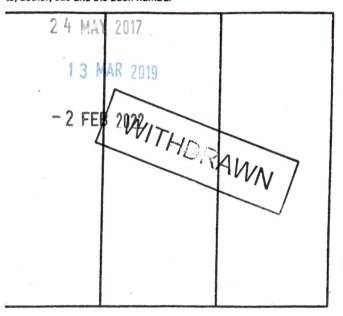

Gemini168

— A BOOK BY —

Andy Lanigan;
D. Moore Linden

authorHOUSE®

AuthorHouse™ UK
1663 Liberty Drive
Bloomington, IN 47403 USA
www.authorhouse.co.uk
Phone: 0800.197.4150

Published by AuthorHouse 01/22/2016

ISBN: 978-1-5049-9678-5 (sc)
ISBN: 978-1-5049-9679-2 (e)

Print information available on the last page.

CONTENTS

PROLOGUE

My memories of Mum's funeral were blurred by time and my inability to confront them without slipping back to the angst-raddled, bewildered fourteen year old I was then. My Dad had requested the mourners to wear bright colours, but the reds, yellows and pinks passed me by, and I remembered only an unremitting monochrome nightmare. My mother's face looked up at me from the cover of the glossy service sheet which Dad had half-heartedly agreed to have produced, despite knowing that she would have hated it. Two dates in June underpinned her picture, 6/13 and 6/16 All the years in between seemed to count for nothing now that she was gone.

I felt sick and dizzy throughout the whole day, watching hopelessly as my Dad stoically coped with the welter of emotion generated by hundreds of shocked and grieving mourners. I remember him staring red-eyed into some remote middle distance as other sombrely-suited, square-jawed men, not all of whom I recognised, pressed his hand and whispered apparent condolences in his ear. I gripped my two brother's hands tightly, trying not to meet their wide eyes as they strove to make sense of what was happening. I remember forcing myself not to get angry at Dad's apparent indifference to us, and wanted to call to him as he went dutifully between weeping mourners, clutching shoulders and caressing cheeks. Eventually, he turned and gazed at us, eyes dimmed with unbearable grief, and my anger left me as I felt the ice-cold waves of despair that rippled around him. I pulled my brothers close and waited for it all to end.

Mum's illness had seemingly lasted mere weeks, yet time passed at an accelerating pace as the gravity of her condition became apparent. I heard fragments of talk about special treatments, drugs and therapy, with fish oil capsules being mentioned at one point. Even my fourteen year old mind couldn't take that in as a serious option, and I closed out all the talk of extraordinary cures in favour of a belief that Mum was invincible, and that she would rally at some point soon. Our life as kids remained fairly normal, and it was only over the final few days that the crushing reality of what was happening crashed into our young minds. With no time to properly say goodbye, and any words muddled by emotion and the numbness of trying to think of what to say, Mum seemed to slip away from us, sending seismic shocks through our depleted family. In the stunned, dream-like aftermath of her leaving, Dad became increasingly detached. He was there, being attentive and consoling, but not like a father should be, more like a professional grief counsellor, with no intimacy or depth to his words. Maybe it was his training kicking in; maybe it was the only way he could deal with the enormity of the events that had riven our family. I was an almost preternaturally aware teenager, and it served my brothers and I well, as more and more responsibility for their well-being passed to me as Dad retreated further into his fortress of grief.

He resumed work after a few weeks, and life became a succession of short stays in various exotic and not so exotic countries, as he took any opportunity, it seemed, to get away from our old home. We grew to quite enjoy it, and did well in the numerous international schools that we ended up in. Dad pushed us all relentlessly here, and days of hard study were followed by the difficult physical challenges of a raft of martial arts training programmes. Time in Brazil was followed by a year in Manila, after which we ended up in Berlin for around 18 months. Six or seven months in London led us then to two years in Paris, where we probably reached the first approximation of happiness that we had experienced since Mum died. We liked the city, and memories of our holidays there as a family helped to make our stay more than bearable. We also returned intermittently to New York, and even to our summer home in Florida, but we were generally peripatetic.

We made friends easily, and forgot them just as readily. We fielded questions about Mum, answering in sparing terms, and deterring any potential pity or sentimentality by presenting a closed triangle of mutual dependency to anyone who dared to offer any. The paucity of any real emotion in our lives had differing effects on us as individuals. Anderson, my younger brother by seventeen months, covered his true feelings by becoming a consummate actor, and it was generally impossible to work out how he felt at any time if he didn't want you to. Easton, almost two years older than me, became edgy and sometimes almost irascible, retaining a youthful humour which almost made up for his other, darker, personality quirks. I gave myself up to routine and responsibility, always looking to break things down to get to the nub as quickly as I could, and assumed the role of my brothers' keeper. Dad was a peripheral figure throughout these years, sometimes almost like a visiting dignitary quizzing our seemingly endless line of nannies about our well-being, only occasionally talking to any of us in any depth. He was still Dad to us, but in a remote and almost disinterested way.

We all eventually got into tertiary education, and as we were living in Edinburgh at the time, I signed up to an IT degree at Glasgow University, followed up by a postgraduate course. Anderson took the opportunity to sign up to the Conservatoire in Glasgow, whilst Easton, being Easton, decided to do a remote degree in International Security from Leicester University. We all graduated in turn, and after three and a half years of almost being settled in Edinburgh, Dad announced abruptly that we were returning to New York permanently. We could all have stayed put, or done anything else we wanted to, but we had always been part of a something, and none of us really wanted to be that far from the other two, so we moved back en bloc, and took up life in a brownstone in Brooklyn Heights. Dad, by now, had reduced his travel and was increasingly fixed with his work at the Institute for Strategic Studies. He remained taciturn and remote, but we saw a lot more of him, and gradually came to understand what drove him, and how he needed to cope with the dark tunnel of grief in which he had been for a decade or more. No other female ever got a foothold in his life. We knew a few had tried to date him - extraordinary, talented and vivacious women working at rarefied levels in his field of work - but he rebuffed all overtures, maintaining an immensely saddening posthumous monogamy, despite eager promptings from his rarely seen male friends, and as we got older, also from us.

The three of us seemed to soak up his attitude, and none of our relationships endured for any length of time. We all dabbled successfully, fitting comfortably into the good looking metrosexual stereotype, but regular dating never firmed up into anything real. Easton in particular seemed to attract female attention without effort, using his personal magnetism poorly, juggling multiples of unknowing and smitten females precariously around his total lack of commitment to any of them. Life was comfortable, in a sterile, vacuous kind of way, but it was about to deal us another blow.

In January, Dad had a meeting to attend in Toronto, and as was normal practice, his bosses chartered a private plane out of Newark airport. I drove him there, hugging him awkwardly before he boarded, watching as the pulsing wing lights disappeared into the dark sky. Sometime around 4am the next morning, I was shaken awake by a frantic Easton, mumbling incoherently and crying. I was still bumping the heel of my right hand off my temple, when Anderson appeared at the door and announced flatly that Dad's plane had gone down somewhere over Lake Ontario. The next few days were traumatic with numerous visits to police stations, a painful, grief-raddled trip to Toronto, and various press conferences all flashing past in a whirl of noise and light.

Dad's bosses, seemingly all clad in generically-cut grey flannel suits, hovered around us with contrived, coldly formal solicitousness, pulling every string they could to ascertain what had happened. They spent hours with us, trying to console and calm us, but also asking us very probing, occasionally intrusive, questions about our knowledge of what Dad was involved in. The end result was that after two months of searching the lake and examining a plethora of radar and satellite tracks, no wreckage or bodies were ever found. Lake Ontario was a huge body of water, the size of New Jersey State, with waters up to 800 feet deep. Many ships and boats had disappeared, but a plane being swallowed up within reach of two of the biggest metropolitan areas in North America was inexplicable. We had no closure: I blocked any talk of a funeral, and none of us went to the Memorial Service that the Institute arranged for Dad. I instructed my brothers not to sign any papers put in front of them by Dad's attorney that would mean any of us even inferred he was dead. We dragged the armour that had shielded us after Mum's death back on, and toughed out an agonizing three months before the grief subsided; a little. Things didn't get to us the way it had after Mum, but we were older, harder, and our relationship with Dad had been what it was; simple as that.

We all went back to work on the same day, and avoided any conversations about the accident, shunning sympathy and comfort just to get back to normality, and that's how things were when I got the e-mail...

CHAPTER 1

The e-mail looked weird. It was the typical phishing type message with a link that would unleash Armageddon on your hard drive. However, it was the sender which caused me to spend nearly fifteen minutes looking at it; not full on fifteen minutes, but back and forwards for about that time. I would normally have deleted it instantly, but had not done so with this one. My security software had not placed it in junk mail either, which meant it had come from an original source.

Gemini168.com had intrigued me and I was now running through all the combinations that this sender's address could refer to: a die-cast model aircraft manufacturer out of Vegas; the obvious star sign, a NASA mission, an observatory, DJ equipment. None of these made any sense: Gemini16801 suggested an auto repair company at Penn State. Not that either, but there was something very familiar and interesting about it, so I clicked the link, risking meltdown of the disc. I hoped the anti-virus would cover me.

Unbeknown to me, the click of this link would change both my life and that of my brothers for ever, for as I pressed my right mouse key over it, far away in Virginia a warning flashed on a PC screen, setting in motion a series of events which would lead us in to deep danger.

The article it threw up in the New York Times was written by a journalist I had never heard of before, Taylor Wheelan. I read as much of the papers as I could in between work and all the sports stuff I do, but had never come across this guy. A search of his name came up with some character in an online game, nothing else, not even this article. Lots of names close to his, Thomas etc, but none with the first name of Taylor: intrigued, I read the article.

'All is not as it seems'
By Taylor Wheelan

Big Pharma, as the Pharmaceutical industry is often known, is a multi-trillion dollar industry spanning the globe and dominated by four main players; one here in New York and the other three spread across Europe...

...So far so standard. The article went on to explain how clinical trials are conducted and how the results are controlled by each country's drug enforcement bodies, the FDA here in the U.S, NICE in the UK, all very routine, informative journalism. However, the third last paragraph was the most interesting section within the two thousand word piece. This is where Wheelan had probably earned his money, a dollar per word usually and he was two thousand dollars better off because of this expose. Here he explained where his investigations had taken him and what he was attempting to reveal.

His article made it clear in some cases the clinical trials were being manipulated and that a number of the drugs were more harmful than the illnesses they were designed to cure. He also indicated that many eminent doctors and some high ranking officials in various countries were being paid to either prescribe the drugs, or to have them listed on the respective countries prescribe-able medicines lists. This had massive implications to the pharmaceutical industry and to some of the biggest companies on the planet; so why had this never been exposed further? Why had there been no further headline making revelations? Why had this not made the TV news or a Public Broadcast expose?

More to the point, why had I been sent this message with this attachment? Why me? What was Gemini168 getting at?

Everything about this message said, "So what?"

I decided it was time for some exercise. Exercise was easy for me to do. I loved it. I enjoyed the feeling I got when I pushed myself harder to achieve more press-ups or some additional suicide squats. Perhaps it was the natural opiates the brain produces when you push your body to the limit that I became hooked on or perhaps I had a problem with my self-image and needed to work out regularly to convince myself I was not losing my edge in martial arts, but whatever the shrinks would say, I could only reply by saying that I love a good workout. With the thought of the body's natural pain killers surging through my brain I spun my chair to head to my little gym area. The thought of Dopamine was definitely still there, but so was Gemini168 and "All is not as it seems." I just could not understand why this story had not gone anywhere and why I had not read anything else about it in the papers. I decided to try and find Taylor Wheelan.

Where better to start than the features desk of the New York Times? I looked up the office online and gave the desk a call. The guy who answered sounded about 18 years of age; perhaps an intern; someone who believed that newspapers and journalism were still going to make it through all this digital evolution and the noble profession of investigative journalism, as we know it, would be in rude health for the rest of the decade: Yeah, I used to be 18 as well…

"New York Times features desk!" He almost sung it.

"Taylor Wheelan please." I tried not to sing it.

"Oh! I don't know that person. What does he look like?" He replied, still melodic. Some sport was in order here: I would not go too far, as by the sound of him he was probably not long out of diapers, but the singing was getting to me: I decided to go for a little song to get him thinking. My song of choice was Jonny Cash, 'A Thing Called Love', and I was going to sing it to him in my best Jonny Cash voice.

"Six foot six he stood on the ground.
Weighed two hundred and forty five pounds,
But I saw that giant of man brought down to his knees by… Can you put me through to the Features Editor, please?"

There was a silence; an intake of breath, and then he said, "Who is calling please?"

Decision time for me; do I give my own name and have to explain why I am calling or do I give a false one and bluff things from there on? My name was okay. What harm could I do if I was just enquiring about an old newspaper article that, once written, went nowhere?

"My name is Bailey Marks... Could I talk with the Desk Editor, please? It is kind of urgent."

"Hold on, Mr Marks. I will try to get him."

As a youngster growing up, I saw my fair share of Spiderman cartoons. I was always intrigued by how accurate a depiction of a newspaper editor his boss was. The person who came on the line sounded just like Peter Parker's boss at the Daily Bugle. Go figure! The image in my head of J. Jonah Jamieson shouting at Parker was growing as the guy on the line said, "Thomson! How can I help you?" I wondered when he was going to start shouting at me.

"Do you know the whereabouts of someone called Taylor Wheelan, who worked on your desk? Not sure how long ago it was he was there, but I cannot find any trace of him and was keen to talk to him about an article called Big Pharma that he wrote."

The reply completely took me by surprise as it was anything but a shout. It was whispered and almost conspiratorial. "The reason you cannot find him is because his name is Thomas Taylor Wheelan. He worked here for a while, but he's been gone for months now. That article I think you are referring to, killed his career. Can't tell you much more here, but if you are looking for him, he does stuff for local charities. I've got to go. Bye."

And with that he put down the phone. It was one of those moments where I found myself looking at my phone, wondering if the conversation that had just happened had taken place at all: a Features Editor on the biggest paper in New York goes from sounding like a gunny sergeant to someone admitting a terrible indiscretion to his parish priest.

Decision time: do I call the newspaper back or start to look up Thomas T Wheelan? One thing was for sure, I was not doing my workout right now and for the first time in years, felt like I might miss it all together today.

Within a short period of time I had tracked down the Thomas Taylor Wheelan I was looking for. He was writing for some charity publications and was, it seems, still based here in New York. After a few more clicks I had a number for the publication he wrote for most often. I dialled the number and got a young female voice. She did not sing her welcome and so spared herself exposure to my 70's ex-convict, country-star, melodic repertoire.

"I am looking for Thomas Wheelan."

"Thomas doesn't work here. He comes in about once a week to talk to Margaret, our head co-ordinator and should be back in tomorrow if you want to talk to him?"

"Do you have contact details for him?"

"Hold on." There was a click and a quiet buzz on the line. She was looking Thomas' details up. There was another click and a voice said "Hello!" This was a much older voice. Could this be Margaret? Margaret was driven, I could tell from her tone. She was sharp and to the point. "You're looking for Thomas? Who is calling?

"My name is…" I hesitated. Something about the way this had unfolded told me that all was not right. From the Newspaper Editor going all "CIA" on me to this woman beginning to interrogate me, I was beginning to get a little suspicious and so when in doubt, bluff. "Thomson. My name is Thomson and I am looking for Thomas to write an article on a charity event happening locally and believe he would be ideal for that."

There was a silence: too long a silence. I could feel my heart begin to quicken. Why was that? There was nothing sinister in all of this, not yet anyway, so why was my pulse quickening. Was it anticipation of getting to the bottom of this email or was it all the cloak and dagger stuff that seemed to be building up? "I really don't know if I can help you. He's very particular who he writes for, he's had some bad experiences… I'll save your number and see what he says. He may call you, he may not, sorry. Bye!" The phone went silent and she was gone.

Time for exercise: I was frustrated at the events which had just unfolded and knew that I needed to work off my stress. A good hour of full body work-out should help and allow me to think things through. I would deal with this tomorrow. I had clients to keep happy and a fair bit of programming to write. It would be best if I just focussed on that and left this email for another day.

One of the benefits of being self-employed is that you can largely choose your times to work. When it comes to IT, no one can tell you what to do. If you are building a database, you are the only one who knows how it is structured. When you consult with a client, you always tell them that what they want is possible. You give them a time scale and you scope out the structure of what is required. You then begin to write the coding and show them what you have done. At this stage you have made some money. The big earnings come when they change their mind and you have to develop the database further. The programme then begins to get more complex as it grabs data from various sources. If you build in enough doors, no one else will be able to navigate through what you have created.

The final money spinner is when you build in a Service Level Agreement. This is where you ask the client to sign up to you having a response to problems they may incur while using your database creation. So if they have a problem with the software or the system crashes, you promise to be on site, or virtually fixing their problem within a certain period of time. The shorter the response time, the more expensive the contract and boom! You are earning while you are sleeping because you set them up on a retainer. It was lonely at times, but when you get into a little group of trusted programmers you can sub-contract out some of the work and then finish it off by installing your own back doors and loops to cover what you have done. Sneaky, but everyone was doing it.

I was just pulling on my gym top when my mobile rang. Time to clear my head and get my best programmer/ IT consultant voice on... maybe a client needed a problem sorted.

I answered my phone; "Is that you Mr. Thomson?" I don't know how long I paused for, but I certainly missed a beat.

"No." I suddenly clicked....this could be my man.

"Sorry, wrong number."

"No wait, are you Taylor Wheelan, Thomas Wheelan?" the words tumbled out of my mouth in approximately the right order. I was met with silence. For some reason, my heart was going again.

"What do you want?" When he first asked if I was Thomson his voice was measured and confident, now it was strained with suspicion and doubt – all too familiar tones around this guy, it seemed.

"My name isn't Thomson, it's Bailey Marks. I want to talk to you about an article." The caution seemed to disappear from his voice, he was sharp, precise.

"Don't say another word on here: Central Park in one hour opposite the Ritz on the benches. I assume you are in New York. How will I know it is you?"

I looked down at my desk. "I will be reading last month's Esquire magazine"

"How do I know it is last month's?"

"George Clooney is on the cover."

"Be there in one hour, or I am gone."

The line clicked and burred softly; he had hung up.

Another hang-up in a day of hang-ups; I pursed my lips and mused quietly for a few seconds; maybe I should've told him I'd be reading Harper's; maybe not....I had no idea what to expect. The rumbling noises of roused brothers from the next room snapped me back to reality. They were going downtown, and I was meeting them later for an early dinner: I'd leave with them, and go to Central Park from there. It would be a push getting across town to the Park in an hour, so I readied myself to leave. 'Oops, can't forget George Clooney.' I said to myself, and I went to join my bickering brothers, clutching my magazine.

We stepped out of the foyer of the brownstone in Brooklyn Heights into the sharp New York sunshine: the green of the early-blooming trees vying for our attention with the rumbling cacophony of traffic from the main road up ahead. To my right was my older brother Easton. A black belt 4th Dan in Bruce Lee's Jeet Kun Do and a level 5 in the Filipino martial art of Kali: in other words, very capable of looking after himself. Standing just over six feet in height, a chest of 44 inches and a waist of 32 inches with guns 'like Navarone,' as he liked to put it, he was in great shape, as befitted his current job as a professional doorman - a filler post, he called it. A crop of blonde curly hair perched precariously on the top of his head, clipped in at the sides, defined his look. We called him Harpo, he loved his look and was very conscious of his clothes – a serial fashionista with a predilection for designer brands. Today he was in Dolce & Gabbana shirt and trousers along with Paul Smith shoes.

I admired him for a number of reasons. The two most important were his speed of decision in any situation, and his ability to use his inherent and pronounced mean streak during a fight. You didn't say the wrong thing to Easton, and people who knew him learned to choose their words carefully. To my left was my younger brother, Anderson. 190lbs and just short of six feet tall with an unruly shock of brown hair. We called him Chico, which he tolerated grudgingly, not being one for nicknames. He was a jobbing actor, and serious about his "craft" as he called it; he had scored a few good parts in his time, and lived the thespian role to the hilt. He was also a black belt in Jeet Kun Do as well as being very proficient in the Filipino art of Balintawak. He was more studied and rational than his blonde sibling, but just as formidable an opponent once he'd been pushed beyond his limit. He too liked his designer labels. Today he was in Ralph Lauren polo shirt and chinos with a pair of Timberland boots.

Me? Six feet one inch, 44 chest and no stranger to a gym. I worked... Well, was in IT - no explanation needed! People called me Groucho, maybe down to the dark wavy hair as well as the fashionable black round rim glasses I liked to wear...and apart from not having the drawn-on moustache and penchant for killer one-liners, I embraced the moniker fully, being an avid admirer of the legendary brothers.

Not wanting to lag behind my sartorially cutting-edge siblings, I was wearing a Corneliani shirt and Tommy Hilfiger chinos; my shoes were by Grenson – we were a competitive trio, in all aspects of life! Like them, I was capable of looking after myself, and being the clever one, I possessed that innate confidence that I could sort out either of my siblings if push came to shove. A black belt in Jeet Kun Do was helpful, however my favourite was Balintawak. I loved the mechanics of that martial art, the way it uses the momentum and the positioning of your opponents to work against them. It is low energy consumption for the proponent and allows the quick neutralisation of any potential threat. I tended to analyse everything, a trait I inherited from Dad, and the stark simplicity of Martial arts appealed to my sensibilities. Dad had made sure that we would be ready for almost anything, and along with our raft of Martial arts, we could shoot many types of guns. I was a competition level archer, while Easton was mean with a crossbow and we all ski raced to a high standard. As well as that, we spoke seven languages between us. We all spoke French, Spanish and German, with Easton being fairly proficient in Italian, and Anderson adding Portuguese and Russian. As befitting my IT geek status, I was a perennial dabbler in Mandarin…. Well, that's what I would tell anyone who couldn't speak Mandarin.

Easton and Anderson decided to get off the subway in Midtown; we had agreed to meet in a couple of hours at the Tribeca for a bite to eat. De Niro's restaurant was worth a visit and you could always sit and star-spot if the conversation became too inane. They said their goodbyes and set off into the noisy diaspora of the mid-morning commute, occasionally bumping shoulders as they loped purposefully down the crowded platform. I watched them, smiling to myself, enjoying the fuzzy, protective, feelings of closeness and love that I felt for them. I was the most important person in their lives, and they were the most important people in mine, although Easton would always say that *he* was the most important person in his life.

I turned and looked at the subway map: about eight stops to go - not long. I could savour the sheer energy and bustle of the people along the way. I loved New York and its inhabitants. I felt totally at home here, as we all did, but our roots were not deep, and the regular moves between different cities and countries during our childhood and youth had honed a cosmopolitan thirst for life, wherever we landed as a family. However, we were British, and remained British wherever we were; that's what British people do, as my Dad always used to say: "They didn't dominate the world by assimilating, did they?" I liked to be profound early in the morning, my thinking tended to be looser and less inhibited then, before the demands of the day drove me back to logic and planning, or geek-dom, as Easton would say.

I stayed on until Columbus Circle. As I exited the subway, the sun was still bright and I strolled to the junction of 59th and 8. I reached the Ritz opposite Central Park at 10.05. I was a little late, my mind had been a bit *too* loose today. I quickly took in the usual joggers, Tai-chi aficionados, dog walkers and the odd early Frisbee thrower. No sign of the person I was looking for. Surely five minutes wouldn't spook them into leaving? Feeling as though everyone there knew why I was there except me, I perched on the edge of a bench and waited for something to happen, self-consciously flicking through my damned magazine. Time passed. I toyed with my phone, adjusted the collar of my shirt, re-tied my laces, and polished my glasses to a gleaming sheen before planting them back on my nose. I held my magazine up like a hitch hiker's preferred destination card. I guessed that anyone watching me trying not to be conspicuous would be shaking their heads ruefully at my consummate inability to do so.

I glanced at my watch. It was now 10.30. I had always thought that punctuality was de rigueur when it came to espionage, or whatever this was, but I had really no idea what to expect. I was busily counting some ants swarming around my boots when two sandaled feet hove into view. I looked up quickly. The man who stood there extending his hand in greeting was of medium height, with vivid blue eyes, and cropped, thinning salt and pepper hair that was barely visible on his shiny, tanned head. He spoke in a surprisingly deep voice.

"Bailey?"
I was momentarily startled by his sudden intimacy.

"Er, yeah, and you are…?"

"Taylor Wheelan. Good to meet you," he replied, simultaneously clasping my hand in a dry, firm grip. The face meant absolutely nothing to me, I assumed that he was the e-mail man. He sat down next to me, looking around the park.

"You need to be more careful, I could have been anyone." I drew a quick breath and replied. "You knew who I was, didn't you, so I guess I'll have to trust that you're you."

Wheelan slipped a pair of shades onto his nose and moved his face close to mine.

"You can't afford to trust anyone, my friend, not now."

I blinked questioningly. He continued, "Your Dad died quite recently, didn't he?" I suppressed my rising frustration and replied coolly, "He… he went missing in an air crash. His body was never found. Why are you bringing this up?"

Wheelan set his jaw, looked around again, and in a low voice, said "Your dad was involved in certain things." He turned away apparently shaken by what he had just said. My patience was wearing gossamer thin. "What do you want? Why did you ask me to come here, and what involvement has my Dad got with anything that you do?"

He scrabbled around in a dilapidated shoulder bag and produced a shiny pamphlet, which he pressed into my hand. I looked at the title page, "Pharma Medical Solutions" and looked back at him blankly.
"And this is...something to do with your article?" I shrugged with my eyebrows, a trait I had inherited from Dad.

"Jesus, you really don't know, do you?" He was perspiring now.

"Know what? You're beginning to rile me, Mr Wheelan, know what? What am I supposed to know?"

Wheelan, clenched his fists, and spoke rapidly. "Your Mom died of cancer, didn't she?" The fragile veneer of politesse that I was extending to this strange man snapped, and I grabbed his neck, dragging him onto his feet.

"No more riddles, friend, or I'll tie a fucking knot in your neck! What the fuck do you want with me?"

Wheelan gasped for air, his thin arms vainly pushing against my iron grip. He was almost inaudible;
"I'm on your side. For Christ's sake, you're choking me!"
I tightened my grip and snarled into his ear
"Take a deep breath. Now I'm going to drop you, and you're going to tell me what the fuck you're talking about!"

I released my grip on his Adam's apple, and he plopped down on the bench, wheezing and retching. My adrenalin rush subsided long enough to realise that several curious park users were staring at us.
"No sweat folks, he was choking on a pretzel." I croaked lamely. "Excitement over!" Unconvinced, the voyeurs went back to their business, unwilling to ruin a good morning with involvement in anything too challenging. The cringing journalist gathered his wits and rubbed his throat, still bearing the angry red weals caused by my hand. I sat, wordless, still pulsing with adrenalin and frustration at allowing myself to lose control.

"You are all in danger," he rasped.

I shook my head in disbelief. "What are you talking about? You need to give me a clue, throw me a bone. Terrorists? Jihadists?"

Wheelan cut his hand across my conversation. "None of them. Your Dad was involved in other things much closer to home, literally… But you obviously have no clue….maybe this wasn't such a good idea. The more I tell you, the more danger you'll be in."

I really had no idea what this man was trying to tell me. I sat and stared at him, working my hands vigorously. He sensed that my blood was rising again, and shoved a card into my clasped fists.

"Go and talk to this man. Tell him you've talked to me. He's the key player here. You'll understand when you talk to him, and even if you don't, it might get you closer to finding out about your father."

"My father was an army veteran who became a business consultant. The sort of person who would ask you for your watch to tell you what time it was. I have no idea what you are talking about!"

At that, he got up, slung his decrepit man bag over his shoulder, and turned to shuffle off. He fixed me with a pitying look. "Your father was an industrial spy for the United States Government - one of the best, and very capable of taking care of himself. He was onto something very big. Do you really think his disappearance was an accident?" He turned and walked away. I was too freaked out to do anything, and simply sat watching his skinny back moving away from me. After a few seconds, he turned and shouted back, "Good Luck, I hope you find what you're looking for."

He held his pose meaningfully for some few seconds, and then turned and continued walking into the bustle of the Manhattan crowds. Well, I mused, what the fuck was all that about? What am I looking for? I looked at the card, "PROF. JEROME FAVREAU, ACADEMIE DE SCIENCE, L'ETOILE, PLACE D'ITALIE, PARIS" stood out proud in black ink on the pale blue card, followed by an endless Parisian phone number. I scraped the fleshy part of my bottom lip with the edge of the card, my mind still creaking with the weight of what I'd just heard. I was rarely lost for words, or actions…. I felt impotent, baffled at being landed in a situation that I couldn't understand. I sat in the sunshine, oblivious to the noise of the birds, the snippets of conversations floating past, and to the distant shrieking of sirens from the city, reaching deep inside myself for some sort of clue as to what I did next. I had to find my brothers and tell them what I had just heard. It wouldn't go down well, my belief that Dad was not dead upset and disconcerted them, but they had to know: time to go.

I sprinted down to the subway to get the C line from Central Park. I knew the brothers were in Midtown and it would be easy and quick to get to them. I had so much to tell them, or maybe I hadn't... Practically barging my way to the front of the platform, I glanced at the timetable and knew, with an exhalation of relief, that I would make the 12.20 train. I glanced around the busy platform; a couple of stressed tourists were pounding down the stairs as the train pulled in. I moved to beyond the yellow line. Why was it there? I mean, nobody gave a shit. I looked around at the throngs of people; suits, shoppers, joggers, workers, all of them lost in their own worlds - a bit like me.

All at once, I had a strange feeling: one of impending violence - something like the one I got just before fighting in a Martial arts competition, fear diluted with adrenalin, and expectation. I felt a presence behind me and suddenly felt myself being propelled off of the platform, arms and legs flailing wildly as I glimpsed the massive bulk of the incoming train crashing along the track. The noise of the engine and the acrid smell of the wires filled my senses as I desperately thrust my legs down, looking for a solid surface. They say these things happen in slow motion. Thoughts of the boys, Dad, and Mum screamed into my head... This was it... I felt myself falling, felt a crunching blow to my head, and the last thing I heard was the whistling crescendo of brakes being rammed on.... then nothing. It wasn't slow for me, it all happened in milliseconds. The darkness came down.

CHAPTER 2

The first Gulf war of '89 – '90 caused big problems for those returning back to a non-combat situation: after they had been in the thick of close quarter fighting, how did they get any sense of normality back into their life? There was a particular, addictive buzz about going out on patrol, not knowing what will be encountered. Insurgents could appear from nowhere dressed as goat herders or lay people. With something as simple as a mobile phone they could detonate IEDs large enough to lift the vehicle you were travelling in clear off the road. The frequency of ambushes was high as was the body-bag count.

Many a combat soldier struggled to settle in a life where they were not on constant high alert. To deal with this they fought each other. Petty squabbles turned in to full-on fights; many were brought up on charges and some were even DD out of the service. On leaving, they got involved in petty crime and in some cases went on to organised crime. By the time the second Gulf war had come around in 2000, the needs of these well trained, combat-hardened individuals were catered for by companies such as Blackwatch.

Blackwatch grew out of a requirement for security to be provided for some of the politicians who would visit the camps in Afghanistan. Many of these visits were pure publicity stunts with the dignitaries requiring vast sums of tax payer's money to get them from Washington to Helmand. Flights on private jets, helicopter rides in Chinooks, fighter jet cover, AWACS cover at altitude, satellite scanning of the whole theatre, not to mention the Intelligence gathering required to ensure the news of their visit had not leaked out. The sums were astronomical. Not forgetting all the Special Forces' personnel put at risk to gather this information,

What better way to minimise the risk whilst maximising the responsibility than to pass this task on to a private concern which could be dragged through the litigation courts if they got it wrong? For the private contractor it would mean having well trained personnel and powerful connections high up in Washington and at the George Bush Centre for Intelligence. Blackwatch Solutions had both.

Major Mitch McKenzie was a born soldier, entering the US Army at 18, and working his way through several units, mostly the Marine Corps, and ranks before spending a long time with various branches of Special Forces. He had hob-knobbed with the CIA in the first Gulf war before running some big special ops in Afghanistan. At age 50 and over six feet, he was still muscular and fit: he exercised daily, an almost religious regime of stretching and calisthenics that set hard a physique which had lost the elasticity of youth. His buzz-cut was still there, and in times of stress, he would run his hands rhythmically over the speckled stubble above his ears, as if coaxing a solution to a problem out of his agile and needle-sharp mind. His most prominent physical feature was a prognathous, thrusting jaw that pointed directly, challengingly, at anyone he was talking to.

He had been photographed with the President and had been a special advisor on a number of movies about the shadowy world of Black Ops.

When the time came for him to re-enlist, he decided it was better to go down the private route instead. He had the contacts as far as specialist teams were concerned and he was a sensitive, political animal when it came to dealing with the boys at Langley and their pay masters at Capitol Hill. His family lineage could be traced all the way back to his great grandfather, who had served with the historic Scottish regiment that his company took its' name from. A name chosen as homage to that regiment, now defunct after the UK government's armed forces rationalisation. He wore his Scottish heritage with an almost Calvinistic zeal, and rarely let the grey areas or blurred lines of life complicate a clear set of values and beliefs which made him at once trustworthy, but also inflexible and at times intolerant.

Blackwatch Solutions was formed within a year of him discharging. It was one of the first corporate PMC's, and Mitch was proud of that. To many serving and recently retired people of his ilk, it was a surprise that he had chosen to leave the services, but when the phone call came in from him asking if they were interested in working in the private sector, many saw it as a badge of honour that he had selected them. When he started discussing salaries with them, many realised it was also a great pension plan and soon it became an aspiration to be involved with Blackwatch Solutions.

It did not take long for Blackwatch to grow into a formidable "Private Army." Special Forces personnel from around the world were looking for ways to use their skills whilst being rewarded at a level that was lucrative to say the least, when compared to the salary offered by their respective governments. Australians, American, British, even Russian ex-operatives made themselves available for the jobs that Mitch could offer them. By the time the US government had decided to scale down its operations in Afghanistan, Blackwatch had grown so large that it had offices in 49 countries and covered all of the world's hotspots. The services on offer now ranged from one-off provision of bodyguards, all the way through to special infiltration operations for various governments which did not want to be associated with the "Kill-list" that they had provided. Insurgent leaders in Africa would disappear, terrorist bomb threats in Bali would be thwarted, mystery viruses would cause the crash of nuclear facilities in Iran, Chinese political leaders would suddenly be associated with the death of a foreign national. No job was too complex for Blackwatch. They had connections around the world to ensure that they were well protected from any scandal that might arise should there be a leak about some African dictator's bank account being raided.

Mitch was at the top of this almighty tree and the view from up there was inspiring....His ego and sense of righteousness meant that the casual snuffing out of an occasional life left no dent on his conscience, and he liked to believe that he was with the good guys....he allowed himself no latitude to ponder on anything. Years before, in Helmand, he had shot dead two 10 year old Afghani boys he had suspected of carrying an IED, but had found nothing when he searched their torn and bleeding bodies. He remembered the way he felt that day, and hated the weakness of it. They would have become killers anyway, he asserted, and blocked the worm-like thoughts of remorse from his mind. He was a good guy, and if the good guys wanted someone terminated, he trusted their judgement. He was irrevocably tied to his paymasters, and there was no money in humanitarianism, was there? Mitch's emotions had been gradually supressed and eroded by years of losing friends and comrades and witnessing appalling scenes of humanity in extremis. Now, protected by layers of organisation and clothed in a sleek suit instead of sweat soaked combat fatigues, he had found a way of being remote from death and all its consequences.

He was reading an email when his phone rang. He checked the number and saw that it was Dan DeMarco, his Head of Operations. Dan was also ex-special forces: A Ranger, he was tall, broad, and had a full head of unkempt, dark hair, which for a man in his late forties was a strange look. Most people who met him believed it was a hairpiece or that he maybe had dyed it. Neither was the case, as Dan was notoriously prickly about his coiffure; about anything in fact, he was a man who never had 'patient and caring' down on any resume. Dan was also a man who liked to be on the move. Mitch knew that Dan would be standing, looking out the window to make this call. He always did when making a call from the office down the corridor.

"We have something you might want to see," said Dan.

Mitch, always one for protocol said, "I will come to you," Dan grunted, "Okay, fine." He rather enjoyed his short walks to Mitch's office, which although austere and soldierly, had stunning urban views and better air-conditioning than his, which was three doors down from it. It was not a big deal for Dan to go to Mitch, but it would look better if

Mitch was coming to him, almost in a social way, than for him to be wandering in to Mitch's office with something as sensitive as this. Mitch wasn't big on conversation, and all of his employees knew to keep superficial stuff to a minimum. All the offices on this part of the third floor were similar: similar size, similar layout, similar decor and similar doors. The military discipline of regimentation hung heavy when it came to designing the internals of Blackwatch Solutions HQ here in Washington.

Mitch routinely counted the doors. No names on the outside meant visitors had an idea of who was behind them. The third teak laminate door on the right was Dan's office. Mitch did not need to knock. As he walked in, Dan was still looking out the window.

"Mitch, I am a little concerned," said Dan, turning as he said it. His hair never ceased to amaze, as it tumbled over a noticeably sweaty brow.

"We got another mark from the guys at Langley. Same source as before, but this one's a little unusual. The mark is an American citizen. Well, half American, half British."

Mitch pursed his lips. "Has it been issued?"

"Yes"

"Is it too late to rescind?"

"Yes, um, well I'm not real sure… It's been authorised, and is in pending status," said Dan. "Would we really want to piss those guys off by not completing? It's a big risk to our business if they decide that someone else can do this sort of thing for them."

Mitch loosened the buttons on his jacket and sat down on the leather faced wooden chair in front of Dan's desk and ran his hands over his head. "Corrupt third world politicians, drug lords in Columbia, the odd murderous Oligarch taking a tumble. There is a sense of justice in that, isn't there? But American citizens? That dictates a whole different set of principles… even if he's half Brit. Some of us are Americans in name only, Dan, and don't hold Uncle Sam so dear to their hearts, but why ask us? There must be easier and cheaper ways of doing the in-house stuff. We went into this thinking we would be dealing with people outside the homeland, not *fellow Americans*."

The last two words were intoned in a mock Obama voice. Dan grimaced testily… Now was not the time for one of Mitch's rare dips into political humour. Mitch caught his mood and reverted to his normal clipped tones. "Which department is it from?"

"That's the thing, Mitch. It is routed from the FDA via the CIA, through our usual contact, Herb Johnson. The two agencies are working on some big drug issue, but I don't have any detail. Even my sources are unsure what they are up to on this one. Could you pull in some favours and get me some heads-up? I will sanction this mark unless you say otherwise, but now we are in a tough situation: if we refuse the request, it won't sit well at Langley. We need to manage this one, or we could find ourselves very deeply in the shit. We know nothing about this guy, what he's doing, what he's done, I've never heard of him. Have you?"

"What was the name?"

Dan leant over his desk, scanning a piece of paper. "Bailey Marks, dual UK /US citizen, 25 years old, current location, yadda, yadda…. That's all I have. Don't know anything else about him, but I could find out for you, if you wish?" Mitch's brow creased. Dan was perplexed. Was that a flicker of uncertainty there? "Mmmm. Negative Dan, you stand easy. I will make that call and find out what is happening between Langley and the FDA - hold the mark until I get back to you, you understand?"

Mitch stood up abruptly and rapped his knuckles on the desk, as if to terminate the discussion.

"I'll see if I can work things out." Mitch turned to leave the office. As he stood in the doorway he turned back to face Dan. "You stall any pressure to complete this mark, okay? Do not pass it on to any of our contractors until I say so."

"Okay, Mitch, you've told me already. I'll sit on it till you say otherwise," said Dan, shaking his head angrily as Mitch's back went through the door. "Fucking stiff-ass-jar-head…. heard you the first time!" he mumbled to himself. Mitch was already gone, striding with intent down the corridor to his office -he had calls to make.

CHAPTER 3

Herb Johnson was a career civil servant. Years of driving desks and sitting at endless meetings had left its mark on him, with a pallid, yellowish face perched on top of a squat, rotund body. He was 55 years old, one year off retirement, but his penchant for three-piece suits, lifted shoes, and aviator style gold rimmed glasses dated him badly. He wouldn't have looked out of place in a Reagan administration photo shoot. He was a paper warrior, a Xerox commando, who gloried in authorisations, sign-offs and protocols, and had no time for improvisation or initiative when there were policies and procedures to follow. He had been in his current job for some months now, and realised early on that he would get no higher in his career than where he was, such was the lack of visibility and profile of his role to other government departments. Someone high up had wanted an accomplished administrator to manage a low-key, distinctly grey element of the Agency. Someone whose proficiency in the role was balanced by a total lack of flexibility or initiative, who followed instructions and got the job done. Herb fitted that template like a glove.

He had a year left till his retirement date, and that was fine, damn fine. He would make sure that he got his place in Long Island off of this, and with that mind set, he filled the role with the minimum of deviation from policy, asking no questions, issuing no challenges to the imperatives that arrived on his desk.

IT was not Herb's strong suit, and because he was barely competent in e-mails and simple formatting, he had put three young guns on his payroll to do the nuts and bolts stuff. Red was an Alabaman, loud, brash and nakedly ambitious, but a real driver in the team. Kyle was a mid-western boy, whose quiet and polite demeanour belied the fact that he was an accomplished hacker and cracker... and possessed of a terrifyingly high IQ.

He also had a really annoying habit of playing his music through the office PA system, but as most of it was from Herb's era, he didn't mind that much, and then there was Wes... Herb was unsure of Wes, a failed applicant for the Agency, he had spent some years freelancing around the Hill, hawking his IT expertise to various government agencies, as well as some distinctly shady private concerns. He was an African American, and sometimes Herb wished he hadn't taken the line of least resistance and employed him at the expense of some outstanding non-black candidates. He had taken him on because of his contacts and wider non-government experience, and although he had justified that decision with some early success against system hackers and internal whistle blowers, Herb still didn't let him do any of the detail stuff.

In recent months, Kyle had been looking after the admin processes with Herb reckoning that, as he had to authorise all input and output here, Kyle would just be a cipher for the information flow. He had done well, and Herb had given him more and more leeway, letting him sign off cash payments and deal directly with the various contractors that were used. The boy had potential, but Herb didn't acknowledge it, seeing Kyle as a guileless, blunt instrument that would keep things simple, and not get in the way of that cherished beach home on Long Island. Wes could burn his ass all he liked, Herb was doing things his way, and if Wes wasn't on the team, that was tough. Things were going pretty well, and the only pubic hairs that occasionally dropped into his coffee cup were caused by the actions of some of these god-damn private military contractors that he had to deal with. Most were ex-servicemen, whose management capabilities were as limited as the bad ass jargon they all seemed to use. Herb hated dealing with these people, knowing that they were contemptuous of his lack of military background, and preferred to let Red and Kyle do the leading edge stuff, happy in the knowledge that Red in particular, loved taking the rise out of these stiff-necked, taciturn amateurs, who he viewed as interlopers in his box-filed, compliant world. They were unpredictable, volatile, and Herb kept them all at arm's length. These guys weren't professional administrators he reasoned, and therefore, not worthy of his time, let the boys deal with them.

Mitch pressed 4 on the speed dial and settled back into his leather recliner to await a reply. The tone rang once, twice, followed by the click of the call being answered.

"Office two, how may I direct your call?" the female voice was clipped, almost robotic.

"Black here, let me speak to Herb Johnson, please" he replied

A short silence was followed by a booming male voice, "Well if it ain't our itinerant Scotchman!"

Mitch blanched; he detested protocol being broken. "Who is this?" he asked testily,

"Not Herb Johnson anyhow. You don't get the big Cajuna on speed dial, so guess I'll have to do... Call me Red."

Mitch had dealt with this guy before...a real pain in the ass cracker from the Deep South. He spoke formally: "Red, I have just had a confirmation for a mark that I need to discuss, can we speak?"

The echoing voice boomed back, "If you stop mumbling in that god damn Langley speak we can, Hell, these phones are encrypted, no need to worry about ears on this line!"

Mitch could barely contain his anger. "Red, we have a protocol that covers our communication, I'm asking you to observe it."

A stifled grunt prefaced another ear-splitting ejaculation. "Have it your way, Mr Blackwatch, proceed."

Mitch breathed deeply and spoke slowly and clearly. "We have a notification for a Bailey Marks. Can you confirm this, and also confirm the source?"

A few seconds passed, with the rustling of paper and tapping of keyboards distinctly audible, before Red replied, "Notification confirmed, source is classified."

Mitch flinched as he took in the reply. "Classified? Can you confirm author?"

Again, the tapping of keys, Red's laboured breathing clearly audible before the curt response came.
"Author classified, source classified. Further information is unavailable; we done here?"

Mitch cursed silently at yet another breach of protocol, but forced out a final comment. "Thank you, call terminated."

He ran his hands over the ripped sides of his head as he tried to rationalise what had just happened. Someone way up had classified the source of the mark. He'd never heard of this before, and his logical, delineated world was shaken. His introspection was broken by his phone ringing. Dan again. He reached to pick up, pulled his hand back, and then finally leaned across and lifted the receiver, "Dan, what can I do for you?"

Dan spoke tentatively, quietly, not at all normal for him. "That mark we discussed earlier, it's already been attempted,"

Mitch sat upright. "Attempted, what... before it was sanctioned?"

Dan's reply was flat and toneless. "I guess so. It looks like he was pushed on to the tracks at a subway stop in New York."

Mitch sprang out of his chair, his voice thundering down the line. "You guess!? And what in the blue fuck does that mean? How did an unauthorised mark get passed out - don't move soldier!"

He tossed the phone onto his desk and barged out of his office, covering the short distance to Dan's office in a few long strides. He didn't knock, throwing back the door to bounce off of its stop. Dan was, as usual, at his window, visibly quailing at what he knew was coming.

"Explain Dan, and explain so I don't have to ask again," Mitch in a rage was an imposing and intimidating figure, even to a Special Forces veteran like Dan. Dan clutched at his unruly mane and held out his hand in supplication.

"Mitch, I have no idea, I..."

Mitch leapt in before he finished. "You have got that right soldier, you have *no fucking idea*!"

Dan leaned back against the wall, subservient and unable to defend himself. Mitch continued his assault. "You are my Ops man. If you have no idea, have you any suggestions as to who I would ask then? Dave in Office 2? Mike in office 4? Or maybe the little Chinese woman who cleans the fucking rest rooms? You will find out what went on here soldier, or you can get yourself a job as a door guard in fucking Wal-Mart. Understand?

"Dan looked at the flecks of saliva on Mitch's quivering lips and nodded weakly, dropping his gaze as he did so. Mitch straightened his tie and swept out of the office, not feeling or seeing the malice in Dan's eyes as they bored into his departing back.

CHAPTER 4

A small pinhole of light grew gradually larger and various fragmented sounds penetrated the silence. The smells of clean linen, disinfectant and, strangely, and overpoweringly, Tom Ford, Tuscan Leather, barged into my nostrils. I forced my gummed eyelids apart, and saw a pink face, topped by a rick of blond hair peering anxiously at me, about 10 centimetres above my forehead.

"Bailey, you're awake!" It had to be Easton. Another, darker, head came into my blurred sightline. "Give him a chance to breathe, Easton. He doesn't need mouth to mouth!"

That would be Anderson then. My senses were struggling to deal with the cornucopia of signals being fired at them, and I closed my eyes tightly and took a deep breath. I exhaled fully, and cranked my sticky eyelids apart. Easton and Anderson were both leaning over my bed. I was in some sort of hospital.

"How are you?" blurted Easton?

I grimaced, and growled: "I'm okay, but my left arm is really sore."

Easton's voice rose, obviously concerned. "Jeez, where does it hurt!?"

I tried to pull myself up, barking "Just about where you're sitting on it!"

Easton jumped up, apologising as he did so. Anderson helped me sit upright, almost yanking my other arm off as he did so.

"Guys, I appreciate the visit, but give me some space for Chris-sakes!"

My two brothers stepped back ashen-faced. "Sorry, we were worried about you." mumbled Anderson.

I was by now in super grouch mode. "And who's had the bath in Tom Ford cologne this morning? MY Tom Ford. I'm choking here!"

The brothers exchanged glances, and decided that mollified silence was their best option. I was sore, had a head like a hung-over bell ringer, but realised gratefully, that I had no broken bones or serious injuries. I had been lucky, and was reminded how lucky by the residual smell of subways and trains that lingered in my nostrils. I remembered being propelled off of the platform, the spurt of fear and adrenalin that had convulsed me, and clawing helplessly at fresh air as I fell to the track. Instinct had taken over, and curling into a tight ball, like some sort of man-sized hedgehog, I had squashed myself into the space between the track and the lip of the platform. Then, after a searingly loud screeching of wheels and grating of brakes being applied, something hit me on the temple, and I passed out after the initial spike of pain. I felt a tightening of my stomach muscles and a tingling in my scalp as the realisation set in that I had been pushed onto the track. Someone had tried to kill me! I groped for some rationale, mouthing incoherent curses as I did so. Someone tried to kill me: my God!

My reverie was brought to a sudden end by Easton, "Bailey, are you sure you're okay? You're mumbling all sorts of shit to yourself."

I crashed back to reality, turning to look at my baffled brothers. I spoke tersely. "What happened after I fell? Were the police called? Did they question anyone? Did anyone see anything at all?"

The blizzard of questions whirled around my perplexed brothers. Anderson stood up suddenly. "You're coming at us here, Bailey. What is it you want to hear?"

Easton chimed in "Why so many questions, we weren't there! The cops contacted us and told us that there'd been an accident. We were just happy that you were okay. Two witnesses said that you tripped and fell onto the track. The cops will tell you when they come to see you."

I latched onto my brothers' uncertainty. "Tripped up? What am I, an invalid!? Accidents don't happen to me. Didn't either of you think it was maybe a little strange? I was almost spread all over the C Line, and neither of you did anything!"

Anderson stuck a finger in my face. "You're being an asshole here, d'you think we should have been there to fucking catch you? You're the one who decided to fall off the fucking platform. Sorry we didn't read your mind and realise you were going to have a brain fuck on the Subway. You tell us what happened. Did you drop some loose change on the track or something!?"

I rose from my bed, straining at the raft of wires and tubes restraining me. "Someone pushed me, I didn't fall, I was pushed....SOMEONE TRIED TO KILL ME!"

I realised that I had yelled the last part of that sentence at the absolute top of my voice when I heard my words bouncing back at me from the cream-coloured walls of the room. I sank back into my bed, suddenly spent. Easton sat immobile, hands gripping the arms of his seat, watching as Anderson moved to the bottom of the bed. The silence was broken by the click of the door handle opening. A white–clad nurse glided into the room, all calm and cool efficiency.

."Is there a problem gentlemen? You are making a lot of noise. We have other patients, and you are upsetting them."

Her eyes moved between the three of us, unblinking and reproachful. Easton cleared his throat and hesitantly replied, "Sorry, we were just happy to see that my brother was okay. We were, err, just celebrating." He chewed his lip as his words tailed off.

The nurse tilted her head and looked at Easton questioningly. "Really? Well, it sounded as though you were about to punch each other out! We have other patients here. This isn't kindergarten!"

She fussed around my bed, again yanking my maltreated arm around as she sought to make me comfortable. "I will call the Police. They asked me to let them know when you came round. You can carry on your conversation now, quietly, please!" She turned on her heel and glided back out of the room.

Anderson cleared his throat quietly, and looked at me questioningly. "Someone tried to kill you?"

I stifled a curse. "We've done that bit, Anderson. Not got it yet?"

Easton barked in defence of his brother. "He's not getting it because it sounds so ridiculous. So someone just decided to kill you? Why would anyone want to kill you - apart from us, right now?"

His lame attempts at humour only riled me more.

"I was pushed. Didn't fall, trip or faint. Don't you believe me?"

The brothers exchanged a familiar, familial look. Frustration surged through my bruised body. "You don't believe me! Jeez, what do I have to do?"

My head throbbed with little ripples of pain, growing in frequency as the volume of my protestations rose. I sank back on the pillows, spearing my bothers with accusing eyes. Easton put his hand on my shoulder. "Look, you're not yourself yet. Get some rest, and maybe things will come back to you."

I laid back, tired and temporarily defeated. Anderson shook his head as he spoke. "C'mon Bailey, you're concussed, not thinking straight."

I felt the genuine concern from both and looked at the ceiling. They were worried about me, and I was too tired to push things. "Let me get some rest guys. We'll talk later. Talk to the nurse and find out when I can get out of here."

Easton ruffled my hair, pulling his hand back quickly as I winced.

"Sorry bro, didn't mean that!"

I grimaced as the ripples of pain pulsed down my neck, grating quietly. "Least you didn't punch my arm."

Anderson shoved the still apologising Easton through the door, waving as he went. "Be in touch, sleep tight."

The door shut with a sharp 'clunk,' and I suddenly felt intensely weary. Maybe they were right, I mused, drifting off into a fitful dose. Sleep came slowly. As the pulses of pain diminished; maybe they were right.

The Police Officers who turned up about two hours later were solicitous and professional, but I had already decided to say nothing, and to go along with what they had told me. I asked about the two witnesses, tourists, apparently, who had seen the whole thing. Lies, obviously - maybe it was one of them who pushed me. The officers were leaving when I had a thought. "Guys, wasn't there any CCTV footage? Every station has it, right?"

The older of the two officers replied. "It has, but something happened to the drive that day, Mr Marks. Nothing was recorded. It happens. Listen sir, 50 people a year are killed on the tracks. We're happy that you are okay. We'll be in touch." They left the room, shutting the door carefully as they went.

My concussion was not serious, and the following morning I was released from the hospital. I still felt somehow remote and physically tentative, and strangely vulnerable as I single-stepped my way down the stairs to reception. My vision was still not completely clear, and bizarre prismatic images sprang up whenever I tried to focus too hard. I reached the bottom of the staircase, and clamped my hand around the rail. The brothers were there, eyes full of concern and expectation. I had called them earlier to tell them that I was being let out, and despite their uncertainty about me leaving hospital so soon, in their opinion, of course, it was good to see them. I felt a ball of emotion well up in my chest.

"Christ, you look awful!" jibed Anderson, grinning sideways at a smirking Easton. No ill effects?"

I coughed to clear my throat and fired back. "Apart from the fact that I can see two each of you, no…! Hope it clears up soon."

Easton shuffled over and gripped my shoulder. You can see TWO of me? God, that must be awesome!"

My jaw tightened as I tried not to smile. "Yeah, and I could still take both of you!"

Anderson grabbed my other shoulder and I was led out of the building by my two laughing siblings, all feelings of vulnerability replaced by that familiar confidence in being with the two people I trusted most in the world.

We pulled up at a small, grey German sports car. "What's this?" I asked.

"My new car," replied Easton sniffing.

I sighed deeply and drawled. "It's a scale model, right? Why not get a full size one?"

Anderson flipped a door open and said in a mock salesman voice, "Yes sir, and it's deceptive. It's even SMALLER when you get in!"
Somehow we all squeezed into the miniscule vehicle, and were driven off by Easton, his mood flattened by our criticism, and apparent in his scowling demeanour.

The car was silent for a time as we drove along the freeway. I became aware of Easton glancing at me occasionally in the front mirror. Anderson sat close to me, his hand resting on my left shoulder. I couldn't take it anymore. "Guys, I'm okay. Can we be normal please? I'm not a fucking invalid!"

As always, my swearing tugged at ancient family protocols, I (almost!) never swore. Easton spoke earnestly. "Bailey, you need to cut yourself some slack. You've had a rough time. We just want to see that you're okay, so don't get down on us for worrying about you."

And like Pavlov's dog, Anderson immediately chimed in. "Why are you being such a hard ass, Bailey? Maybe we should have let you take the bloody Subway."

Our ken-speckle upbringing meant that we moved freely between British, American, and the odd French conversational expression - which made for some strange, hybrid slanging matches between us.

I felt a rising knot of frustration in my throat. "I spoke to the cops, but did you at least try and find out what really happened?"

Easton gripped the wheel tightly as he spoke. "C'mon Bailey, don't go there. You had an accident. We spoke to some senior railway people and the Police. There was no CCTV footage of that night, but people saw you fall."

I sat forward. "No CCTV footage? How was that? Every station in New York has round the clock CCTV – how come there was none that night? Who saw me fall?"

Easton's speech faltered. "Tourists apparently…. and the CCTV had been out all day, something wrong with the hard drive, they said."

I bit hard on my bottom lip, something I usually did when I was about to lose it. "Good to know that my dear brothers have bust their chops in trying to find out what happened to me. I could be dead, and you two have really gone balls out to get to the truth, haven't you?"

My voice had gained decibels as well as almost an octave. Anderson, inches away from my face in the claustrophobic back seat of the car, eyeballed me challengingly and spoke in a soft, assertive tone. "You're *not* dead Bailey, and we did try to find out what happened. Why would these people not tell us the truth? We're just happy you're okay, bro. Is there something that you aren't telling us?"

As always, Anderson's words damped down the dangerously combustible situation. I relented, and sat back in my seat, a dull, gnawing angst coursing through my body. I had no idea what to do; the brothers: I couldn't tell them everything right now, especially as I had only a scintilla of an idea as to what was happening. My mind then emptied, and absolute clarity came into my thoughts. "We need to go to Paris!" I blurted out. Easton almost swerved off the road, as he fixed his gaze on me in the mirror, while Anderson looked at me the way he used to when I was trying to tell him that I hadn't taken cash from his pocket - when I had, of course.

"There's a professor there that could help us find out about Mom, I read an article the other day... "Anderson cut me off." Jesus Christ, come on Bailey. How will it help us? Will it bring her back? Will it help us miss her less? You've got to let go, bro. Mom and Dad are gone, we need to deal with it!"

My voice rose suddenly. "I am dealing with it. I want to find out why Mom died. Why she didn't get proper treatment? Not just for me, for us and also for other people who might need help in the future. You both know how I feel about Dad I won't believe he's dead until I have absolute proof."

"And what exactly do you want Bailey?" roared my enraged brother. "His fucking bones in a bag? Because that's all that will be left of him. The US Government has told us that our Dad is DEAD Bailey, but that's not good enough for you!"

He slumped back in his seat, emotionally spent. My beliefs, or obsessions, as Anderson called them, always caused major grief for us all. I bit my lip and toughed out the silence that had fallen between us: "I'm going, whatever you two do." I asserted quietly.

"Lot of memories in Paris Bailey, some real good ones." Easton's voice tailed off.

"I need to go, there are things we need to find out" I reiterated.

"What do you mean by we, Kemo Sabe?" inquired Anderson archly, humour returning to his tone. We all loved the Lone Ranger, and I got the in-joke. Anderson had calmed down, and was looking at me knowingly.

"Well, I can't go on my own, can I? Besides, French isn't my best language!" I looked pleadingly at Anderson.

"Not making much sense with your English either at the moment Bailey, are you?" he quipped. Paris held much that was precious to us as a family; when we were a family. We visited often, sometimes with Mum to see Dad at his work, or just to vacation after Dad moved back to the States. We had many great times there, appreciating the city more as we got older, feeling comfortable and at ease as our grasp of the language and the geography grew. All of that was dampened by the fact that Mum had shown her first signs of sickness there, but we cherished the family times that we had, and still loved the city and the way it made us feel. I still had nothing that I could use to get the brothers on board. I looked at them both anxiously.

The brothers looked at each other and then at me. "We'll come... erm, because you've asked us to," said Anderson earnestly. "We probably need some time away. Be good to get away from here for a spell."

I took a long, relieved breath, then, suppressing my desire to hug them both, settled for a perfunctory tap on each of their shoulders, unable to break out of my innate British reserve.

"I'm not working anyway, so I'll use it to build some characters," said Anderson airily.

Easton guffawed. "Acting's not working, it's... acting!" he giggled.

"Yeah? Well, when I have to hold doors open for brainless socialites and beat up on drunks, I'll worry about *my* job!" fired back Anderson.

Easton turned to continue the spat, and almost ran a red light. "Guys!" I bellowed. "Enough already! We need to go and get packed and ready. Let's can the fraternal stuff until we get on the plane?"

The brothers' eyes met, silently agreed a truce, and the rest of the drive home passed quietly, shoulder to shoulder in Easton's toy automobile. God only knew how we would get through the flight!

CHAPTER 5

Paris in the springtime. The sunlight rippled over the burgundy canvas canopy of the Cafe Tapas where the three of us sat, immersed in that knowing silence that perhaps only siblings can enjoy. We had checked in at The Hotel D'Autriche, on the Cite Bergere. Crummy, dingy; yes, but a place which held precious memories of family holidays that seemingly happened in some mythical past age.

I sat running my finger around the rim of my coffee cup, looking at my two brothers, and for the umpteenth time, marvelled at how they had turned out. Easton, betraying his immaturity, had crammed a whole croissant into his mouth, smiling hamster-ishly as he attempted to swallow it. Anderson squinted disapprovingly at his brother's table manners, sipping his mineral water then sighing audibly as Easton coughed sharply, sending crumbs shooting across the table. I gazed at him nonplussed. Dad would have been proud – 'would have been?' What was I thinking? He was out there somewhere, wasn't he? I had to believe. I damped down the anger which always sprang from thinking about him, and about the things I should have asked him when we had him, I re-focused on the brothers. Easton, croissant now satisfactorily, if messily, swallowed, wiped his hands with his napkin and sat back in the rickety wicker chair. "Now what?" he ventured in his usual staccato manner.

Anderson glowered at his brother over his sunglasses. "We wait. We haven't finished our drinks," he said querulously. I loved the synergy between the two brothers, one all speed, dynamism and instinct, and the other more sober, thoughtful and in need of a plan.

"Come on Bailey, what are we going to do?"

Easton could be trying. I took a sip of my latte and put on my stern voice. "We have plenty of time before we need to be at l'Etoile. Now let me finish my coffee. Calm down!"

Easton made that annoying raspberry noise which was his forte, exhaling through flapping lips and growling at the same time.

"Sometimes I can't believe that we are related" Anderson was fond of using this witticism, and Easton always, Pavlov's dog-like, rose to it.

"We're not. We just happened to share the same womb," he smiled as Anderson's brow furrowed.

Then I saw them; a group of men had emerged from a junction in the road and were walking down the narrow street towards us. All my senses were on alert, and my misgivings went critical when the lead man looked at us, turned to the others and beckoned them on.

I placed my cup on the table, dropped a 20 Euro note on the saucer, and stood up slowly. The brothers needed no prompting, quietly pushed their chairs back and moved towards me. These guys were not tourists, and I guessed by their accessories, fixed looks and stiff body language that they weren't out for a promenade du jour. They were coming to us, nothing surer. I tapped the brothers' arms to get their attention, and we moved out into the middle of the street. Years of training took over, and I felt that tingle of anticipation in my arms and throat. Anderson stood tall, breathing very slowly, flexing and un-flexing his fists, whilst Easton, not one for latent menace, shamelessly tightened his guns and winked at me. I wondered if these guys knew what they were taking on. We edged along the cobbles towards the men; a spasm of doubt shot into my head, and was quickly ejected. We had trained for things like this, and we knew we were good, but how good were these guys?

Even for Paris this street was narrow, which was a good thing considering what was in front of us. We were in Rue de Trevise, which snaked up a slight hill for about half a mile as it twisted up from Rue de Bergere over to Rue de St Cecile, but at this stretch it straightened out for about 300 yards. The tight confines of the street allowed two thin strips of barely passable sidewalk. To our left was an endless line of parked cars, to our right a row of shops and offices. This was an old part of the city and the shops and offices had small doors and windows. Solid sandstone bricks made up the structure of the buildings, which were about three or four storeys high, trapping noise and leaving the street washed in the mid-afternoon sun behind us.

It was all very quiet at this time in the afternoon, with the only other people around being the late-lunching office or shop worker. In front of us now were seven men. Up close, they looked VERY like Eastern Europeans, perhaps Polish or Lithuanians, or maybe Russians. Their look was generic: bald glossy heads, limited necks - almost flared ears. They were not in good condition, with the incipient guts and love handles of out of condition doormen, not one under 200lbs, I mused. They obviously enjoyed the indulgences of life, food and drink, but bizarrely, all seven of them were showing off their ample figures by wearing skinny jeans and tight white crew neck t-shirts. That clinched it, they MUST be Russian - not a good look!

They had the facial features of American pit-bull terriers and the glowering demeanour of pall bearers at a Mafia funeral. The whole scene would have been quite comical were it not for the fact that they were all carrying weapons. Pit-bull one and two had baseball bats...tapping their tips menacingly on the ground in front of Easton. I had three almost directly in front of me. The one right in front of me had a very elderly machete, and the two behind him had batons of some sort. The one in front of Anderson was carrying a knife with a five inch blade and one behind him, incongruously, what looked like a garden hoe. Because the sidewalk was so narrow they had to line up in three layers to come at us. There was not enough room to assault us in an arc. Due to the line of cars and the row of buildings, they did not have the chance to circle round us. In addition, the sun was at our backs and therefore shining in their eyes. They were obviously amateurs, I felt a little disappointed. This should be easy, I thought, so we might as well have some fun. The chances of us walking away unscathed were high.

Anderson spoke first: "Privet, tovarishch, ya mogu pomoch'vam!?" the greeting was unanswered. Mmm, maybe not Russian. Then Anderson went again, this time in English, "You guys got real shiny heads. How do you do that?"

The group were about eight feet in front of us and the random, throwaway question seemed to snap the monolithic band of resolve binding them together. Sideways glances and questioning frowns flickered from pit bull to pit bull. The logical side of me put this down to their limited understanding of English. The dark side of me put it down to the fact that they probably had a very limited blood line and struggled to differentiate their uncles from their fathers. Easton spoke next. He was clearly fixated by the similarity in appearance of these seven men, "We are three brothers." Why was he speaking in a cod Russian accent? He was on the edge. "Are you guys brothers, related? Clones maybe?"

Baleful glares again rippled round the pit bull coven. I could not resist the temptation to drop a line on them. "Where are the Seven Brides? Mind you, where would seven ugly sons of bitches like you find Seven Brides? Unless maybe you've all got sisters!" That one hit a tender spot; some of them spoke English alright. One of them took a step towards Easton - oh dear; It all happened very quickly from that point on. Easton moved in. Pit-bull one swung the baseball bat in his right hand back and balanced himself by stretching out his left hand in front of him. Easton took another step towards pit-bull one leading with his left hand. He placed his left hand inside the elbow joint of pit-bull whilst grasping his left hand and pinning it against his own chest. This was all done very quickly and allowed him to deliver a head butt right on the nose of his opponent. As pit-bull fell back, Easton moved with him, never letting go of his grips. This allowed him to push his opponent into pit-bull two behind. As number two was raising his bat, Easton punched him with the heel of his right hand upwards to the bottom of his nose. Getting this wrong, killed the person being hit. Easton had to get it right. Over-doing it would force the bones of the nose into the brain. Death would be quick. If that was your goal then you gave it everything you had. It was not Easton's objective. He merely wanted to immobilise this guy so his take-down blow had to be precise. It was, and pit-bull two was finished.

Pit-bull one was still putting up a fight, albeit, a limited one. He needed another slap and so Easton drove the heel of his right hand into pit-bull's left ear. Pit-bull one went down like a wardrobe, bouncing once on the sidewalk, emitting a low, sonorous moan that terminated abruptly as his tongue slid down his throat.

To my left Anderson was dealing with blade wielding pit-bull - number six of seven. The knife was in his right hand as he made a lunge at Anderson's throat. Anderson quickly dipped his head down to the left avoiding the arc of the blade, allowing him to bring his left hand across his face to push pit-bull's right hand further away. In one swift move he brought his right hand up to the elbow of pit-bull and pushed his arm further away. He then ran his right hand down pit-bull's forearm and gripped his hand and the blade. Then a hard heel of his left hand to pit-bull's right elbow broke his arm and released his grip on the blade.

Pit-bull six was the first to make any real noise during all of this and he let out a loud, feral scream. The natural amphitheatre of the buildings caused the sound to echo somewhat, but as it rose it was lost to the sky and did not attract any attention. A quick recoil of Anderson's left hand allowed him to strike pit-bull on the right corner of his jaw and he went down as if he had been paid to take a dive in the third. Anderson now had a weapon. Pit-bull seven was raising the baseball bat with both hands over his head. With the blade still in his right hand, Anderson stabbed him under his right arm-pit. There is danger with this move in severing the brachial artery. The person will probably bleed out and be dead in about three hours if they do not get help. At this point Anderson was not counting nor was he being considerate with the blade. He missed the artery, but pit-bull seven was not down yet. He was howling mad though, so using the butt of the knife handle, Anderson delivered a hammer blow to pit-bull's jaw, breaking it in the process and dropping him on the spot.

I had the elderly machete to worry about. It came in a wide arc from my left at neck height. I stepped inside pit-bull three's curving right arm grabbing his elbow with my left hand, pinning his left arm to his own chest with my right hand and head butting him on the bridge of his nose. A quiet "umff" noise came from him. I could smell his rank breath. His right arm tensed. This allowed me to twist left and push down on his arm, pulling him off balance. I ran my left hand down his forearm and gripped his hand and the handle of the machete. I twisted counter-clockwise and he let go of the blade. I now had the blade in my hand with the butt up facing up. I swung it to the right side of his head hitting him hard on the temple. He toppled over to his left like a child in the playground. One staggering step and he was on the sidewalk prostrate behind the advancing Easton.

Number four pit-bull was wielding his baton in his left hand. My left hand was down to my right side having just dispatched pit-bull. I still had the machete in a dagger like grip and so I slashed up the way aiming for the fingers of his left hand. I was never going to miss with a blade this big, even if it was as blunt as a plank of wood. He let out a pain-raddled scream. The arc of blood splattered across pit-bull five behind him. Pit-bull four dropped the baton and it rattled on the sidewalk. The heel of my right hand caught him square on the chin and he fell back into pit-bull five. Clearly all of this activity in front of pit-bull five was having an emotional impact upon him. As I advanced one step towards him, stepping over pit-bull four, his eyes widened. He dropped the garden hoe, spun on his right heel and took a large lumbering step in an attempt to run away from us.

Easton, now to my left, having despatched his two pit-bulls, took two quick strides and was close enough to click the heels of pit-bull five; a little school boy cheek goes a long way. The last standing pit-bull was no longer standing. It had taken us about fifty seconds to drop all seven of them. The intense violence of that short time span hadn't generated a drop of sweat from us, and as we all quickly checked, it seemed that not one drop of blood or spec of dirt had touched our prized clothing. Anderson jumped a little as his shades dropped onto his nose from where he had perched them on his head. Easton guffawed at his obvious discomfiture, quickly losing the mood as he spied an infinitesimal drop of blood on his left boot.

"Shit…that'll never come off!" He turned towards the remaining, submissive pit bull. "What have you got to say about THAT? Asshole!"

Now the three of us approached him. He was cowering with his back to the sandstone wall of a designer clothes boutique. Easton, ever the fashionista, ignored pit-bull and pressed his nose against the clothes shop window.

"Nice shirt." Pit-bull turned his head in Easton's direction, which made Anderson and I laugh out loud.

"Don't think he means you, Borat." said Anderson. The shaven head turned querulously, sending an angry look, and of course it told us that this pit-bull also understood English.

"Who sent you?" I asked.

"No one," he replied, large bloodshot eyes darting, anxiously from brother to brother.

"So you guys were just out robbing tourists then?" fired Easton, almost absent-mindedly pressing his nose against the shop window, the steam from his breath fogging up the view. He stepped back and wiped away the marks of his own breath, then pressed his nose back against the window. He did not even look at pit-bull, but stared intently at a garish silk shirt which dominated the store display.

"Yes," said the man with the shiny head. Anderson put his left arm on the wall above pit-bull's head and leant in closer to him and growled sotto voce-

"You don't dress like muggers. Even the local "crims" wouldn't be seen dead in your get-up. This can be done easily or painfully. I am going to count to three. If I get to three I am going to do some wood carving on your head, buddy. Understand?" as he said this, Anderson raised the point of the knife to pit-bull's cheek, just under his right eye. Pit-bull blinked; a good sign. Anderson was really acting here, but the pit-bull did not know that, and he stared, slack-jawed at the blood smeared knife.

"Artilleryman." Said the fashion victim sitting in front of us.

"What?" said Anderson.

"The Artilleryman Bar." Said the pit-bull. "An English person. I do not know his name, but he spoke English very good," he said in his Eastern European accent.

"What do you mean, 'very good?'" asked Easton, nose still against the window. I could see an attractive girl looking out from inside the fashion shop shifting uncomfortably in her seat behind a desk. The silk shirt was forgotten as he stared at the attractive shop assistant. She was getting nervous.

We would have to be quick before she called the Police, or in case she had done so already.

"Good English. Good English - English from somewhere very clever. He has been taught very good."

The Eastern European accent was getting stronger now. He was getting worried. Perhaps about how much information he had given us. It was time to move this on – quickly.

"You mean he was well spoken – educated?" I asked. The pit bull's ashen face creased. "Yes. Very well spoken," he said. It was obvious he was just a paid man, not privy to any deep information. These guys probably made a living doing low-level hits and beatings for minor criminals…or educated Englishmen

it would seem, but why did they come after us? And who would want us roughed up?

"Guys. We should move," I said. "The girl in that shop has probably phoned the cops and they will be here soon. Don't want to spend time with the Paris Police explaining this whole situation. If this pit-bull here wants to do that, then he is welcome to give it a go, but I'm thinking we should split. What say you all?"

Easton was now drumming his fingers on the window of the fashion shop. He was either considering a purchase or trying to get the girl inside to wave at him. My guess was the latter. He pushed off from the window and walked past us heading south. The pit-bull hardly had time to register relief before I spoke "Take a deep breath." The Pit Bull obliged, then I dropped him with a clenched fist to his solar plexus. He slumped against the shop window, gasping asthmatically.

"Breathe out now, there's a good fellow!" The immobile, inert shapes of the pit-bull pack littered the sidewalk. I quickly checked the one Anderson had stuck and reassured myself that he wouldn't bleed to death before help arrived.

I looked for Easton, who was now moving away from us. "Where are you going, Easton?" I asked.

"For a drink in a bar," he said. "A very English bar, right here in Paris."

It clicked instantly for me. Sitting opposite the Pantheon in Paris was the Artilleryman Bar, a well-known, if slightly seedy, English pub.

Anderson, arms folded, looked at me and growled. "So we're going to an English bar in Paris to find a well-spoken Englishman. Way to go bro!"

I took off my glasses, and took out a cleaning cloth. "The youngster is onto something," I said, polishing the lenses assiduously whilst following the already disappearing Easton.

Anderson flung his arms open in a gesture of resignation. "I just can't believe we're related!" he bellowed after us.

I exchanged looks with the grinning Easton, and we replied in stereo, "We're not, we just happened to share the same womb!"

Anderson barely suppressed a reluctant smile and shuffled after us, muttering incoherently. Our first day in Paris had been eventful. It seemed that certain people knew that we were here, but we didn't even know *why* we were here. Things had moved so fast since I had read *that* e-mail just over a week before. How could we make any sense of it all? I lost myself in a reverie, following in Easton's slipstream as we made our way through the quiet, early afternoon streets. I rolled my conversation with Wheelan in Central Park around in my head again and again. So far he had been on the money, I *was* in danger, and but for incredible luck in New York, and the sheer amateurism of our recent playmates, I might be dead, or at best in intensive care. I stole a glance at my brothers, and felt a spear of angst as I realised that I could have gotten them killed as well. I felt the acid in my gut as I realised that we were in something swirling well over our collective designer coiffures.

We didn't have Dad to guide us, to deal with whatever was going on. We had lived a kind of vicarious life for years, always wondering what Dad did, imagining the situations and dangers he faced, but this was happening to us. This was real, and I couldn't understand why I wasn't sitting in a corner with my shirt pulled over my head. The brothers had pulled up to wait for me at an underpass. I shook my head briskly, took a deep breath, and joined them for the final leg of our journey.

CHAPTER 6

The bar was dark and cool, a welcoming ambience after the short walk in the bright sunlight. I eased into a chair, and looked at a dog-eared menu as the brothers moved in next to me. Easton, as was his wont, noisily dragged a seat across the wooden floor to join us, wedging Anderson against the bar in the process. "Jeezus, can't you do anything quietly?" groaned Anderson.

"NO!" bellowed Easton mischievously. Several addled drinkers amongst the sparse clientele lifted their heads woozily to check out the fuss.

I scanned their faces quickly, and seeing nothing to concern me, ordered some drinks. We were all teetotal, so three Perriers were disdainfully dumped on the bar by the saturnine, black-clad barman, his disgust at us not ordering anything stronger apparent. He was English, I guessed, with a slab of thickly-gelled hair stuck on top of a long, angular face, but he took my order in French, and asked for payment in French. Easton took a gulp of his water and belched loudly, Anderson looked at him with barely-concealed contempt.

"You might want to take off your shades Ando. You look a bit of a jerk in this light," said Easton perkily.

Anderson slowly removed his shades and folded them methodically before putting them in his shirt pocket, shaking his head malevolently as he did so.

I engaged the taciturn barman in conversation. "Get many English people in here?" He lifted a towel and wiped the bar top apathetically. "Not talking then, mate," I persisted.

"It's an English pub, innit? So we get loads." he replied, revealing an East London accent.

"Any in today?" I pressed.

He scowled, as though answering me was causing him some pain. "Every day. Like I said, it's an English pub."

"What about Russians?" I continued.

He stopped wiping the bar top. "What are you, the local diversity officer? I dunno, we get all sorts and all nationalities in here."

"Just making conversation friend."

My retort went unanswered as the barman busied himself with some glasses, looking up at the flickering flat-screen TV a metre above his head as he did so. I picked up on some item of news scrolling across the bottom of the screen, some incident on the Metro. Apparently someone had been killed.

My mind started to wander when Anderson eased himself in front of me at the bar and tried another tack.

"Look friend, we've just had some trouble, and we think some of the guys involved may have been in here. They meant us real harm."

The barman made a dismissive noise from the back his throat. "Really? You don't know my customers. If any of them wanted to do you over, you wouldn't be able to come looking for them, trust me. Now why don't you finish your little fizzy drinks and do one!"

I set my teeth and pulled out a business card. "My number is there, if you remember anything. Good talking to you." I turned to move away from the bar.

The barman flicked my card off of the bar with a horny thumbnail, and I watched as it arced away into the gloom of the body of the bar. The barman set his hands akimbo on the bar and hissed menacingly. "Now piss off, the lot of you, before I get the fucking Police Nationale, understand?"

I had barely opened my mouth to utter an as yet unformed retort when I felt Easton's right hand fly past my head, grabbing the barman's left hand and pinning it to the marbled bar surface. My mouth quickly closed as I saw Easton's other hand grab an ice pick and swish it down in one flashing movement to hover about a centimetre above the barman's quivering paw where he had flattened it to the cool surface of the bar.

"Easton, no!"

Anderson reacted at last, trying to pull Easton away, but the earlier fight had left Easton pumped, and the venom dripped from his words as he rasped into the by-now terrified barman's face. "You little prick, I'll stick this arm to the bar, then rip your other one off and shove it so far up your ass that you'll be able to clean your ears out from the inside!"

Anderson looked at me hopelessly and took his hands off of Easton's arm. He was in the zone, and right now his mean streak was as wide as the Champs Elysee. This was dangerous, and flying out of control.

"Come on Easton, let it be!" I bellowed, grabbing his left hand as it held the ice pick rigidly above the helpless barman's sweating limb. His eyes seemed to glow in the gloom, but he wasn't seeing or hearing me. I had resigned myself to taking Easton down when the barman decided to faint, crashing down on the layered lines of glasses stacked beneath him. The noise snapped Easton out of his red zone, and he looked at us with his familiar startled brows-down look.

Large men in black were making their way towards us through the murk, and, having taken the ice pick out of Easton's hand, I helped Anderson propel him towards the exit doors. We burst out into the street, squinting, our eyes protesting at the sudden explosion of light. Two Policemen gazed at us questioningly from across the sidewalk, and seeing them, the black-clad gents pursuing us seemed to morph back into the dark interior of the bar. The Policemen stared at us for a few seconds, and then walked off, arms moving in typical Gallic conversational mode.

Anderson looked at me, and we both looked at the panting Easton, who had gone from psychopath to naughty ten year old in the blink of any eye. After a few portentous moments, he straightened up, adjusted his designer collar, and said innocently, "That went well."

"Sometimes you're just not too bright!" I growled.

Easton blanched somewhat, but then after running his fingers through his blond pelt, fished the pair of shades out of Anderson's pocket, perched them on his nose and looked at us both challengingly. "I would never have done it. He was jerking us around, but I would never have done it," he said submissively. Anderson made the move. "Let's see if we can make it to the Etoile without getting killed or arrested." None out of two so far, and we still had no idea why we were here.

We walked in silence, with Easton lagging just behind us. "Just far enough to avoid conversation," smiled Anderson. I looked back at my incorrigible sibling, and felt that deep protective angst that I used to feel when he was in third grade. The shades hid his eyes, but he was still mollified, and his gait lacked its usual swagger. We moved on through the bustling, lively streets, enjoying the spring warmth and the familiarity of our surroundings.

The Etoile was a superbly modern edifice, yet completely at one with the rest of this stylish city. I gazed admiringly at the building's symmetry and the gleaming superstructure, mentally congratulating whoever had conceptualised and designed this extraordinary construction. We walked into the air-conditioned atrium, where an immaculately dressed woman sat behind an impossibly elaborate desk holding a phone whilst typing furiously on a silver laptop with her free hand. Anderson spoke, in his clipped and correct French.

"Bon apres-midi, nous sommes ici a voir Le Professeur Favreau, et..."

"Please," the woman interjected in English, "Take a seat. I will have to call someone."

Anderson, abashed, looked at me quizzically. "Is there a problem?" he said.

"You must wait!" came the curt reply.

Anderson persisted, "Look, I am British, but I can speak good French."

The woman barely looked up from her typing. "I also speak good French, and I am Romanian. Now please take a seat."

We all sat down on the brown leather sofa which faced the desk and listened as she spoke in rapid, unintelligible French to someone on the other end of her phone.

"Didn't get any of that, did you?" inquired Anderson. I hadn't. French was not my best language. What was going on?

The receptionist clattered the phone back into its holder and stood up. "Jeanne Salas, the Professor's aide, will see you now. Please remain here, and she will come." At that, she sat down and resumed her typing.

"Having a bad day, I think." Easton spoke for the first time since we arrived. I shrugged an acknowledgement to him, and leaned back on the sofa to await events. The sound of high heels on marble, punctuated by bursts of male and female conversation, heralded the arrival of two formally dressed men, and a tall dark-haired woman in a pinstriped business suit who stopped at the desk as the two men approached us. The taller of the two wore a fashionably rumpled dark grey linen suit, combined with a lilac shirt opened at the collar. The other a steel blue mohair suit, with a pale blue shirt and burgundy tie ensemble. The bigger man looked us over and spoke in heavily-accented, but perfect English.

"You are here to see Prof Favreau, I believe. Can I ask why?"

I stood up. "Why do you want to know? Who are you?"

"I am Capitaine Papin, from the Prefecture de Police and this is my colleague, Lieutenant Dumouriez," he said, without ceremony, "and we are here investigating the death of Prof Favreau. Your names, please."

I looked at Anderson and Easton, and back to the detective. "Dead? When did this happen?" I said, trying to remain composed.

Jeanne Salas, whose puffy eyes and flushed cheeks now became noticeable, moved slowly forward and said in a halting voice, "It happened about an hour and a half ago. He was killed on the Metro."

Before she could finish, the shorter of the men, Dumouriez, who also reeked of tobacco, stepped forward and announced flatly, "We don't know how it happened at the moment, but he somehow landed on the track, and the train hit him."

The skin on the back of my neck crawled, the TV news flash in the Bombadier! Surely not. I felt a tightening in my throat. Anderson knew what was on my mind. I had survived my brush with death in a subway, here was someone who hadn't.

Papin then spoke. "Again I ask, names please, and what was the purpose of your meeting?"

I took the lead. "I'm Bailey Marks, and these are my brothers, Anderson and Easton. We had arranged a meeting to talk to him about some research we are doing."

Papin regarded us with an inimitably Gallic stare. "The Marks' Brothers - like the old American comedy performers?" He smiled humourlessly, quickly returning to serious business. "Passports please." We handed the documents over without demur. Papin flicked though each one, glancing at each of us in turn. "Research? Are you scientists?" inquired Dumouriez.

I replied quickly, "No, I'm in IT, but I am working in web design with a pharmaceutical company at present."

Papin gave the three passports back to me, accompanied by a quiet "Merci"

Dumouriez took out a card, passing it to me as he spoke. "Gentlemen, we will need your details, and your movements as we are conducting an investigation here. My colleague will take them from you."

He whispered something to Papin, shook the visibly wilting Jeanne's hand and strode off.

Easton had moved to Jeanne's side, and he gently guided her to the sofa, where she sank down and burst into tears, all reserve and protocol submerged in an outburst of grief.

Papin completed his note-taking. "She has already answered a lot of questions. I would suggest that you do not put her through any more. We will perhaps contact you soon if we have anything that we need to ask you. If you leave Paris, please inform us. Good bye." I took no meaning from his tone, and nodded silently as he left the atrium. Anderson had already joined Easton and Jeanne on the sofa. I asked the receptionist for some water, which she quickly supplied from a vending machine on her side of the desk. I held the cup to Jeanne's lips and she sipped some of the cold liquid, taking a breath as she finished.

"Monsieur, we are all in shock. We only heard of the Professor's death less than an hour ago. I cannot accept it, he was such a gentleman. Forgive me, it is very difficult for me." Her voice tailed off as a wracking sob convulsed her slim frame, and as Easton instinctively put an arm around her, she did not pull away or react, resting her head on his broad shoulder. She regained her composure momentarily. "We tried to contact all the Professor's appointments, but we had no contact details for you. I am sorry."

"Please, it's okay," soothed Easton. "Don't talk if it is too hard for you."

I had to ask. "We saw a news report on TV about an hour ago about an accident on the Metro. Was that Professor Favreau?"

She wiped moisture from her eyes, which were almond shaped and such a deep shade of brown that the pupils could hardly be discerned. "Yes, they are saying it was perhaps suicide, but I cannot believe that. He had so many reasons to live, to work." Another ululating sob cut her words short.

Anderson touched my hand. "Come on Bailey, no more questions. She's too upset, we can come back."

Easton, now holding Jeanne's hand, as well as supporting her head on his shoulder, looked at me reproachfully. "Yeah, enough Bailey, she can't take much more of this."

Easton had a knack for generating almost instant trust in complete strangers, and I sensed that this strikingly beautiful and vulnerable woman was about to become a willing victim. The receptionist had come over to us, and helped Jeanne up, prising her hand from Easton's. He reluctantly let go.

"Messieurs, we are closing the building because of the situation. You will have to go now."

"Jeanne, can we call you later? I need to know that you are okay," Easton interjected almost frantically.

Jeanne looked at him with those dark, reddened eyes, and said quietly, "Yes, I will get in touch. Please, what is your name again?"

"Easton, Easton Marks, these are my brothers Bailey and Anderson. We're at the Hotel D'Autriche on Cite Bergere. This is my cell phone number." He handed her a card. Her hand touched Easton's lightly as the card passed between them, and I realised, startlingly, that she for some reason, trusted him, and us. She looked back briefly as she was led away, pushing her hair back from her face as she did so, those eyes still glistening with a meniscus of unshed tears.

We shuffled out on to the street, all three trying to rationalise what had just happened, and indeed everything that had happened over the last few hours. Anderson spoke first. "What about that, Bailey? Another accident at a subway station, I..."

"I had no accident, I was pushed!" erupted out of me, an ejaculation of frustration and confusion. "Still not believe me? Maybe you would if I was dead as well!" I was angry beyond logic.

"Come on, we do believe you. Anderson didn't mean anything by it!" pleaded Easton. The brothers were not used to me showing such raw emotion.

"Look, I almost got killed; deliberately killed, and now someone we were coming to see has been killed. He's a high profile guy and people knew that he would be meeting us. Something really deep is going on here, and we need to waken up to it!"

Anderson and Easton stared at each other, aghast. I (almost), never lost my IT geek cool.

"Okay Bailey, you tell us what's going on here?" Anderson was not known for lateral thinking. I took a sharp breath, and grated through clenched teeth. "For Christ's sake Anderson. Someone has tried to harm me twice and all of us once. What have we done? Who have we pissed off?"

Easton stood in front of me, arms folded. "Maybe we'd understand things better if you told us what you know, and why you brought us here."

He and Anderson stared at me guardedly, as if I had just committed some deep indiscretion. I sighed, looking at my two beloved brothers, realising that I had brought them here on little more than trust, and that I would have to tell them. It would be a relief, a catharsis, thank God!

"Okay boys, let's have a coffee, and we'll talk."

Easton's mood rose immediately. "Well, let's find somewhere that we haven't had a fight in or been chased out of then!"

Anderson chuckled sardonically, "I quite enjoy this. We could do a new kind of Rough Guide: Places to fight in and be chased out of in Monmartre. Beats the shit out of boring visits to the Sorbonne or Les Invalides!" The spell was broken, I had them again. We walked off, joshing and roistering like 15 year-olds on a school outing.

CHAPTER 7

We pulled in at a cafe on Boulevard Auguste Blanqui. Anderson and I sat down and scanned yet another generic menu, whilst Easton stayed upright, his bulging arms folded in a macho show of belligerence as he machine-gunned the clientele with narrowed eyes. Anderson sighed "Sit down Easton, you look like some dumb-assed meerkat!"

Easton reluctantly pulled a rickety plastic chair back and eased himself slowly into it, still swivelling around the cafe. "We need to be sharp, Ando, we're marked men!" he ventured earnestly.

"Well, Marks' men, at any rate, that right Harpo?" grinned Anderson.

Easton hid his smile by smoothing his hand over his mouth, and looked at me expectantly.
"C'mon Groucho bro, you need to talk to us." He punctuated the end of the sentence by rapping the table with his knuckles.

"Yeah, well you need to listen, because a lot of it doesn't make any sense," I stated flatly. I stopped talking as coffees arrived, and then leaned forward as the waiter moved away.

My phone rang. I looked at the number flashing up on the screen - didn't recognise it.

"Answer it," said Anderson wearily, pushing his chair back from the table.

I pressed the green icon. "Hello?"

An accented female voice came back at me "Bailey Marks?" I replied in the affirmative. She continued, "I am Hasar Tresfor." I looked at my brothers and held up my left hand, shrugging to signal that I had no idea who was on the other end of the line.

"Okay, how did you get my number?"

"From your business card. You were in the Bombardier Bar a short time ago."

Her English was formal, but perfect. However, I couldn't place the accent. I spoke carefully. "Really? Seemed the barman wasn't in a calling card mood, he threw it away." Her voice came back quickly, clear and sharp. "I know. I heard you talking to him, and saw the blond one attack him."

I swallowed hard. "A misunderstanding, language problems," I lied.

"You have no need to be wary, Mr Marks. I'm not the Police, and I know that you are probably British, as is our day barman... but he is a jerk, and I really don't care what happened to him today."

I glanced at my frowning brothers again, and responded guardedly. "Okay then, you saw us at the bar and found my card. Why have you called me?"

There was a brief pause, "You are in danger. I heard one of you say that you had been attacked. Well, I heard men talking about some sort of fight, or ambush, a couple of days before you came in. One of them was English."

I caught my breath, fending off Easton's anxious signals with my left arm as I cradled the cell phone in my right. "A well-spoken, well-educated Englishman? I know it's hard sometimes..."

She interrupted before I could finish patronising her. "I went to university in York, Mr Bailey. I speak English very well. He was obviously well spoken, but I cannot say anything about his education, except that he speaks good Estonian."

I glanced at the brothers. "Put it on speaker, Bailey. We can't hear a thing!" pleaded Anderson. I shushed him away, and returned to the conversation.

"So you overheard these guys talking about beating us up, just in a regular conversation? Not really concerned about keeping it secret, were they?"

The girl clicked her tongue, her obvious frustration lancing through the speaker. "Yes, Mr Bailey, I did, but they patronised me almost as much as you are doing – they were speaking in a different language, not French or English."

I gripped the cell phone tightly. "What language? Could you tell what it was?"

Her laugh tinkled down the phone "Mr Bailey, you are slow today! I have told you that your Englishman spoke Estonian. They were talking in Estonian!"

I took time to respond, already way behind in this unequal conversation. "And you understood them because…"

My voice tailed off, and she took the silence as a prompt. "Because I am Estonian, Mr Bailey, and so were the men your Englishman was talking to. Only we Estonians and a few Finns speak it. It is a very unique tongue, related to no other so these oafs felt it was safe to talk openly. "What chance would there be of another Estonian speaker being in an English bar in Paris!"

She sounded almost cocksure now, and I found myself warming to this disembodied voice "Well, you got that right, I suppose," I said lamely.

She laughed and uttered some indecipherable sounds. "Sorry, I didn't get that," I replied.

"Mr Bailey, that was Estonian! There is no supposing about it!" she rapped back. Unbelievable, who was this person? I looked sternly at my giggling brothers who had picked up the last part of the conversation and were enjoying my discomfort.

I was about to speak again when she interjected with real urgency, "I want to help you, Mr Bailey. These are bad men, and they make a living from beating up anyone they are paid to. People are frightened of them."

"Well, Mslle, they'll not be earning any money for a while, we dealt with them. Hasar, could you meet up with us? We need to know everything you know. We have no idea why people want to harm us. You could help."

Static buzzed on the line for a few seconds, but she came back with a firm response. "Yes, I will be at the seats behind the fountain in Rene Viviani Square at 10am on Wednesday. I will see you there."

My ear felt thick and numb. I stood up. Anderson looked at me incredulously. "You're not going Bailey. We don't know her from Adam. It could be a set-up." Easton, heaving his muscled frame out of his chair, moved beside me. "I'm with him Anderson. We've got to go for this."

Anderson, arms outstretched dramatically, addressed us both with some venom. "Bailey hasn't even started to tell us anything yet, and you want to go running into another potential fuck-up without any real reason! Any which way you want, this thing is fucked up. Why are we here Bailey? What's going on!?"

Easton shuffled agitatedly and suddenly reached down and grabbed his brother's head, pulling it close to his as he spoke. "Ando, you're such a fucking ACTOR! Come on. We need you!"

Anderson was unmoved, and winding up to a real frenzy. "This isn't Saturday night on some fucking club door,

Easton, and it's not some game on your fucking PC, is it Bailey? This is real, and you've put us in harm's way without telling us why. Not good enough bro, not good enough. You knew what you were doing when you talked us into coming to Paris!"

I suddenly felt crushed and hopeless. Anderson's words were soaked in real bile, and I had no answers to give him. I had dragged the two most precious people in my life halfway across the world on a barely-informed hunch. I had failed them. I flopped down into the plastic seat, my purpose and resolve temporarily gone.

Easton looked at me with real concern in his eyes. "I hope you know what you're doing Bailey, but I'm with you!" he bellowed.

I rubbed my face, shoving my glasses off of my nose as I did so. "Easton, Anderson's right. I don't really know why we are here. It may lead us to Dad somehow... Jeezuz, we had to come, don't you see?"

Anderson and Easton exchanged looks. Anderson spoke first, eyes wet with emotion. "Dad? He's dead Bailey. Don't you get it, he's not coming back!?"

My hand slid down my face. "He's not dead. I can't believe he died. He's out there somewhere, just don't know where."

Easton sprang to my side and grabbed my shoulder. "Not dead? What!? What aren't you telling us?" Easton was like a darkening storm cloud. "Bailey, why are you talking about Dad? Why were these guys at the café trying to take us down? Jesus, Bailey, what's going on?"

I felt the brothers' rising panic, and suddenly rediscovered my backbone. "Dad wasn't a business consultant. He was an industrial spy, working for the government; OUR government, and he was involved in a major investigation when he went missing." The brothers were now quiet, looking at me with anxious, uncomprehending eyes. My turn. "Let's go back to the hotel, we need to talk." Two mute nods finished the conversation, and we started walking back, Anderson and Easton just behind me still sullenly silent.

The long spring night was only just beginning to darken when we got back. The female concierge stood up when she saw us and beckoned us to the desk. I walked wearily over to the reception area.

"M'sieur Marks, I have two messages for you. Can you take them please?"

I took the notes from her hand, unfolding the first to read it. It was from Dumouriez, the Policeman. Just what we needed!

"That one is from a Lieutenant Dumouriez, he is a Policeman!" the concierge snapped.

I looked at her through narrowed eyes. "Really, want to tell me what it says? "I riposted. She started to say something, then folded her hands and shook her head. Dumouriez wanted us to go to the local office to answer some questions. The tone was not pressing, but this was not what we needed. Why now? I crumpled the note up and stuffed it in my shirt pocket, and then opened the second one, staring challengingly at the hard-faced concierge as I did.

It was from Jeanne Salas, and she wanted to meet us to talk, urgently, it appeared. Why didn't she call Easton? The brothers had moved to my side. "We're in demand guys, seems that everyone in this city either wants to kill us or talk to us."

Easton nipped the note from my fingers and rapidly read it out loud. "Shit, she did try to call me. I didn't recognise the number. Sorry guys." He dipped his head in apology, looking to Anderson at the same time.

I stepped up to the reception, and spoke brusquely, "Which note came first, the Policeman's or the girl's?"

The concierge looked at me haughtily, and said, after a few seconds, "The Policeman was here first, the lady called about an hour later. I hope there will be no trouble, we have a reputation to consider."

Easton moved me out of his way as he pushed up to reception. "Reputation? Really? I'd rather spend the night on some piss stained bench down by the Seine than here. Yeah, I'll post it on Trivago for you!"

The concierge smiled weakly and carefully walked backwards into the adjoining office. Easton was a silver-tongued devil at times, but I was too tired to lecture him on tourist etiquette and nodding to Anderson to follow, I strolled into the lounge, and sat down on the Chesterfield which formed the centre piece of the room's furniture. Anderson and Easton sat across from me and leaned forward expectantly. I started talking.

CHAPTER 8

Kyle's ubiquitous music swirled round the office, setting Wes' feet tapping, while Kyle himself silently mouthed the lyrics as he typed, transfixed to his PC screen. Other people seemed to have bigger distractions to help them though the day.

Herb Johnson was lovingly unwrapping his breakfast as Red walked unannounced, as usual, into his office. "Would you barge in on me on the john as well?" he said caustically.

Red guffawed, "Sorry, need to talk. You need to hear this." Herb glowered momentarily, but his mood lifted as he laid his hot savoury bagel out on his desk, complete with a side order of fries.

Red gawped askance. "Fries? You sure have some unusual morning tastes, boss. Fries for breakfast!?"

Herb didn't look up as he replied.

"Well, you good old boys eat that grits shit, don't you, so we're kinda even on the weird food thing, ain't we?"

Red grinned, but with no warmth.

"We're getting some razz from the cheese eaters about one of our subs, boss. Seems the Blackwatch boys have let things go some, that psycho limey is running around Paris racking up stiffs."

Johnson looked up, licked some errant ketchup from his fingers, and looked intently at Red. A square, muscular body was topped by a craggy, florid face, framed by his eponymous carrot-red hair. Herb spoke. "Red, you got all sorts of qualifications from two universities, and a business school, that right?" Red nodded in affirmation, unsure of where the conversation was going. Herb picked up a knife and carefully sliced through the bagel as he spoke. "So why, with all these letters after your name, do you still talk like some cracker pig farmer from Shit-ville Alabama? Razz? Cheese-eaters? Stiffs? Let's have it in English Red, American English."

Red shuffled his feet, his normal bravado wavering. "Got it," he murmured.

Herb sank his teeth into the bagel, chewing luxuriantly as he spoke again. "So, can you handle our Scotch boy, Red? Or do you want me to straighten his jar-head out?"

Red bristled "I can handle it, just thought you'd want in on the loop."

Herb took another bite. "Maybe Wes could help you out?" he said slyly.

Red snorted. "Wes? Yeah that'll be the day!" At that he turned and bustled out of the office, leaving Herb alone with his bagel.

Wes was sitting staring at his screen when Red's slipstream dislodged some papers from his desk. "Hey Red, where's the fire? Anything I can do?"

Red glanced at his junior colleague dismissively. "Yeah, you can pick up those papers, boy!" His reply stung Wes, and he fired back, "I'm not your boy, and quit riding me because Herb trod on your ass. I was asking if I could help!"

Kyle did not even deign to look up from his screen, shaking his head at such a pointless waste of energy, but he didn't escape Red's ire. "Turn that god-damn music down, Kyle. I can't concentrate with all that noise goin' on. Can't you wear headphones?" Kyle smiled guilelessly at his colleague and turned the volume control down. Anger somewhat vented, Red lifted his feet onto his desk as he picked up his phone and pressed the speed dial.

Wes glowered at his erstwhile colleague, and returned to scrutinising his screen. "Shit-kicker," he intoned noiselessly, as he thought dark thoughts. Wes was light years ahead of Red in IT expertise, but not as forthright about moving his career on. He glanced at Herb through the gap left by the almost-closed door. His boss was absolutely focused on demolishing the last of his morning bagel, and wouldn't have noticed an elephant sitting its butt on the edge of his desk. Wes grimaced; he had almost made it into the Service, and now he was a gofer for the CIA's version of Homer Simpson, and had to put up with Red's know-all Southern shit day after day. He stared at his other, bespectacled workmate's reflection in his PC screen. He didn't get Kyle, not at all. He was polite, helpful, diligent, and just plain ass-clenching boring. Wes fancifully imagined Kyle's body being driven by a tiny alien in his skull, like some MIB character...or maybe he was not human at all. Herb loved the guy, and all the big stuff was pretty much nailed between him and Red. "Time to boost your resume, make a move, make it happen Wes," he mouthed to his flickering reflection on his PC screen, deciding at the same time to listen intently to the conversation that Red was about to have.

Mitch was reading – an oft-revisited tome called "Jackboot," describing the history of the German soldier. He revelled in the tales of ascetic discipline and selflessness shown by German troops down through the two World wars. They were professional soldiers, highly motivated units who followed orders without demur, unlike the mass of conscript citizen soldiers of his own country and Britain. These guys, properly led, would have won both wars, he mused. USA's best were very good, and Britain's were even better, but these were small elite components, and the general standard of the rest was nowhere near them, with the Brits again being better, if reluctant, warriors. He turned a page, ready to immerse himself again when his phone buzzed shrilly. He saw that it was from Office 2. "That asshole Red had better follow procedure this time!" He intoned, to no-one in particular.

He put the receiver to his ear. "Black here, proceed," he said smoothly. His voice echoed back to him; god-damn-it, the stupid son-of-a-bitch was on speaker! He was just about to express his outrage at another blatant breach of protocol, when his head was filled with Red's nasal southern drawl.

"Look here Mr Bee-lack, seems that some of your guys are kicking up a storm in old Paree. The um, operators that you subbed the mark to have been causing all kinds of shit to hit numerous fans."

Mitch's rage dissipated as he digested what Red had related. "Unsure of your message, can you clarify, Red. Maybe use some more clichés?" he almost stuttered that.

Red came back instantly. "Clarify? Well, how does one unauthorised mark being completed, followed by some half-assed mobsters failing to complete another sound? Always happens when you use that pencil-necked Limey...you know, the guy you said you would never use again after the snafu in Sierra Leone? Your guy has taken out a high-profile research professor, a member of the Academie De Science, no less, and sent a posse of eastern European numb nuts after your last mark. They took it on in broad daylight in the middle of the city - hell, they could have sold it on pay per view, only they got smeared all over the sidewalk by the mark. Clear enough now?"

Mitch had drawn blood as he bit his top lip. He answered thickly, "I will review process urgently, and provide all relevant information when..."

Red cut across him, all pretence of formality gone now. "Whatever, but you need to pull this guy's neck in. We're getting real heat from the cheese-eaters about this. The last mark issued has now been rescinded, and you'll have to get that to the Limey. Looks like he's gone native on you. I'll leave it with you. Keep me posted, unless you want me to deal with it?"

Mitch started to reply, "Negative, I'll deal with it."

Red muttered something that Mitch didn't catch. "Say again, Red …" Then the call ended abruptly. The jerk had hung up! Mitch smashed the receiver down on his desk, splintering the case and sending shards of plastic across the desktop. He composed himself momentarily, and slowly and methodically pressed the internal line to Dan's office. "Mitch?" came the fraught reply. Mitch fought back his volcanic anger. "Dan, come in here now please."

Seconds passed, and the office door opened slowly, followed by a white-faced, tonsure- ruffling Dan. Mitch stood up slowly. "Sit down Dan, I need to speak to you." Dan pulled a chair towards him, keeping as far away from Mitch as he could, and sat down, cowed by Mitch's icy formality. Mitch closed the blinds and turned to face his, by now, quivering Ops Manager.

"Sierra Leone, last fall Dan - remember? Wasn't real good, was it? Your Limey ran around like a fucking bounty hunter taking out every mother he could, didn't he? He almost cost us our jobs, our fucking lives!" Mitch's voice was thunderous, filling the confines of the office. "I instructed you to cancel our partnership, and never to use him again, did I not?" Dan's eyes followed Mitch's circuits of the office helplessly. He nodded weakly. Mitch leaned across the desk and pushed his formidable chin to about 10 centimetres away from Dan's sweat-filmed brow. "So why the fuck is he now running round Paris like Colonel fucking Kurtz? He's killed a fucking professor, a member of the Academie De Science, and he's using hired street heavies- to cream off as much cash as he can for himself, no doubt. You think before you answer me, Dan. Your ass is on the line here!"

Dan's eyes fixed on the window. "I didn't sub him the job. He messed up in Africa, you told me not to and I didn't, but he's an educated guy, a Sandhurst man, and I think he's worth another shot Mitch."

Mitch rubbed his razzed temples furiously. "So because he's a good guy, and speaks like Daniel fucking Craig, you just thought you'd go against a direct instruction from your superior and give this fucking psycho another chance to screw up everything we've built here. This guy is a rogue operator - the kind that screws things up for every other PMC. The Czechs won't let him train his guys there, even most of the South Americans won't touch him!"

Dan retorted, "I didn't issue him this mark, Mitch, What do I have to do?" The stony set of Mitch's face did not move one iota. Dan gave up, clamped his mouth shut and waited passively for whatever was to come.

Mitch growled in a low voice, "I'm taking some time Dan. You mind the store… and you put a moratorium on any more of these contracts until I get back. Call our guys now, understand? I'll bust your Ranger's ass if there are any more foul-ups."

"Affirmative, Mitch." Dan was barely audible. Mitch glanced at his watch, took a long, lingering look at Dan's pale face, and swept out of the office.

Dan exhaled audibly, "Fucking jarheads; all the fucking same," he murmured as he picked up the phone.

CHAPTER 9

The rain spattered noisily on the bay windows of the hotel lounge. I sat listlessly trying to read a coffee stained-copy of Le Monde, silently cursing my bad French. Anderson and Easton hadn't appeared for breakfast, and I guessed that they were still sore at me and what I had told them. "Can't really blame them," I mused aloud, which garnered a curious look from a middle-aged woman sipping her café latte at the next table. I caught her eye, and she looked away hastily, froth perched on her upper lip like a cream moustache. The drab weather pretty much mirrored how things had been since I had told the boys what I knew. Maybe they felt that I had let them down, lied to them, I didn't know, because both of them had gone silent on me, which they knew I couldn't stand.

My efforts at reading the paper lost all momentum when I saw that it was from the previous day. I scrunched the broadsheet up in frustration and rammed it back into the magazine rack that I had taken it from - another bemused look from Ms. Cream Moustache. I looked at her directly and pulled my lips wide with my fingers, dangling my tongue as I did so. She immediately stood up, clattering her cup down on the table and hastily exiting the restaurant.

Mission accomplished, I pulled out my lap top, plugged it in to a power socket on the facing wall and waited for it to load up. A bulky, bearded man, maybe a Hasidic Jew, judging by the long side curls, moved past me and sat on the seat that Cream Moustache had vacated. Typical, I thought, can't get a quiet moment anywhere, I signed in and started browsing the web, looking for something to kill the time until my brothers appeared.

After a few minutes, I felt a tap on my shoulder. I turned quickly, I hated strangers touching me!

The bulky, bearded man spoke in a deep, curiously accented voice.

"Excuse me, is someone sitting here?" the accent was almost Ruritanian.

I answered curtly, "No buddy, same as the other 10 empty tables."

Seemingly undeterred, he asked again. "I can sit here then?"

I noticed he had large, kind looking, brown eyes. My black mood lifted a little - I could only be miserable for so long. I relented, "Okay pal, go ahead."

He smiled, and squeezed his ample frame into the chair. "Sank you berry much!" I suppressed the overwhelming urge to smile at this outrageous cod accent...who was this guy!?

Feeling strangely comfortable in this stranger's company, I carried on surfing as he typed furiously on an ancient laptop. I decided to have some coffee, and turned to look for one of the morning waiting team. My look was answered, after a minute or so, by a dishevelled, unshaven waiter, who mumbled incoherently to himself as he shuffled off to get my coffee. Personal hygiene was obviously not high on this guy's priorities. "Well, as long as he kept his fingers out of my coffee. I was jolted back into the present by the hirsute stranger abruptly standing up, folding his laptop as he did so. He inclined his head slightly. "Goodbye, Sank you again."

'I stood up, talking after him. "Hey, no sweat pal." I watched him walk out of the restaurant, taking in his slightly shambling gait. "What a guy," I reflected vaguely. I was momentarily struck by the way the guy moved; what the...? I was having another profound morning. I resolved to get back to surfing. I pulled my laptop close again. It took a few seconds for me to notice the silver data stick protruding from one of the USB ports. How did that get there? I was meticulous about all things IT, and didn't normally use data sticks; so it wasn't mine: the beard guy! I jumped out of my chair and moved quickly through the French windows facing on to the street. The sidewalks were now swarming with morning commuters, and my frantic scanning of the masses of pedestrians revealed nothing.

I returned to the restaurant and grabbed the soporific, unkempt waiter as he listlessly waited for some bread to drop from the grill. I spoke in my shaky French, "The big guy sitting next to me, where did he go? Did you see him?"

Two reddened eyes stared back at me, and I caught a whiff of his foetid breath as he replied. "No se" The Spanish threw me a little, and I repeated the question in the same language, to get the same, vacant reply. Shaking my head,

I cursed quietly, and went back to my seat, eyeing the data stick warily.

Anderson and Easton were walking slowly toward my table, both wearing their generic glum faces. "Hey Ho," I thought, seems I had already met the only person in the world that morning that wasn't pissed with me!

The brothers sat down silently, interspersing knowing mutual looks with reproachful glares in my direction. "Morning boys, sleep well?" I breezed.

Anderson growled a retort. "About as well as we could, wondering if we were about to be whacked in our sleep!"

Easton, his shirt collar askew, also chipped in. "Yeah Bailey, what you got for us today? Will it be a sniper, polonium in our coffee - or maybe an exploding croissant!?"

I sighed ruefully, and spoke in measured tones "Guys, we're in this now. I hate the fact that I put you in danger. Hate it that I can't tell you any more than I can, but hate most of all thinking that you don't trust me anymore!" Another look passed between my sombre brothers. Anderson spoke first. "Come on Bailey, of course we trust you….but maybe you could've looked into things some more, found out what was going on before you brought us here."

I held my arms wide in acceptance of what had been said, "Guys, I only knew what I knew, and I just needed you with me. I'd never do anything to hurt either of you. I looked out for you guys, I still look out for you, that's what I do."

Easton was trawling a spoon carefully around the contents of a sugar bowl, carefully heaping it up, and then flattening it in sequence. He talked without looking up from his task. "Bailey, you mean more to us than anything else on earth, but you need to stop looking out for us and accept that we're not in fifth grade anymore. We want to help, and we can look after ourselves."

I struggled to hold in my mounting emotion. "Sure you can," I said as I reached over and flattened Easton's errant shirt collar. "It's hard to let go, and I will try, but you'll always be my brothers." The memories of the years we spent growing up as a tight, mutually needy triad were still raw, even now.

We sat looking at each other, the air thick with feeling, no one willing to speak in case their reserve cracked. I swallowed hard, setting my jaw, determined not to blink away the moisture which filled my eyes.

Anderson matching my resolve, spoke softly. "You were there for us all through the years after Mom. I had no problem with that. You knew what to do, what to say, you kept us in line. We'll never forget that Bailey, but we can't handle whatever we're mixed up in now. We need to go to the authorities; talk to this Dumouriez guy."

Shit! I'd forgotten to reply to his message! This was going nowhere. I rapped the table, startling my siblings. "And tell them what? How can we tell them about Dad? We don't even know if he's dead or alive, hiding out somewhere, and what about the Professor? Where does that fit? He knew something, and the same people who killed him think that we know something as well. We're in danger, we've got to keep with this - no-one else can do what we can do."

The brothers sat without expression as I spoke, and that didn't change at the end of my rant. Anderson picked up a chocolate cookie and peeled off the foil wrapper. He started nibbling off the chocolate obsessively as he spoke. "How can we do this, Bailey? One or all of us will get hurt or worse. We have no idea who these people are, or why they're doing what they're doing." He flicked the now chocolate-less cookie into an ashtray, shaking his head.

I leaned towards the brothers. "We meet the girl tomorrow, and take it from there. She might be able to lead us to this Englishman, and then we ask him some questions. Things could change if we know why he's tried to take us out."

Easton stood up suddenly. "Okay, so we find this guy who's tried to have us killed, and ask him real politely why he did, and he'll tell us? Yeah, way to go, why not. We'll try that." I was about to bite on Easton's cynicism, but Anderson spoke before I could react.

"Alright, we'll meet her, but we don't leave the hotel today and we don't contact this Dumouriez guy unless she gives us something that the Police can follow up." I nodded in agreement, sighing inwardly with relief at the brothers' sudden acquiescence. It would be a long day, but we all needed some down time to think things through. We still just about together, however strained things had become.

I didn't really want go poking around or sightseeing in any case. We had some coffee and slipped into our normal conversational mode. The tension in me eased, so I left the brothers talking animatedly about their favourite Hulot movie and slipped upstairs on the pretext of needing a nap. I wanted to see what was on the silver data stick.

I set the load up in motion. Lights flickered and the quiet hum of the machine's fan floated round the room. Script began to unroll on my screen. 'What in God's name? It was an on-line copy of the Queen's Courier, a local New York newspaper: I read the lead story:

"POLICE WERE CALLED TO A HOUSE IN QUEEN'S YESTERDAY AT AROUND 4 O'CLOCK AFTER NEIGHBOURS REPORTED A DISTURBANCE AT THE APARTMENT IN LITTLE NECK. ACCESS TO THE PROPERTY HAD TO BE FORCED, AND THE BODY OF A MAN WAS FOUND IN THE KITCHEN. POLICE AND PARAMEDICS WERE CALLED, BUT THE MAN WAS FOUND TO BE DEAD AT THE SCENE. POLICE WOULD NOT GIVE OUT ANY INFORMATION OTHER THAN THE MAN'S AGE, WHICH WAS 48 YEARS. NEIGHBOURS SPECULATED THAT THE DEAD MAN'S NAME WAS TAYLOR WHEELAN, AN UNEMPLOYED JOURNALIST WHO HAD LIVED AT THE APARTMENT BLOCK FOR 8 MONTHS. THE CAUSE OF DEATH IS UNKNOWN AT THIS POINT. POLICE HAVE SET UP A CRIME SCENE CENTRE, AND ARE APPEALING FOR WITNESSES TO ANYTHING UNUSUAL TO COME FORWARD."

I sat stock-still, trying to rationalise what I was reading. I grappled with the wild thoughts that crashed into my head.

There was zero chance of that article being on my PC. It must have been on the data stick. Why did the Beard leave it with me? Did he know why we were in Paris? How could he know? I sat in my chair, stupefied. Wheelan dead? I checked the date of the story; the day after I had been pushed on to the track in New York. I shut down the PC and sat back in my seat. I should have been dead as well. What was going on?

I snatched the stick up and stuffed it down the side of a suitcase. I had to tell the brothers, but tell them what? I had pushed their belief in me to the limit over the last few days, but they needed to know. I slept fitfully that night; my head swarming with random fragments of situations, possibilities and outcomes. Easton always told me that I thought too much. God, if only he knew...

CHAPTER 10

The day was damp and grey, fitting the mood as we ambled, without enthusiasm, along the Quai De Montebello towards our meeting place on the Seine. The river looked brown and glutinous, and the smell of bad water clung to everything around it. Arriving at the park, Easton walked purposefully ten or twenty metres on, coming to a stop at two bollards joined by a chain, folding his arms as he looked back at us. Anderson stayed with me, sitting down alongside me on the edge of the monument, pulling out a copy of Le Monde and fussing with the flapping pages as the wind caught it.

Another meeting where I had no clue as to what my rendezvous looked like. I was still learning at this particular game, and I hoped that my lack of savvy was not going to prove terminal today. I glanced at my watch - we were early, so I craned my neck to get a glimpse of Anderson's paper as we waited, but rapidly got bored and started playing with my phone. I idly browsed through the functions, snapping on the Bluetooth screen. I noticed the usual clutch of available pairings, shaking my head at some of the lame device handles. One jumped out at me "168....168....the e-mail number! What the Hell!"

Now totally spooked I stuffed my phone into my coat pocket and concentrated on scanning the crowds of people passing by. Sure, someone was watching us... but who? The place was black with people. This meeting hadn't been a good idea, Anderson was right, we were out in the open now. I had been a fool. I looked over at Easton. We had to get out of here.

A blonde, well-built girl came strolling towards us in to the park carrying a takeaway coffee cup. I caught her blue eyes even from a distance, and also noted that she was wearing winter boots. A scarf fluttered from her neck, setting off her pleasant, open features. She paused briefly at the pedestrian crossing, and then only metres away from me she suddenly veered off towards Anderson.

Her voice was clear and crisp, "You're the actor, aren't you?" Anderson lifted his eyes from the paper and looked the girl over.

"Yes, I am the actor...and you are?"

"Hasar Tresfor, "she breathed, in a school-girl-ishly-smitten voice. "I saw you in that zombie film, you were very good. I want to act as well!"

Anderson coughed self-consciously; accepting plaudits were not his bag. "Playing a zombie doesn't really count as acting, kinda comes natural to me." He mumbled.

She laughed. "No, you were good! Believable, and I..."

"I'm Bailey" I interjected, "and the guy minding the store up there is Easton" flicking a look at my arms–akimbo, watchful brother. "You know Anderson, I see, so I'll take a rain check on further introductions. You came to tell us something?"

She shrugged, and sat down next to us, unwrapping her scarf and sipping her takeaway latte. "Three brothers, all called Marks, like those old film stars. That's funny!"

I was in a hurry. Yeah, we laugh about it all the time." My barely hidden sarcasm didn't faze her. She smiled, without reproach, then breathed dramatically, "You are all in danger."

I looked at Anderson and caught his wry twitch. "Hasar, we get that, we really do, but we need to hear what you know about this Englishman you heard talking to the heavies in the bar."

She looked mildly surprised that she had not revealed something extraordinary to us, but soon recovered her poise. Talking between sips of coffee, she spoke clearly and rapidly, "He is a PMC and uses the bar for meetings. I have seen him a few times, mostly with other men. He met some Estonian men recently, and that was when I heard that they were planning to hurt you - although I did not know it was you then."

Anderson looked at me inquiringly. "PMC?" I knew what she meant.

"Private military contractor," I answered.

She nodded in agreement. "Yes, he is an ex-British paratroops soldier, he always wears the tie."

I needed to move this on. "So what was he talking to the Estonians about?" She, at last, finished the coffee and placed the cup on the ground. "I know that he paid them 21,000 Euros to deal with you, in advance."

When you split it between the seven pit bulls... Anderson was quick to come to the same conclusion. "Three grand each - is that how much we are worth?" he snorted.

Hasar spoke again. "His instructions were to kill you, and hurt the other two badly, and to make it look like a random street fight - he repeated that a few times."

I felt a spasm of something travel up from my boots and through my stomach, I fumbled for some sense in what she was saying, but before I could speak again, she continued, in a low voice. "They have already killed someone, they pushed him onto the subway. They were laughing when they were telling the Englishman."

Anderson looked at me, appalled. So they had murdered the professor, there could be little doubt about it.

I swallowed the lump that had lodged in my throat, speaking slowly "Hasar, you will be in danger now too. These people tried to kill me in New York, the same method that they used here – the subway. They seem to know a lot, and I think that they will know that you have met us. Would you tell this to the Police?"

She tossed her hair back and said emphatically, "No, I would not. I am leaving Paris today to go to London. I have friends there. I want to get into acting." She looked at Anderson, "Perhaps you could speak to some people for me?"

I shook my head despairingly. This girl had no sense of danger. Anderson cleared his throat. "I don't know many people in London, but I suppose..."

I cut him off. "Hasar, it's not quid pro quo here. We appreciate what you have given us, but you need to tell us anything else that you know. We need to get to this Englishman."

The girl's eyes widened as I spoke. Her voice lost some of its assurance. "I am sorry. I should not have asked. I thought that you could help me."

"We can help you get out of Paris." I said it without really knowing how that could happen. She talked as she prepared a roll-up cigarette. "Well, there is something else you should know. They talked about your father."

Anderson and I had been looking at Easton, and her remark snapped our focus back to her. "Are you sure, are you sure you heard that?" I had unconsciously grabbed her hand as I spoke.

She pulled her hand away. "Of course I did, maybe you patronise me again!"

I felt a surge of doubt, don't want to piss her off now. I lowered my voice. "Sorry, I'm not. We haven't seen our father for a while, so please, tell us what they said."

She finished rolling her cigarette, and I waited frustrated, as she took three or four attempts to light it with an ancient disposable lighter. She drew a long pull, and exhaled deeply. I was now seething. "Hasar, please..." She flicked her hair back, pulling an errant piece of tobacco from her teeth as she did so.

"The Englishman looked after your father, or he said something like that."

She paused. I was frantic now. "Looked after my father!" What did that mean? I was anxious not to spook her. "And, what else Hasar?" Then I heard Easton's voice, and caught his movement on the edge of my peripheral vision. I turned to look at the girl and saw a small round hole appear in her throat, followed seconds later by a barely audible noise like a muffled drumbeat.

Anderson, moving in seeming slow motion, started to stand up as Hasar's hands went to her throat, pulling her shirt open as blood began to flow from the open wound. He grabbed the girl as she lurched to her feet, her attempts at speech being stopped by blood gurgling into her vocal chords.

Easton flashed past me, his eyes bulging. His right index finger pointed at an outhouse to our left. I turned to look in that direction, my legs still paralysed by what had just happened, and saw a man in a suit, about 15 metres away, pointing a gun at me. Movement returned to my legs, and I sprang up and ran towards him. Dad had always told us – run away from anyone with a gun, but instinct had taken over, and I knew that Easton was in front of me.

The man cocked his head. He was going to fire… "Easton, get down!" I bellowed. Easton turned to look at me, and then seemed to be swatted over by a giant invisible hand. "Easton, you okay? Easton!" I gasped, and sprinted to where my brother had crashed to the ground. Blood streaked his blonde mane, and his hand was splotched with crimson as he ran it around his head.

He was talking. "I'm okay man, you get him! I'm okay," He pushed my hand away as he spoke. "The girl, how's the girl?" I tried to co-ordinate my out-of-control senses, and glanced back to the monument where we had been sitting.

Anderson was on his knees, holding Hasar's prostrate body across his legs. He looked up, shaking his head as he did. "She's gone Bailey."

I looked back to see the gunman still standing there, apparently unconcerned that many people were looking at him, imprinting his sallow features on their brains. No fear, no panic. Jesus what sort of guy was this!? I stood up slowly, and started to walk towards the smirking killer. I saw that the gun was a Beretta, fitted with a silencer, and that he was pointing it straight at me. I carried on walking, adrenalin blotting out fear and common sense, oblivious to the shouts and screams of the scattering crowds. He was going to kill me, and I was walking straight towards him. I heard at last the seemingly-muffled, but recognisable, shouts of warning from my brothers.

The gunman laughed out loud, and pulled the trigger. I froze. Nothing happened. The gunman's face contorted as he wrestled with the cocking mechanism. He turned and ran down the slope to the walkway that ran along the river, and I, taking a deep gulp of oxygen, sprinted after him. Anderson's voice penetrated my bubble of madness. I looked back to see Easton sitting on the sidewalk, with Anderson holding his shoulders. He was waving me back, but there was no chance of me going back now, and I turned and resumed my pursuit. The gunman had an untidy stride, and I gained on him by the second. He looked back constantly, his previous arrogance seemingly gone, still grappling with the cocking mechanism as he tried to put distance between us.

Shocked pedestrians and street artists recoiled as we surged past, knocking over tables and signs as we went, unaware of the shouts and insults of outraged waiters and impervious to the douches of foamy cappuccino as takeaway cups flew onto the pavement. Police sirens sounded in the distance as we reached the underpass at the Pont de L'Archeveche. The crowds had thinned to zero, and I was alone with Hasar's killer. He pulled up, wrenched at his gun again, and smiled grimly as he pointed it once again at my rapidly approaching body. I suddenly realised that I was going to die that grey afternoon on the Seine, and as my legs lost all traction the distance between us narrowed to barely 20 metres.

An instant sweat soaked my shirt and dripped down from my temples, filming my glasses as it did. Idiotically, I took them off, but I could still see my man clearly now, a dark, stubbled face framed by cropped black hair, two brown eyes burning malevolently into mine down the barrel of his gun. I put my hands up instinctively - Dad would be pissed at my sheer stupidity, my brothers would never see me alive again. I thought fleetingly of mum…of Hasar…and that I had no real idea as to why I was going to die.

He spoke in a heavily accented English. "Stay there boy, you are next!"

I felt all fear dissipate. "Why are you going to kill me? What have I done? What do I know that is so important?" I was scrambling for reason and, after all, this was my last moments alive.

He smiled thinly. "It does not matter to me, and it will not matter to you. Time to die!"

I saw him raise the gun, and vowed not to blink. Just then, a tall, athletic man with cropped greying hair and a prominent jaw emerged from an opening behind the gunman, and tapped him on the shoulder. The killer turned jerkily, unable to react as the stranger clamped his left hand on the gun, and coiled his right arm round his assailant's neck. In one clean movement, the stranger's knee came up into the small of the gunman's back at the same time as the right arm wrenched his neck back. A dry snapping noise broke the silence, and the gunman's eyes bulged as his body slid down the leg of his attacker to the ground.

Stunned by what was unfolding, I was planted to the spot as the stranger took the gun from a lifeless hand and emptied the magazine, the cartridges bouncing randomly across the paved walkway. He then reached a gloved hand into the lifeless man's jacket and pulled out a leather wallet. I watched, spellbound, as he pulled some cards from it and stashed them in his lapel pocket before throwing it onto the chest of the man he had just killed.

The stranger stared at me - now what? He spoke. He was American. "Get going. Get back to your brothers and get out of Paris. These guys will try again, and you have the cops all over your ass as well. Don't waste anymore time. You could have been killed - chasing a man with a gun is stupid, suicidal. I'm sure your Dad would've told you that!"

I was astonished. "You knew my Dad? Who are you? How do you know my Dad? And how did you happen to be here?"

He grinned. "Way too many questions. All you need to know is that my name is Mitch, and I'm on your side. You and your brothers need as much help as you can get. Take this." He lobbed a cell phone towards me, which I caught in shaky, twitching hands. "I'll get to you through that. These guys are tracking your own mobile, take the battery out and lose it-now!"

He turned away. I suddenly realised that I had seen him before - I shouted after him, "Hey, you were at my Mum's funeral, weren't you?"

He paused, looked back at me, and nodded his head. "Yep, I was there." He looked at me for a few seconds, and then spoke softly. "I'll get back to you soon, now get out of here." He gestured with his hand, and then strode off, leaving me to deal with the enormity of everything that had just happened, spiced with another tantalising fragment of truth.

My reverie was destroyed by the sound of a voice screaming from above me. I stared up, befuddled, barely registering that it was Anderson. "Bailey, get up here, we have a car, come on..."!

I felt as though I sleepwalked up the steps, following Anderson's beckoning arms towards a white Audi A6 sitting at the roadside. A dark haired female called to me from the driver's seat. "Get in! Hurry!" I caught sight of a bloodied, but alive, Easton lying across the back seats. I suddenly realised that the woman was Jeanne Salas - the dead professor's assistant who we met on that day at the Etoile. How did she get involved in this? She called again, this time echoed by Easton leaning out of the back window.

"Bailey, wake the fuck up and get in. Come on." Anderson pushed me through the open car door, to land next to Easton, who was pressing a wad of tissues against his still-bleeding head.

"You okay?" I asked urgently.

He nodded energetically. "Yeah, I always leak like a stuck pig from my head, but he only clipped me - I'm okay man."

I clasped Anderson's shoulder, "Hasar, where is she?"

Anderson looked me in the mirror and said flatly. "Not good news, Bailey, we couldn't do anything!"

My mind was at once destroyed by a sudden anger. "What? You just fucking left her there? For fuck's sake, why did you do that?"

My grip on Anderson's shoulder had scrunched his shirt into a ball. He thrust my hand away angrily. "She was dead. The cops were everywhere. We had to go. How would we explain this one, Bailey? Another murder?"

Easton spoke urgently, although he was in pain. "Jeanne called me about five minutes before Hasar was killed. She's been trying to reach us. I told her where we were. She pulled up just before the cops turned up. We had to go Bailey, the girl was dead. It's fucking awful man, but we had to leave her!"

I put my head in my hands in abject grief. Anderson turned and grabbed my hair, pulling my head up. "Bailey, we need you. Come on! Jeanne has something for us."

She had remained silent during our conversation, but now talked rapidly as we turned over the bridge and cruised through the damp streets. "I called you because I think I know someone who can tell us why Professor Favreau was killed, and perhaps also why people are trying to kill you." Her dark eyes looked at me earnestly via the mirror.

I looked at Easton, who nodded reassuringly. My voice was croaky. "Go on, tell us, and hopefully you won't land up the same as Hasar for telling us."

Anderson glanced back at me reprovingly. Jeanne spoke, "The Professor was working with a Professor De Vico from Rome on a paper that was going to expose dangerous drug testng by a major international drugs company. He had evidence that carcinogenic drugs were being released on the market even after some tests on volunteers were stopped because of the side effects. We believe that at least four fatalities have been covered up."

My scrambled mind cleared rapidly - Big Pharma, Taylor Wheelan.

She continued, "I think the Professor was killed by people who do not want this information made public, and from what Easton has told me I think the same people are now trying to kill you, and maybe killed that poor girl today because they thought she was working with you."

I was in shock, and needed time to come out of it. I offered no comment, sinking back into the seat, resting my head on Easton's bloodied shoulder.

Anderson broke the silence. "Drive, let's get out of Paris. We'll talk when we put some distance between it and us. How did you take that guy down Bailey? He looked... dead."

· God Almighty, I hadn't told them! "I didn't; a guy came out of the shadows and took him out before he could shoot me."

"What? Who was he?" blurted Anderson, astonished.

Easton, as usual, jumped in before I could speak, "Some dude comes out of nowhere and takes him out? Tell us Bailey, and no bullshit!"

"Let me speak you guys, for Chris-sakes!" I exploded. Silence broke out. "He knew our Dad. He was at Mum's funeral, I recognised him. He knows people are after us, and he gave me a phone to keep in touch, and he says he's on our side." I ran out of breath as I finished and my words tailed off wheezily.

Anderson vented his anger. "Son-of-a-bitch! Drive Jeanne, get us out of here!" Easton touched Jeanne lightly on the shoulder to underpin what he had said, and the car accelerated smoothly onto the Quai de la Corse. I closed my eyes. The rhythmic swaying of the car and barely audible French voices on the car radio were numbly comforting, and I almost fell asleep. If only; maybe it would all be a dream; maybe.

CHAPTER 11

Mitch had strolled the kilometre or so back to his hired BMW after his encounter with the gunman, and sat there passively observing the frantic events catalysed by the recent shooting. He stayed put for an hour or so, and then drove the short distance to Rue Des Ecoles. He parked up, flicked the handbrake on and undid his seat belt. Pulling the cards he had taken from the dead man's wallet, he locked the car doors internally and began scrutinising them. "Radu Munteanu, Hmm, probably Romanian." The next card was red cardboard, with white lettering, and a crescent moon of the same colour. "The Domebache Club, Mall of Berlin, Potsdamer Platz, Berlin." There was a mobile number scrawled on the reverse. He flicked onto his car-phone function, and typed the number in. He paused as a Police car crawled past, and then pressed the green call icon on his dash. The dialling tone tolled sonorously round the car interior. Then it stopped, and a clipped, impossibly English voice came through the speakers.

"Why Mitch, the Mean Marine! How kind of you to call me - I thought I was persona non-grata after our little contretemps last year! This is a pleasure!"

Mitch's jaw muscles rippled involuntarily - the Limey! He composed himself, modulating his voice as he spoke. "Ex-Captain Fenwick, late of 2 Para. You've changed your number. Understandable after your exploits in Sierra Leone, but kinda nice to know you kept mine. How's business?"

A pause - then the voice wafted through the speakers again. "Good, Major McKenzie, very good. I have some new friends now who seem to have stronger stomachs than your Langley Farm boys, Business, pardon the pun, is booming!"

Mitch sighed. Americans had problems with British humour - if it could be called that. He decided to go in low and heavy. "I ran in to one of your guys in Paris today, interesting meeting."

Another pause - the uncertainty oozed down the line. "Really? And how would you know it was one of my people Major?"

Mitch grinned. "Well, let me see, maybe it was the way he was running round in broad daylight shooting at people in front of hundreds of witnesses, or the fact that he was Romanian, or the fact that I was able to take him down without creasing my suit."

The clipped tones wavered a little. "I see. So you took him out did you? How very American of you Major, another notch in your little belt of righteousness for you to convince yourself that you're different from all us other hired killers."

Mitch felt the venom in his voice. "You were called off your last mark, Fenwick, and you pushed it through. You've taken out a professor and you've murdered an innocent girl. You're out of control. I'm calling you in, and Dan won't help you."

Fenwick laughed thinly. "Not up to you, Major. As I said, I've got new friends now, and they don't care to be lectured on morals by washed-up Gulf vets like you. I'm annoyed at you Mitch. Radu had promise, and he has a brother who won't be very happy with you, but don't waste time on Dan, he's not involved. Far too loyal to you, typical no-initiative American. Anyway, I need to go. Pressure of work and all that."

Mitch's tone hardened. "I'm telling you to come in, Fenwick. Come in now."

Fenwick's snarl matched Mitch's. "Listen, you're not in this game, and you have no hold over me. Understand?"

Mitch stared at the dashboard as he answered. "Then I'm coming after you, and none of your half- assed, bargain basement heavies will save you."

There was hesitation, but the voice remained defiant. "I welcome the chase; goodbye." The phone clicked off.

Mitch pounded the steering wheel impotently. The Englishman was not intimidated, and he realised he would have to take him out, or be taken out. He rammed the car into drive and careered away from the kerb, urgent now in his purpose.

CHAPTER 12

Herb sat languidly flicking through a realtor's survey of Long Island properties, clucking happily at what each new page revealed. "That one's mighty expensive," he thought, but no matter, he would be there with the rest of the rich folks soon enough. Just a few more months, just a few more...

His idyll was fractured by Red's braying voice. "Boss, got to talk to you. We've had another killing in Paris that we think is linked to the others."

Herb stood up, pulling his voluminous pants high around his waist. "What you talking about? Who the fuck is authorising these? Was it the Englishman again?" he growled.

Red nodded once, his normal bluster missing. "We think so boss. This time a young, female student was taken down in broad daylight. She was Estonian, and was with the Marks boy and his brothers when she was killed. Looks as though they killed the guy who did it. He was found dead about a mile and a half away, with a broken back and neck."

Herb stared through his thick spectacles. "These boys can handle themselves, can't they? Got anything on him, name, whatever?"

Red flicked to a screen on his PC. "He's a Romanian, worked for the Englishman for a long spell. Don't see him getting his severance pay any time soon."

Herb ignored the lame attempt at humour. "Where's the Scotchman? Why didn't he pull the plug on the mark? You did tell him to, didn't you?"

Red was agitated now. "I did, as soon as you told me to. He's on leave, I can't raise him."

Herb leaned on his desk, glowering. "Leave? No such thing in our business, Red. These dumbass razz-heads should be available at all times, part of the deal. Now go find him, and find out what is going on, and make sure you hold any further payments to Blackwatch until you do."

Red nodded once, and practically ran out of the office. Herb waited till he was alone and then clapped his pudgy hands to his head. "Jesus, these fucking cowboys are going to burn my ass!" He waddled through the office door and made straight for Kyle's desk. The comings and goings had roused a soporific Wes. What was going on? He quickly pulled a pile of papers together and made straight for Herb.

"Could you sign these, boss, just routine stuff?"

Herb waved him away. "Put 'em on my desk, I'm busy here."

Wes smirked as he turned away and entered Herb's office. He placed the papers on the desk top and tip-toed around the table, watching Herb intently through the partially-open door. The jerk had left his PC on sleep. Wes sensed an opportunity. A flutter of panic pulsed through his body as Herb got up and walked towards the office, but soon subsided as he realised he was only getting another chair to place next to Kyle's. Breathing deeply, he tapped the return button, lighting up the screen. "Right," he thought, "let's go." He clicked on the top icon. "Properties in Long Island" flickered onto the screen. "Asshole!" he thought, moving on to the next. He skimmed through five or six innocuous spreadsheets, hardly daring to glimpse occasionally at Herb, who was by now totally absorbed in his work with Kyle.

Wes continued to plough through the rows of icons, not really knowing what he was looking for. He spotted an icon that was a jpeg of what looked like a beach house. "What the hell was that?" Wes clicked on it and watched as the screen filled with what looked like a bank statement Wes, puzzled, noticed that all the pay-ins were odd amounts, all under $100. He scrolled back. "Holy Shit!" there were pages and pages. He hit the last hyperlink, and the screen went to the final page. Wes sucked in his breath as he read the final line - $335,617. "Wow." he whispered to his reflection in the monitor. "Funee-monnee..." He scrolled back, and panned across the page to check who was paying in, just about every PMC they were dealing with was listed - what was going on?

He peered at the pulsing screen. These were lists of payments to PMC's, but all the original amounts had been rounded down to the nearest 100. He had seen this before when he worked in banks: the son-of-a-bitch was skimming.

Wes worked feverishly, sending the screen to his e-mail, and then wiping all traces of the message. This was huge. Wes could not take in what he had found. This was his chance. The sound of a chair scraping back jolted him back to the now, and he quickly grabbed the pile of papers that he had brought in, and stood nonchalantly stroking his chin as a choleric Herb stomped back into his office.

"You ain't been here waiting for me all this time, have you? I can sign those anytime. Now go and help Kyle with what I've given him!"

Wes sighed resignedly. "No, Mr Johnson. I just brought some more in - missed them on the first trip."

Herb didn't hear any of what Wes had said, and pushed himself angrily into his chair, mumbling expletives to himself.

Wes looked contemptuously at his blustering boss as he walked to Kyle's desk, intoning quietly to himself "Asshole, you got some explaining to do!"

Kyle spoke quizzically. "What's that Wes? Didn't get that buddy?"

"Nothing man. Just saying Herb's got some work to do," he replied airily. "So what you got for me Kyle? Herb says you need a hand!"

Kyle pulled the empty chair back and beckoned Wes to sit down. "Gotta put some of these PMC guys in their place buddy. Let's go!"

CHAPTER 13

Jeanne had taken us by a circuitous route to her neat apartment in Montparnasse. My brothers sat squashed uncomfortably on her two-seater couch as she dispensed coffee and water, occasionally dabbing at the pink weal on Easton's head with a cloth soaked in antiseptic. I stared out of the window, expecting Police cars, or worse, to arrive at any time. The trauma of Hasar's killing still gripped our psyches, and conversation was hushed and halting. I was anxious to see that Easton was okay. The bullet had scored a deep track from the side of his forehead to his ear, but injured though he was, he was obviously alert and lucid, rebuffing my questions with curt, monosyllabic answers.

Anderson had sponged Hasar's blood from his hands as soon as he had reached the house, but was still feverishly rubbing them together as he sat staring at some vague spot on the facing wall. I tried to keep a hold on my shredded nerves, having faced death yet again, but my outward calm was not fooling Jeanne.

"Bailey, you must try to relax. We need to decide what we do now. What's happened cannot be changed."

Her earnest, soft voice was soothing, and I managed to get some focus. "You are in danger by simply being with us Jeanne. Two people have died for the same reason, and I can't protect you. We need to go on alone. You don't need to be in this."

She reddened, and barked back. "The professor was a good friend, and I am not going to walk away from his murder, because he *was* murdered, and probably by the same people who are trying to kill you! Now I will go on alone. You won't stop me, but we can help each other."

Easton looked up, his milk-white face accentuating the garish gouge on his head. "We need to help Jeanne, Bailey. She might lead us to what is going on here, and we're not doing real well on our own, are we?"

Anderson chimed in. "She's right. The one thing we can't do is to walk away now. Whoever they are will come after us anyway... and Jeanne is probably already on their list."

I knew that this was probably true. "This guy gave me a phone and said he would contact me on it. He wants to help us. He and Dad probably worked together. Question is, should we trust him?"

Easton looked at me blankly "Why can't you call him? Call him now? Why have we got to wait?"

Frustration rose in me. "Because I haven't got his number. The directory is empty. The guy's obviously a professional, the way he took the gunman down, the way he spoke...."

Jeanne interjected. "The police will find us soon, that's for sure. They will work out that we are together and come for us. We must move now!"

I groaned as I remembered the message from Lieutenant Dumouriez. They would have been to the hotel by now, asking questions of our cheerful concierge. Jeanne was right, they would find us soon. I had barely begun to think of how to deal with Dumouriez when a strange ringing filled the room. A phone. I didn't recognise the tone - why was everyone looking at me? It was the phone that the stranger had given me at the riverside! I fumbled clumsily in my pocket, almost dropping it as I eventually clawed it out of my coat. I peered at the unfamiliar keyboard, pressing the green phone icon hesitantly. I held the device to my ear, and stupidly said "Hi, Bailey here."

A clipped, disdainful voice barked down the line, "Why don't you tell me where you are as well?"

I cursed my gaffe, and tried to sound in control. "Well, I knew it was you."

A guffaw was followed by a curt question. "And who am I exactly?"

I glanced quickly at Jeanne and the brothers, shrugging hopelessly as I answered. "Mitch? Okay. I have no idea, but thanks for saving my life."

The tone was softer as he spoke again. "It is Mitch. I need to see you. Where are you?"

Easton was drawing his hand across his this throat while shaking his head forcefully.

I spoke quickly. "Flat 3, 40 Rue Liancourt. It's in Montparnasse,"

"I know where you are, be there in 10." The phone went dead.

Easton stood up, hands on his head, "You've just told him where we are. He could be anyone!"
"He saved my life Easton, he wants to help us."

Jeanne was unimpressed. "I hope so. He might be coming to my house to kill us all." I grimaced awkwardly.

Anderson, still rubbing his hands together spoke without looking up. "To paraphrase, Bailey, sometimes you're not too bright!"

I leaned back against the wall, arms folded defensively, hoping I had made the right call. The safe world of IT seemed far away and I yearned for its certainty and predictability.

Half a world away, Cal's IT world was about to change irrevocably.

CHAPTER 14

The morning had passed slowly. Wes fretted as he waited for Herb and Red to go out to their regular Tuesday lunch. He sat and listened as they exchanged testosterone-fuelled sound bites, punctuating the punch lines with hoots of forced braying laughter. Kyle looked over knowingly, flicking his eyebrows as he walked past on the way out. "Not joining us for lunch, good buddy?"

Wes smoothed his hand over his mouth as he answered. "No, I'm not done here. Got some work to wrap up."

Herb appeared, pulling on an ancient raincoat, followed by Red, grinning as usual in that infuriating, smug way that so riled Wes. "Work to wrap up? This boy's a machine, Red. He's working on a promotion or maybe a raise!" snorted Herb, thumping Red's shoulder to get his attention.

Red's eyes narrowed and speared down his nose contemptuously. "Reckon we'll have to let the youngster do some bigger jobs now he's got to grips with the simple stuff." Wes looked at Red and forced a bored yawn, simultaneously delivering the finger from under his desk. The honking, forced laughter faded as Herb and the others moved off down the corridor, disappearing totally as the outer door closed.

Wes breathed deeply, and pulled his keyboard close. His finger pressed the "Off" switch on Kyle's music player. "No noise. Sorry Kyle, but your sounds are too retro for me dude!" Enjoying the silence, he typed rapidly, pausing occasionally to listen for any warning of people coming back into the building. He finished the message, and then input the security address he had found. He looked at the screen, hands clasped, for some seconds. This was it. This would get him out of this goddamn crappy job, and this would finish that tub of lard's career. His cursor hovered over the "send" icon as he deliberated. Sucking in a mouthful of air, he clicked it, and the message went. 'God Bless America,' he intoned and then erased all trace of his message. All done. He had no idea what would happen now.

CHAPTER 15

We all jumped as the buzzer sounded on the intercom. Jeanne answered. "Hello, who is it?" The intake of breath was clearly audible, followed by a curt American voice.

"Let me in. Introductions later."

I nodded to Jeanne, and she pressed the door release. She walked to the apartment door and opened it slowly. The tall figure of my rescuer from the river bank stood silhouetted against the light.

"Mitch?" I said tentatively. He nodded, and walked into the already crowded room, where Jeanne gestured to him to sit. He eyed the tiny couch, already groaning under the combined weight of myself and my brothers, shook his head dismissively, and stood facing us, arms folded.

His eyes ran round the room, scanning the brothers and lingering a little longer on Jeanne. He spoke to Anderson and Easton. "You must be Bailey's brothers."

Easton snorted loudly. "Hey, good spot. You sure picked that one out!"

Mitch lowered his jutting jaw and stared straight at Easton. "I remember you all from your Mom's funeral, although your two brothers seem to have grown up some since then. What happened to your head?"

Easton's cheeks had flushed ominously. "I got shot," he mumbled hesitantly.

Mitch tutted. "Yeah, going after a man with a gun with nothing but your pecker in your pants - smart move, almost as smart as your brother was before I saved his butt."

Easton suddenly stood up. His mind wrecked by a sudden squall of anger at this mysterious interloper. "That right? Well, who the fuck are you? What were you doing down at the river anyhow? How do we know you weren't after us?"

I tried to calm my brother down, but he was already neck deep in rage.

Mitch looked at me intently. "You're Harpo. Think that's what your Dad tagged you. Dumb in the head as well as in speech."

I swallowed hard. "Don't think you should have said that," I whispered, and at that, my brother launched himself across the room at the perplexed American. What happened next took seconds, as an explosion of violence filled the tight confines of Jeanne's apartment. Easton had left the ground like some human missile, and he seemed sure to plant his foot squarely in Mitch's chest. The American's arms unfolded and swept down in one fluid movement, smashing down the kick, and tipping an astonished Easton's body forward. Mitch swivelled at lightning speed, grasping Easton's head in both hands and yanking it downwards. I watched, startled, as my brother executed a parabola and smashed down on the slatted coffee table in front of the couch.

Easton's head hit the wooden floor with a dull thud, breath whooshing out of his lungs as his back and shoulders then landed on the floor. The noise was thunderous, amplified by the close confines of the room. I couldn't stop Anderson either as he leapt at Mitch, arms wind-milling rapidly. Mitch blocked Anderson's frantic attack with strong arms, and then brought his knee up to smash into Anderson's stomach. My brother shot a stricken look at me as he crumpled down on top of the gasping Easton, and then vomited copiously over the floor.

Mitch stepped back and turned his eyes on me, adopting a defensive stance. I held up my hands, knowing that any move I made would simply add to the pile of broken bodies on the floor.

Jeanne shouted suddenly, "Stop. Stop it now! Enough!"

Mitch straightened up, fixing his tie as he did so. This guy was good. My brothers could handle themselves, and he had slapped them down without unbuttoning his coat.

Jeanne pushed her way past Mitch to help the prostrate brothers, spitting angry words as she did. "Get out of my way, salaud! What are you? You want to help us? Maybe now you want to destroy my kitchen?"

Mitch stepped over the shattered coffee table, hands rubbing his cropped temples as he did. He stood in front of the small electric fire that was the centrepiece of the room and spoke slowly and deliberately. "You are all lucky to be alive, especially you Bailey. Any self-respecting contractor would have finished you off in New York. Someone high up in our Government wants you, and probably now your brothers, dead. Fortunately for you, they gave the job to people who weren't up to it."

I looked askance at my two brothers and Jeanne. "The American government wants us dead? Why? What have we done?"

Mitch pursed his lips. "I'm not sure. They passed the contracts to terminate you to us first, but I recognised the name, and challenged them."

Easton, by now sitting up, fired back. "To you? What does that mean? You kill people for cash?"

The arms folded again, defensively. "I run a business which carries out contracts for various government agencies, and we do occasionally terminate people. Usually people who need to be terminated in the interests of national security."

"Assassin!" erupted out of Jeanne, "A paid assassin. Did you kill Professor Favreau?"

Mitch rocked on his heels uncomfortably, chastened by the venom in her words. "We're not murderers. We act in the National interest." His voice wavered. Jeanne, Anderson and Easton began to fire questions and accusations, their voices becoming louder and more strident as they spoke. I had to stop this. I bellowed as loudly as I could "Guys, he saved my fucking life. I would be dead otherwise. Let him talk!"

The subsequent silence lasted only seconds, broken by Mitch's subdued voice, speaking as he stood imposingly at the front of the room. He gestured apologetically at the splintered wood of the table.

"Sorry Mam, I didn't mean to wreck your apartment."
Jeanne glowered at him and said nothing. Easton had managed to pull himself to his feet, but any thoughts of exacting revenge on the tall American had been put aside. He knew that this middle-aged man was a fearsome opponent and contented himself with helping a dazed Anderson to the couch. Not a normal scenario for my bad-ass brothers, I mused.

I decided to be direct. "You worked with my father?"

He nodded cautiously, and then, surprisingly, enlarged on this affirmation. "Your Dad was with me in Iraq and Afghanistan. I suppose I worked for him at the time. He was with the agency. I was just a Marine captain. He picked me out to join a team to work up country. We did a lot of good things together."

"Like killing Afghan peasants, no doubt!" erupted out of Jeanne.

Mitch looked at her curiously. My time in France had taught me that French people in general were not known for their love of all things American.

"Ever been to Afghanistan, mam? Ever seen how women were treated by the Taliban? Ever been to a village where all the men had been executed for…?"

Jeanne flapped her hands in front of her face, shaking her head. "No, of course not, but you can't replace one gang of murderers with another and justify it because they're not Muslims!"

Mitch's eyes narrowed and he started running his hands rhythmically over the short hair at his ears. "Mam, I had to swallow a lot of crap when I was in the service, listening to uninformed, card carrying-liberals calling me and my country down, and dripping their crocodile tears all over the graves of thousands of dead Americans …and Brits….and it would have been worse if we'd done nothing. What's done is done. The Afghan people have to die for their country now, and stop blaming others for the shit it's in. If they want the Taliban back, it's up to them. If they want to keep what they've got, it's up to them. I 'm happy that no more Americans will die to keep them free. We did what we had to, and people like you simply have no idea - with respect."

Jeanne's neck had reddened deeply, her dark eyes were filmed with moisture, but she remained silent, clasping her hands tightly together as she sat.

I broke the silence again "So when was the last time you worked with Dad?"

Mitch's posture loosened somewhat, and he coughed softly before he answered. "About a year before your mother died. He told me he was getting out to spend some time with his family, with you. Guess it didn't work out."

"You heard about the plane crash, didn't you? Have you any idea what he was working on then?"

Mitch's eyes flickered, and he avoided my gaze as he answered. "No, not specifically, but I do know that the plane going down was no accident." He seemed to be shocked by what he had just said and he quickly glanced at all of us in sequence to gauge our reaction.

I looked at my brothers, and back to Mitch. "So it was taken down - who by, and why?" I tried to control my shaky voice.

He walked over to the tiny apartment window, and prised the blinds apart with his fingers. "Your Dad was working on something with the FDA, and he was obviously getting close to something."

Anderson spoke for the first time since the fight. "These drug cartels have power, but surely they couldn't take out an American government official... in America?"

Mitch scratched his prominent jaw. "You're right, but your Dad... it wasn't that sort of drugs bust he was working on. He was investigating some major corporations."

"Drug companies?" I blurted, "Big drug companies?"
Mitch nodded. "One of them, that's certain. Look, we were asked to do some work for a government department, and the work had been authorised at a high level. I tried to

stall it, but the work was passed on to another PMC. People have already been killed: the Professor, the girl...."

"And the journalist whose article lead us here. Guy called Taylor Wheelan," I interjected.

Mitch paused, his brow creased. "Really? Didn't know that one - Taylor Wheelan. He was a War co in Iraq; embedded with your Dad's unit - your Dad saved his life at Falluja. They kept in touch after the War, and he's dead?"

"Maybe he was working with my Dad, putting out what Dad was turning up?" I ventured.

"I only had one meeting with him, but he obviously knew more than what was in the article he gave me."

Mitch was almost dismissive. "Look, whatever happened to Taylor Wheelan was probably just part of the chain here. There have been two attempts on your life. Someone high up wants this whole thing erased from the disc guys, and they've hired a PMC called the Englishman to do the job. This guy is rogue, uses cheap local resource - luckily for you. He has no scruples or morals, and that makes him more dangerous than..."

Easton filled the gap, "Than you?"

Mitch smiled, a twisted rictus. "Yeah, much more dangerous than me. I need to take him out, and then get back to the States and get to the root of this."

I took advantage of the subsequent silence. "Are you saying that a government department gives all this the green light? Surely that can't be. Would someone not pick it up?"

Mitch looked at me condescendingly. "Ever heard of Contra-gate, Ollie North? All sorts of stuff is going on without official sanction. Public denial usually means tacit approval! DC is full of public servants building private empires."

I sucked in breath through my clenched teeth, regretting my naivety.

Jeanne spoke softly. "We are going to Rome, there is a Professor there who I think was working with Dr Favreau on a paper. Maybe the Doctor confided in him about the illegal drugs testing. His name is De Vico, He might tell us enough to understand why Dr Favreau was murdered."

Mitch pondered that for some seconds. "You can do that Mslle, but I'm going to Berlin. That's where I can find the Englishman, he recruits his operatives there. Why don't you two come with me? I could use the muscle." He looked challengingly at Anderson and Easton.

The boys gawped vacantly at each other, unsure of what was happening. Mitch spoke again, "You guys took down seven heavies between you…not bad for amateurs. I need that back-up, and I can't bring in any of my own people just now until I know who I can trust. No guns, I'll handle anything in that league. Bailey, you and Jeanne should go to Rome. Maybe something you get from this De Vico guy might help me when I get back to the US. The Englishman will be too worried about me, and what I'm doing to come after you."

None of us spoke, such was the authority in Mitch's voice - was he an asset or a liability? I suddenly remembered Dumouriez. "Half of Interpol will be out looking for us. What can we do about Dumouriez?"

Mitch smiled again, a more expansive sight this time. "Ah, Lieutenant Dumouriez….late of the Daguet Division. Served with him in the first Gulf War. Good soldier. I've already spoken to him. They won't bother us. We should be more worried about the Englishman. The French can't overtly help right now, not after all the shit we've dumped on their streets."

We all listened meekly. This was a serious player, but it felt kind of good as well. He was a professional; an animal, but he was our animal and we needed all that he could give us. I was convinced - we needed him in our tent pissing out.

I decided to wrap things up. "Okay. Rome for us, Berlin for you guys."

Mitch eyed me, as if I had any real say in things, and barked, "I'll keep in touch with you; do NOT call your brothers on any account, okay? Mslle, I'll happily pay for a new table when all this is over!"

Jeanne flicked a sideways look at me as she answered. "You are too kind. I am sure I can manage the 50 euros it will cost in Ikea." Somehow, I guessed that buying a table was never going to fix the rift between these very different personalities - time to move.

CHAPTER 16

Wes stared at the mirror. God, this felt like a date! He had dressed soberly, going for an all-black ensemble that was functional and clean. He ran his comb through his tight curls one last time and checked out his look. Mean and efficient, oozing integrity, he thought, just the look he wanted to convey. He was doing the right thing, and it felt good. He had been startled by the swift reply to his e-mail, but his excitement had been tempered somewhat by the location of the meet. The Lincoln Memorial was hardly the edgy, out-there venue that he had expected, but whatever, he was going to be there, and he was going to bust this embezzlement thing open like a watermelon. He had decided to drive to the Federal Bank, and then walk the rest of the way down the wooded pathway that led up to the Memorial. He wondered fleetingly if he should take anything, but as he had stored all the information needed on a data stick, he decided not to.

"Let's go Wesley, Y'all have a good time now!" he fired at his reflection in the mirror, signing off with a mock salute.

The drive downtown was uneventful, the late spring days were long, and he realised it would still be light at the meet time. No matter, he wanted to see this dude eye to eye anyhow, wondering if they would send a big hitter to take his story, maybe one of these slick agency climbers that he used to aspire to be.

"These guys want to talk to you, Wes. You're gonna get profile now!" Another conversation with a mirror. He needed to calm down. He parked his retro Mustang awkwardly on Virginia Avenue Northwest, then set off on the short walk to the Memorial. There were still knots of people around, people heading for home after an extended day, perhaps, but they thinned out as he got further along the path towards the memorial, with only the ubiquitous black squirrels keeping him company on the last few yards. The reflecting pool had been drained as some sort of repair was going on, so the memorial was unusually quiet.

Wes noticed that there was absolutely no one around as he started climbing the steps up to the Lincoln statue. He felt a sudden cold spot ripple up his spine, and lost his previous bravado. "C'mon man, let's do this, you're doing what's right…no fear!" He didn't quite convince himself, but relaxed enough to make it the rest of the steps. There was no one there. He checked his blue Adidas watch. He was on time. He walked uncertainly over to the Memorial, and propped his back against the giant right foot of the statue and settled down to wait.

Time passed, and Wes became increasingly agitated as the daylight streamed into a misty dusk. He had checked his watch twenty or thirty times, but he had no idea what to expect, or how things would happen. "Well, I'm not moving till either it gets dark or some mother-fucker shows up," he assured himself. Then he heard footsteps, two or three sets….looked like he was getting a committee. He stood up and stretched, rubbing his numb backside and fixing his black coat as the steps grew close. He strained his eyes as two shapes morphed out of the thickening mist. Wes walked towards the pair, speaking tentatively as he went. "Hi guys, thought you weren't gonna show up, I was getting worried for a spell…."

A tall, dark haired man, clad in a black suit stepped into his line of sight. He spoke in a strange accent. "You have reason to worry friend. No one likes a teller of tales."

Wes stopped in his tracks, his legs suddenly turning to concrete, the hairs on his neck and arms bristling. He tried to talk, but his tongue was clamped to the roof of his mouth. He back tracked slowly, his legs refusing to answer the impulse to run that screamed through his body. The dark-haired man walked towards him purposefully, his dark eyes unblinking. Wes then caught the face of the second man. He stared, uncomprehending, and at last found his voice. "You? What the fuck are you doing here? Help me man, this guy is freaking me out. Tell him who I am! Tell him we work together!"

The suit nodded to the second man and turned to look at Wes again. He spoke again. "I know who you are, Wes. You are a fucking rat who has tried to shit on his friends, aren't you?" He pulled a gun from his coat pocket.

Wes went into shock. "Wait up, what are you doing? What's with the gun man?" He mouthed to no one in particular. The second man smiled malevolently, his words sibilant and menacing "Psychic as well. Wes, eh? You never made it in the Bureau, did you? Bitterness is destructive, buddy, don't you know? Terminal in your case."

The suit raised the gun and squeezed the trigger - double-tap. Wes felt the red hot coals piercing his body as the bullets hit him, followed by the icy stabs of pain. He fell to his knees, his ears flooded with the roar of impending death, still staring at his erstwhile colleague. His mouth filled with a copper-sulphate taste - blood - as he tried to talk, and as the suit raised his gun to fire again, he pitched forward onto the cold stone. The second man waved the suit away. "He's finished. What have you got we can leave around? - make it look like a mugging that's gone wrong. After all we are in the murder capital of the USA." The suit nodded and pulled Wes' car keys and wallet out his coat, tossing them on the ground, and then scattering some cards from the wallet onto the bleeding body.

The second man pulled his coat tight. "Leak plugged, I think. Let's get out of here. We got other stuff to do."

The suit picked up the spent cartridges. "Be good to get rid of this piece of shit gun...I was worried it wouldn't fire. Wasn't worth the $20 dollars I gave that guy for it."

The second man nodded. "Yeah, make it look like some strung out-junkie nailed him – like the way you think man!" The suit bowed mockingly, then put the spent cases in his pocket. The two men strolled away from the Memorial just as the first drops of Wes' blood followed them down the steps.

Herb sat at his desk, gloomily flicking through a wall calendar. He glanced out at Wes' empty desk, the chair empty, the PC screen darkened. The Police had called in first thing that morning to tell him that Wes had been found dead, mugged apparently, at the Lincoln Memorial. God knows why he had been there. Wes wasn't a history freak… maybe he was cruising? Nah, he wasn't gay either. Herb felt mildly guilty at his lack of concern. Hell, he didn't know Wes that well, he couldn't fake it.

His contemplation was punctured by the arrival of an ashen-faced Red. "I just heard boss. Terrible, just terrible. Wasn't a real friend, but never wanted any harm to come to him."

Herb realised that Red was genuinely upset, deepening his guilt further.

He stammered awkwardly. "Er, yeah. Listen, his Mom lives in Richmond, could you send her a condolence card, maybe some flowers? …be a nice touch."

Red drew himself up and answered affirmatively. "Yes, sir, be a privilege. I'll get on it now." Herb watched, perplexed, as Red practically ran out of the office. "Damnest thing! Thought Red hated the boy," he muttered sotto voce. "And where is that son-of-a-bitch, Kyle?" He pushed his chair back and stomped around the silent main office wondering if he should get the internal security guys involved. That might unveil his little scam with the PMC's. Best leave it for a little bit, but there was a danger that his little empire might come tumbling down. He would give it until end of day, and if the internal investigators didn't come to him he would decide whether he would go to them or just play this incident off as a tragic accident and Wes was yet another victim of the soaring rise in violence in America's capital city.

All that said, nothing would get done in the office today. "What a pain in the ass!" he bellowed as he barged into his office. He pulled his seat up and flicked the start button on his desktop. He cupped his jowly chin in his hands while the screen lit up, muttering darkly to himself.

The desktop filled the screen, and he signed in. He had mail; he clicked the pulsing icon. He watched with increasing alarm as the screen filled up. It was the spreadsheet from his scam, detailing every cent that he had creamed off! Jesus, who the fuck had sent him this? Who had it to send him? Cold globules of sweat broke out on his forehead, and his stomach seemed to contract to the size of an orange. He peered at the sender – georgirom@hotmail - who was that? He pushed back in his seat, dabbing his clammy forehead with a Kleenex. Someone had made him - how could they know? Wes, Kyle, Red? Who...?

He would be finished. He would go away for this, and not to fucking Long Island! He sat and pondered the enormity of what had happened He chewed his bottom lip, bouncing a pencil repeatedly on the desk. He had to move fast. He pulled out his cell phone and scrolled through the index, pressing hard on his selected number.

The ring tone bleeped once or twice, and eventually a cultured English voice answered. "Hello Herb, not your normal call, is it? I take it we have a problem?"

Herb gulped for air. "Yes we fucking do, and you're it... "Who authorised all these marks?"

The voice at the other end of the phone drawled emolliently. "Why you, of course. They've all come through your office and had your authorisation on them."

Herb was sweating heavily. "...but I didn't call all of these."

The reply was matter of fact, emotionless. "We have all the appropriate authorisation codes – yours, so what are you saying, Herb?"

Dabbing a kerchief at his moist features, the agonised public servant swore silently. "Look, that doesn't matter. I gotta breach here, I've been compromised, and that means you have as well! Someone has accessed my private files."

A snort of laughter snapped back down the line. "Calm down, Herb. We've taken care of it, just like you asked us to."

Herb snapped the pencil in disbelief. He had no idea what was going on. His stomach was churning in panic. "You mean you took out Wes? Jesus Christ! So it was him that hacked me."

The voice turned querulous. "For fuck sake, Herb, have you no idea what happens in your office? I will speak to my man in Washington. He'll look after you, and anyone else he has to. I have to go, give me a call when you are back on this planet."

The phone went silent Herb slouched in his seat, bathed in sweat, his head full of jagged shards of glass What was going on!?

CHAPTER 17

The more time I spent with Jeanne, the more I felt as though I had known her for all of my life. We talked easily, shared a love of martial arts, good clothes, and had the same unnatural love of all things IT. The first part of the train journey south from Le Gare du Lyon passed painlessly as we talked about, well, everything. I told her about Mum, Dad, and tried to explain why we were the way we were as siblings. She was a consummate listener, and I took full advantage. I wound my neck in after about an hour's worth of monologue, worrying that I might have put her into some sort of catatonic state.

"God, I'm sorry, I must be crushing you under all this family angst!"

She laughed sweetly, dismissing my concern with a shrug of her arched eyebrows. "Bailey, don't worry. I could listen to you all day! You tell a good story, and you are funny!"

I felt about 16, like some wobbly-kneed fifth grader, but after all we had been through over the past week, I reckoned I deserved it. She was great company, so what the hell. I never had any real concept of what it was to really value and need someone other than my immediate family, so this was a new, exciting, almost intoxicating experience.

She laughed as she talked. "Your brothers, the look on their faces as they went away with Mitch. They looked like boys being taken to the dentist. It was so funny!"

I sat watching and listening, enjoying female company as I had never enjoyed it before. Our lives had been so steeped in testosterone after Mum, maybe that's why we found it hard to commit to anything deeper than physical sex. I noticed Jeanne looking at me questioningly. I had been a bit too lost in the warm grip of her company. The vista rolling past our windows had grown hillier and greener, and the late afternoon light made us squint as we took the views in. I said I would get Jeanne some coffee, and she pulled a magazine from a day bag to pass the time until I returned. I walked awkwardly along the carriage as it swayed around a bend in the track, taking a first look at some of our fellow passengers as I went. We had been so absorbed in each other that we had barely noticed anything about the other train travellers.

As I waited on our drinks, I scanned the seats around me. Prim, elderly couples, the odd earnest student reading a travel book, some assorted suits invariably messing around with smart phones or peering studiously at tablet screens, and two shaven headed military men, sitting sipping beer. I noticed the flash "Legion Etrangere", and the bright yellow foulard, or shoulder scarf. They were Foreign Legionnaires. They both looked at me as I walked past. Jesus, I hoped they had tickets - for the ticket inspector's sake.

I felt a vibration in my coat pocket. Shit, I hadn't shut down my personal phone as Mitch had demanded I do. I pulled it out quickly, and fumbled for the off switch, cursing my apparent inability to manage a simple task. I pressed repeatedly as all sorts of screens tried to load. "Jesus, just go fucking off!" People in the queue behind me craned their heads to see what was going on. I smiled nervously, making to throw the phone out of the carriage window. The other queuing passengers remained stony faced, they needed their coffee, and I was in their space. Suddenly the Bluetooth screen popped up. I cursed again, "What the fuck…Come ON!" My ranting ceased abruptly as I looked at the Bluetooth screen. There was a device on the connectivity screen. 168!

At the riverside, just before Hasar was killed…168! I looked down the queue, and along the rows of seats. Someone was with us on the train, and it was my stupidity that had let them in. A few people stared back, unsettled by my apparent rudeness, but most merely caught my eye briefly and went back to whatever they had been doing. Not for the first time in recent weeks, I had no idea as to who or what I was looking for.

I walked quickly away from the buffet bar, oblivious to the assistant calling after me. Jeanne looked up as I approached our seats, her brows lowered. "No coffee? Have they sold out?" She asked earnestly. I had left it at the buffet counter. Damn. "Erm, no, I kinda went off the idea."

Jeanne laughed. "The coffee was for ME, Bailey. Is my company getting to you?"

I lowered my voice. "Jeanne, someone –" I was interrupted by a man's voice.

"Sir, you have forgotten your drink." A swarthy, casually dressed bespectacled man stood over us, holding the steaming cup of coffee. Jeanne reached for it, explaining, "Thank you sir, but it is my coffee. My friend has had a little memory lapse."

The swarthy man smiled, but his eyes remained fixed on Jeanne. "Ah, I see, I would not forget anything a beautiful woman like you asked me to do….and it would be champagne that I brought."

Jeanne was a little taken aback by the sudden outburst of smarm, but thanked him politely and closed any further potential conversation down by looking away and out of the window. I caught his gaze, noticing that he hadn't blinked at all during our conversation, and also thanked him. He stood for a few seconds, looking at us both.

I spoke slowly. "Thank you again, now if you don't mind….." His continued staring went beyond curiosity, and I felt anger rising. I stood up, moving clear of the seats. "Look, friend, we want some privacy here. "What say you move on?"

The interloper muttered something and moved away from our seats, looking back balefully several times as he did.

Jeanne whispered to me in a low voice, "What was that? What was wrong with him? Strange man, He looked like you. Same hair and glasses, and wearing blue shirt and Chinos just like you!"

Unimpressed by her comparison, I gave the guy the once over. Hmmm, a very superficial resemblance, and my glasses were bespoke Prada, unlike his chain store efforts. I waited until he had left the carriage and pulled Jeanne to me. She gave a little exhalation of breath as I pulled her close. "It's okay. I need to tell you something."

"Really?" she said huskily. "I thought you were going to kiss me…"

I hesitated. Her face was inches away and the mingled smells of perfume, soap and clean hair suddenly invaded my senses. Her olive cheeks were flushed and her eyes looked like black glistening pebbles. A strange feeling swirled around my insides. It was as though no one else was really there, and we were somehow alone on this crowded train.

Jeanne's liquid voice pierced my reverie. "Bailey, you are creasing my coat. Let go."

I crashed back to reality and realising that I had gripped the collar of her coat, I let it go. "I'm sorry Jeanne, I…"

She interrupted, placing an elegantly manicured finger on my lips as she did. "No, don't apologise for doing nothing…perhaps next time?"

I looked into her impossibly dark eyes, feeling their pull, and nodded. "Erm, yes, perhaps next time."

She sat back, running her hands through her hair luxuriantly. "I look forward to it," she said warmly.

Jesus, I felt as though I had ingested 10 litres of Helium. I had to get a grip. "Jeanne, someone is on the train tracking us. We need to be careful, sharp. We're being watched - probably even now."

She looked around quickly, and spoke quietly across the table. "Do you think it was that strange man with the coffee?"

I shook my head. "No, too obvious. He's just a voyeur, and you can't really blame him, you are very beautiful." I felt a pang of embarrassment at what I'd just said. I was an IT geek for Chris-sakes!

She flushed slightly, coyly pinning strands of her hair behind her ears. Her hand brushed mine as she spoke. "Thank you Bailey. I am so happy that you have said that. Now let's try and enjoy the journey. We will look after each other."

I was already enjoying the journey, more than I had enjoyed any other journey in my life...

CHAPTER 18

The train pulled into Marseille on time, and we sat taking in as much of this exotic, cosmopolitan city as we could through the dirt-streaked carriage windows and railway station structure. I had never been to Marseille, but Jeanne had worked in the city for a time, so I listened intently as she recounted some of her experiences there. I wished we could just get off and spend some time together, without thinking about what had happened over the last week. I realised I hadn't thought about Dad for a few days. Not knowing whether to be angry at myself or not. He was alive, I was absolutely sure about that, but if he was, why wasn't he helping us, or why didn't he at least try and get in touch - maybe he had been injured when the plane came down. Shit, I was gone again, mind going through the same stuff over and over - my bubble of temporary bliss had burst, and I felt that familiar stone in my gut.

Jeanne prodded my cheek. "Hey, where are you? I was talking to you!"

"Sorry Jeanne. Got tied up in old rope. Sorry!"

She looked at me with those incredible eyes, her forehead lined with concern. "Listen, why don't you get us some wine and cheese? I'm hungry and you haven't eaten much since we left Paris."

Wine and cheese it was then, so rising from the seat and stretching my tight legs, I strolled off toward the buffet car. My protesting muscles reminded me about how much exercise I had missed over the last week, and I resolved to get some in whilst we were in Rome. I missed the high, and, well, I wanted to look good for a few reasons, looking back at Jeanne's smiling face as I walked. The realisation that we were probably being watched re-emerged like nagging toothache. A train load of witnesses was hardly going to worry people like the gunman in Paris if they decided to make a move. I needed to stay sharp.

I wasn't a wine guru, but I took what looked like a decent red, and picked up a small net bag of mixed cheeses along with some small, hard brioches to take back to Jeanne. After walking a few metres down the carriage, I realised that I had forgotten napkins. This woman was doing strange things to me!

As I walked back towards the buffet, I saw a bearded, stocky man, his eyes covered by aviator sunglasses. He held out a pile of napkins. "You forgot these Monsieur." "Thanks buddy, I'd forget my eyeglasses if they weren't on my face!"

He responded jovially, in kind. "Yes, the things you lose if you don't concentrate. You had better get back to your lady before someone else does!" A tremor of *something* ran through me - deja vu; I'd probably seen him earlier. Shit, I was hallucinating now. Jeanne popped into my head. Better get back quickly, she might be getting tetchy.

Still smiling to myself, I set off again. Someone was at the compartment door. It was the man who had brought Jeanne's coffee earlier. What did he want? His back was towards me, and he was talking to Jeanne. I called brusquely. "Hey buddy, what can we do for you? He turned and looked at me, he had a small bottle of champagne in his hand - asshole! I bustled up the corridor. "Time to tweak this jerk's collar!" I intoned.

As I approached I saw that the two Foreign Legionnaires I had noticed earlier in the buffet car were coming from behind him the opposite way. One walked into our compartment, and the other, without warning, crashed his fist into the hapless lothario's face, shattering his glasses and snapping his head back violently. I heard Jeanne shouting angrily, over the top of a loud, heavily accented man's voice. Dropping all my food and drink, I raced down the corridor. The first assailant had picked up our inert Romeo by his bloodied shirt collar, but dropped him on the floor as he saw me coming. He eyed the heap on the floor, and then glared at me malevolently, calling to his companion as he did. I ran straight at the man in the passageway, frantically streaming my potential moves as I did.

The uniformed thug crouched in readiness, as sounds of an increasingly violent struggle came out of our compartment. I thought fast, he would be expecting an untrained brawler, so I had to surprise him. The small top window to his left was open as was the door to our compartment. I launched myself, grabbing the two handholds, pulling my legs in front of me as I lifted off. The thug's eyes squinted, and his mouth fell open, he wasn't expecting a move like that and he was totally unprepared for the full load of me crashing into his chest.

His body closed like a book as he was knocked over, a feral grunt escaping from his lungs. I managed to pull myself up instantly, landing on both feet. One down. Bang! My head exploded in a miasma of flashing lights and spears of pain. I tried to focus, swinging my arms wildly as I did - another sickening blow to my gut almost forced my stomach out of my lolling mouth. I vomited, instantly collapsing to the floor. I looked up and saw the blurred shape of a large man standing over me, his foot raised. I fought to regain my senses, to try and defend myself against what was coming, but I was dazed, disorientated, and couldn't avoid the stamp when it came. A dull bludgeoning pain shot across my chest and I rolled over on my back, still dimly aware of the ominous shape hovering over me. I felt my glasses being taken off. He was going to finish me...

I heard a female voice, Jeanne's? I glimpsed a long slim leg arcing across in front of me, followed by a strangled yelp. My vision cleared a little. Jeanne had round-house kicked the second Legionnaire in the throat. I watched, incredulous, as she brought her hands down in a chopping motion on the back of my attacker's thick neck; his body crumpled to the floor. Jeanne cried out and dropped to her knees, cradling my head. My legs were inextricably mixed up with the other three bodies on the floor and I kicked them away one at a time, rising, shakily, to my feet.

No bones broken, I thought, but my nose had been bloodied, and I was still badly winded. Jeanne wiped my nose clean with one of the napkins I had been carrying and cleared the traces of vomit from my mouth.

I closed my eyes to try and stop the synapses of pain pulsing around my head. "Jeanne, pull the emergency cord, pull it now!"

She looked at me blankly. "What? Why? What are we going to do?"

"Jeanne, just pull the fucking cord!"

Shocked at the venom in my voice, she gripped the communication cord and yanked it towards her. There was a cacophony of brakes, engine and human sounds as the train screeched to a halt. I opened the carriage door manually, and screamed at Jeanne. "Help me push them out!" Grabbing the legs of one of the unconscious Legionnaires, she knew what I was doing, and grabbed the top half of his body. He fell to the trackside with a muffled thud, and immediately started coming round. We pulled the other Legionnaire over the still-unconscious body of the lothario, and without ceremony, pitched him on top of his companion.

Out of the corner of my eye I saw train staff quickly approaching along the passageway. "Jeanne, we need to wake your boyfriend up. He's our alibi" She nodded, and started to dab at the man's bloodied face with a wet napkin. The two addled Legionnaires - that weren't - had come to, and were looking groggily up at the train. One reached into the pocket of his combat pants. Shit! He had a gun. I prepared to jump down, but pulled back as two gendarmes arrived in front of the train people. The two thugs, seeing the timely arrival of the Officers, spoke rapidly in an unrecognisable language and ran from the train, jerkily and haphazardly at first, but gaining speed as their faculties returned.

"Careful, they're armed!" I shouted to the gendarmes.

They duly took cover below the windows, pulling out their own firearms as they did. The Legionnaires had reached the road. We watched, appalled, as they forced a car to stop and pistol-whipped the unfortunate driver to the ground. As one levelled his gun at the train, the other jumped into the driver's seat, roaring away as the gunman rolled in beside him.

The gendarmes leapt from the train and sprinted across the grass towards the disappearing car, flattening to the ground as shots came from the speeding vehicle. A last effort from the would-be Legionnaires. Jeanne and I looked at each other, isolated in the chaos of shouting Policemen, agitated passengers and roaring car engines. I winked at her, smiling, and she winked back - we had some explaining to do.

CHAPTER 19

Anderson and Easton sat silently in the luxuriant back seats of Mitch's BMW, occasionally making eye contact and gesturing to each other. This guy was a machine. They had been eight hours on the road without a break, and in Mitch's case without a word. He had decided to drive to Berlin, wanting to avoid any possible risk of being traced through public transport routes. The brothers, still wary of their saturnine driver, had acquiesced without fuss but were now growing increasingly restless.

Easton whispered out of the side of his mouth. "Anderson, I need to pee. "We'll have to stop. Ask him to stop."

Anderson grimaced as he replied. "Bro, my bladder's the size of a football, but he'd probably ask us to pee out of the window."

Easton grinned, temporarily easing the pressure on his urethra, and then whispered quietly, "Think he'd notice if we pissed down his neck?"

Anderson laughed silently, his body shaking. "Stop it for Chris-sakes Easton. I will piss my pants, and everyone else's pants as well!"

Mitch's clipped voice came over the seats. "Now then boys, if you want to pee, just put your hand up. We'll pull in at the first gas station. In the mean time just think of the Hoover Dam. "Works for me."

The brothers sunk a bit further into their seats. Anderson chuckled. "Well a least he talked! Where are we anyway, Easton?"

The clipped voice butted in ahead of Easton's reply. "Braunschweig, still got about three hours to go."

Anderson murmured his thanks, and elbowed Easton in the ribs, setting off a bout of sibling joshing. Mitch watched the brothers through the mirror. He liked them, liked the way they rubbed up together, and he would need them soon enough. Time to pee, he decided, and swished the car across two lanes to get to the upcoming fuel station. They sat and had a coffee in the garage cafe with Anderson patiently trying to get more than monosyllables out of a visibly relaxed Mitch.

"So you're an actor?" he asked Anderson.

"Yeah," he replied airily. "You might have seen me. My last series was on Fox."

Mitch clicked his lips, shaking his head at the same time. "Don't do TV, my friend. You could tell me anything, no need for escapism in my life."

Easton took a long draught of his coffee, and then spoke. "Hey, a philosopher! And I thought you were a just a hired killer."

Mitch's face darkened, and Anderson spluttered into his tea. "Come on Easton, why'd you say that? This guy is on our side, and he saved Bailey's life. Stop trying to bust his balls. Calm yourself down man!"

Easton played with the rim of his cup, obviously regretting what he had said.

Mitch pointed that long jaw at him. "Listen, you little cherry. I do what I do, and have long since gotten over whatever any fucked-up, liberal know-nothing thinks about me."

Easton, bluff as ever, fired back. "Hey, I may be fucked up, but I'm so not a liberal!"

Mitch didn't smile, fixing Easton with a long, sinuous stare. He leaned forward, now looking at them both. "We are going to be in harm's way very soon, and there'll be no time for your little turns of badinage. I'll need you to get my six, and I'll have yours, so if you boys haven't got the juice for that, I'll go on myself, got it?"

"Six? What does THAT mean?" Easton was not up on military jargon.

"It means my back, your back," the exasperated ex-soldier rapped back.

Anderson, flustered, spoke before Easton could dig any deeper. "Look, we are grateful for Bailey's life. Can't tell you how much, but cut us some slack. We've never been in anything like this before. We know that we are in real danger, but we want to help, and we want to find out what happened to Dad." His voice faded, and his head drooped.

Mitch pulled back, speaking softly. "Your Dad was a good man. I trusted him with my life, and if I can help you get what you want in any way, I will. Something rotten is going down here, and it stinks all the way to Langley. Things will never be the same once this has come out, believe me. I just need you to do as I ask and help me close it down." His tone had been earnest, conciliatory even, and the brothers listened in complete silence.

"We're in, we want to help," whispered Easton, as Anderson nodded in mute agreement. Mitch reached over and shook both their hands firmly. "Not be the first time that I've depended on a Marks, you're your father's sons."

The soft silence that followed was punctured by Easton's brash tones. "So it's kinda like one for all and all for one!" Anderson glanced nervously at Mitch, waiting for a reaction.

Mitch sat back, folded his arms, and laughed heartily. "Yeah, something like that. Now get to the john and let's get moving!"

Easton couldn't resist; "Peeing on command? C'mon Anderson, git that bladder emptied boy!" Mitch laughed again, it was time to go.

CHAPTER 20

The train had been stationary for about two hours. We had both given statements. We had basically told the truth. I had gone to help my doppelganger after he was attacked by the two soldiers. The dazed and severely shaken lothario had backed up our versions to the letter, adding that they had been abusing Jeanne when he had happened along. We made no mention of anything else. The Police were solicitous, and apparently not shocked by the behaviour of the Legionnaires-that-weren't. I knew the Legion was a law unto itself, but didn't think they stretched to abduction and shooting at policemen!

The train rolled away again after about another hour, and I felt the pain of my beating fading as the scenery opened up along the Mediterranean coastline of the Cote D'Azur. Jeanne just kind of fitted in with the lush blues and greens of the landscape, and I soon slipped into a light sleep. I opened my eyes occasionally, just enough not to be noticed, and caught Jeanne looking intently at me. That felt good, indescribably good for someone who had drifted through life with no commitment to anyone outside of his siblings. I drifted off into sleep again, with the Mediterranean sun dappling my bruised face.

The rest of the journey passed without incident. Destinations rolled past, Nice, Ventimiglia, Genoa, Pisa, Firenze. I found myself wishing that I could just repeat the whole journey on a loop, so deeply was I taken with Jeanne. The hours disappeared, as we talked about life, ambitions, likes, dislikes - no awkward silences, just easy conversation between two people on the edge of maybe saying something deep. We talked through the darkness, looking at the lights of faraway towns, trying to imagine what was going on in them. Was I a closet romantic? Whatever, this journey was one of those stolen moments in time that I would remember forever, like the days in the Hamptons with Mum and my brothers...yep, this was that good.

I awoke with a tremor from a long sleep about half an hour out of Pisa. Jeanne was still out, sleeping in that still, placid way I had come to know, so I got up and went for a walk along the corridor. I felt stiff and out of shape. Usually I would train for martial arts three times per week; that would involve a workout and then drills on moves. Having been in Europe now for three days, I had been in two fights. One more and I would have done a full week of training. Somehow I had a feeling that I had not seen my last action on this trip. I thought of the brothers, and hoped they were okay - knowing what I did about Mitch made me feel that they would be.

CHAPTER 21

We pulled into Rome Termini train station on a lovely late spring afternoon. As we walked out of the front entrance many great memories of trips here with Dad and my brothers flooded back. My first view of the Coliseum, the Spanish Steps, Piazza Nevona. Rome was a living museum. I cried when I first stood on the Eastern platform of the Coliseum. I felt then that spirits of many fallen foes still danced in the arches and catacombs.

We decided to kill some time before heading to our meeting venue, a square which I knew well and was looking forward to seeing again. We walked off heading west towards Piazza della Rotunda where one of Rome's most famous buildings was - so popular that the French copied it and we had gone to a bar not far from that one in Paris - The Pantheon.

We meandered through the virtual Art Gallery that is Rome, passing the Basilica del Sacro Cuore di Gesu on our right. Our route took us along Via Marsala, turning left onto Viale Enrico de Nicola, round the Fontana delle Naiadi at the Piazza della Republica and eventually to the Trevi Fountain. Although not yet summer, the tourist season was well under way. The crowds were twenty deep at the fountain and negotiating the throngs was not easy. As we got level with the statue of Venus, we were forced up to the top level of the steps due to all the bustle and throng of those trying to get a good photo. Jeez, I hadn't seen so many iPhones since I was at a Bon Jovi concert in Madison Square Garden!

As we got to the South Western corner of the fountain we had to turn sharp right. Somehow one of the many street artists of Rome had captured a great spot to set up his paintings. He was busy; selling the usual pictures of all the main tourist sites and some of the ubiquitous Vespa scooters. He wore a coat that was a little heavy for the season, but I remembered being caught in some really heavy rain on a number of occasions in the city at this time of year in the past. Perhaps he was showing good judgement.

We pushed through the crowds and turned left onto Via dei Crociferi, where many years ago we had purchased a football to play with on our family travels. Our destination was only a short walk from here and we were in good time to meet Professor De Vico. As we turned into Via dei Bergamaschi I could see the doors on the opposite side of the square where we would find the Professor's office. This was the Piazza di Pietra and we were heading for the Centro di Documentazione on the far side.

Walking across the square, memories came flooding back of meandering through here with Dad and my brothers. We had taken the small football and had a little kick around in this very square. At the far end of the square I could see a grey haired man, probably in his late forties, kicking a ball with his two young boys. Playing with them were two centurions. The Roman soldiers were there for the tourists to be photographed with, just as in Times Square you will find Shrek and Snow White.

I remembered one time using the rest rooms in the McDonalds on 42nd street, and as I was pulling the door to leave, in barged Batman. I was startled. "Even Batman has to take a piss!" he said. Four thousand miles away from that and you had centurions playing football here in Rome. There is something about the Italians and football. When we played in this same square, many years ago, I remember a number of people getting involved. There was a business man who came out of the same doors we would be entering to meet the Professor. He saw us playing and got involved. He was clearly in his fifties, wearing Gucci loafers and a very expensive suit. None of that however exemplified his love of the game as much as the fact that the guy he was with was obviously his body guard and the large BMW sitting in the corner was his chauffeur driven car. On another occasion the ball strayed over towards the small cafe in the middle of the North wall of the square. A very elegant lady in a tight red, knee length dress wearing slender high heels stood up and hoofed the ball back at us. It was destined to nestle in the top corner of our imaginary goals had Easton not stuck his head in the way and sent it skyward, close to the top of the four storey buildings around us. Spontaneous applause broke out for the lady in red. She bowed slightly and sat down again to her espresso. God, the Italians loved football, even more than their food!

Jeanne tapped my shoulder. "Hey, I am here too!"

I had been on one of my solo nostalgia trips again. "Sorry Jeanne, there are lots of memories here for me."

She smiled apologetically. "Of course, I am sorry to be selfish. Come, take my arm!"

We walked up the ramp to the double height doorway at the Western end of the square and entered Palazzo Ferrini. On entering it took a little while for our eyes to adjust to the stark contrast of the darkness inside. A reception desk loomed in front of us occupied by a striking dark haired woman in business attire. I approached. She raised a finger and I realised she was talking on a hands-free headset. She finished and said, "Preggo."

"Dove posso trovare Proffessor De Vico."

"Vai al terzo piano. Il suo ufficio si trova alla fine del corridoio." Third floor at the end of the corridor. "Grazie mille."

We headed for the elevator and alighted on the third floor. The walls were marble, no doubt from the quarries in the north of the country. Our footsteps clicked and echoed on the ornate marble floor. I was hopeful that this meeting would be fruitful and give us some answers to the many unanswered questions that we had. Who was behind the killings? Why were possibly the same people trying to kill my brothers and I? What was the connection to the newspaper article I had read? Jeanne looked at me reassuringly, calming my racing thoughts.

CHAPTER 22

Herb had been practically incommunicado since he had read the e-mail, and Kyle and Red were giving their choleric boss a wide berth. Red found it particularly hard, as he would rather talk than breathe. He looked at Kyle, who was as usual, immersed in whatever was on his PC, mumbling along to his music.

"Hey Kyle, turn that shit down and talk to me. What do you think is going on with our man? Don't think he's still cut up about Wes, do you?"

Kyle's glacial blue eyes didn't move from the screen, but he did tweak the volume down. "It hit him hard Red, think he feels bad about all the shit he gave Wes before he was killed. He's not totally inhuman, but he'll get over it."

Red was determined to talk to someone. "God-damn it Kyle, one of us has been killed and our jobs could be on the line here. He's given us nothing to do all day, nobody's talking to us, and someone will pick up that we're soaking up pay checks for doing zip! I like this job, I've got plans, I want to move up. Don't you ever think about things like that between times staring at that fucking PC!"

Kyle took off his glasses and gave him a long, unblinking look. "You need to calm down Red. What's riling you? Who's going to fire us? Hardly anyone knows we're here, so if you're looking for promotion, get a job as a mail man, or a pizza chef. We're under the radar, and we won't get fired, but we sure as shit won't get promoted doing this either. We facilitate murder and mayhem Red - don't forget that."

Red had listened open mouthed as his previously pliant, almost anonymous, colleague ripped into him. He stammered as he tried to reply. "Where did that come from Kyle, where you been hiding that? We work for the government. People know what we do, they must. I didn't bust my ass studying for seven years to end up in a Black Ops hole!"

Kyle pushed his chair back, turning fully to face his simmering colleague. "Worried about your resume Red? Well don't, because you couldn't put any of what you've done here on it. You did the job interview. You signed the NDA and secrecy agreement. Wise up Red, there's no more rungs on this job ladder."

"My worry is that instead of getting fired we get terminated one by one! Who would know? We officially don't exist buddy!" Red folded his arms emphatically, head shaking. Kyle was about to reply when an ashen-faced and noticeably thinner-faced Herb appeared in the office. "You boys got nothing to do? Too much jaw, jaw going on, get to work! Turn that music off Kyle. This isn't a fucking call centre!"

Red stood up, arms held out as he spoke. "Well actually boss, we haven't got any work to do, you haven't given us any for days." Herb's hackles rose visibly as he spoke. "Do I have to give you work? You have a brief. You're empowered to use your initiative. Now do it. There are shit loads of loose ends to tie up. Remember Wes isn't here now, and there are lots to pick from what he was on. I don't hear Kyle grouching. He knows what's to be done. Maybe it's time for you to move on Red, if reading Intel reports is too small potatoes for you!"

Red was having a bad day. "I'm sorry. I guess I'm still spooked about Wes. I'll get on to phone traces right now."

Herb snapped back: "Good, and if any other work comes in, I'll pass it through Kyle, okay? Now let me know as soon as you find anything interesting in the transcripts."

Red nodded weakly, and sank back into his chair.

Kyle looked over at him, tight lipped. "Sorry man, I got to go with what comes down, you know that. I'm sure this won't be for long," he said apologetically. Red lowered his head into his hands and looked down at his desk...this had been a bad day.

CHAPTER 23

Professor De Vico's appearance didn't fit his telephone voice. We had chatted briefly when I set the meeting up. His voice was gentle, like that of a sage septuagenarian grandfather, and I visualised a grey haired, cardigan wearing bookish don. However, my suspect judgement let me down again, and in front of Jeanne and I stood a svelte, middle-aged hipster. He had thick, black-rimmed Prada glasses, a trimmed goatee beard, and long, just greying, dark curly hair. He wore a tight, slim fit, navy blue suit. Todd lace-ups finished the look.

As he shook our hands he fixed us with a warm steady gaze, but on looking at Jeanne, he held his eyes just a little longer; he admired her Gallic beauty, I could tell. In Rome, men will walk past a woman they find attractive and place a business card in front of them. The men hope that if they do this to enough women one of them will call his number. Professor DeVico was not one of those men. He was an admirer of beauty, but not a stalker of it.

"Let us find a good place to talk," he said. I expected him to take us to an office somewhere. "My favourite Espresso is served in the cafe outside," he said, sounding every bit the

Barista aficionado. Who could argue? He was a Professor and an Italian.

We exited the building and headed to the very cafe where the lady in red had smacked the football back to us all those years ago. I looked to my right and took in the sights. Hadrian's temple loomed large. The marble columns were just beginning to crumble but still looked beautiful. The centurions were doing a roaring trade with the iPhone wielding tourists. The football family had gone.

As the Espressos arrived Professor De Vico sat patiently waiting for me to talk. I explained about our desire to track down information concerning Professor Favreau in Paris and how I believed that his death was not suicide. He seemed a little doubtful until I told him about my New York experience with subway trains. He became a tad more animated.

"What exactly do you want from me, Mr Marks? The Professor and I were sometime colleagues, and his death was of course very sad, but we were not friends."

I measured his words. He didn't seem to be that broken up about Favreau and as for his question, I really did not know... I asked him the most obvious thing. "Can you shed any light on why someone might want to kill Professor Favreau? What was he working on that was so concerning for someone that they did not want him to meet with me?"

De Vico took a noisy slurp of his Espresso, as Italians do, and spoke earnestly, his features set. "You say you read an article about how some drug companies were manipulating their clinical trials? Might I suggest that your journey here has been in vain as I know very little about these things, and that perhaps you should be concentrating on what you say was in the article. You may want to look at how the pharmaceutical companies are funding the research and who with."

"I understand that Professor, but it would take me years of research to get to the bottom of any of this and having almost been killed myself and knowing that at least three other deaths are linked with my... my quest, if you like, I can't help feeling I don't have that long to find things out."

"Forgive me Mlle. Salas? Is that name correct? Can you not be of some assistance to our trans-atlantic friend here?" Jeanne who had been leaning forward during all of this, sat back slowly. Her brain was in motion and she was beginning to think through some questions for Professor De Vico.

"I would not know where to start here, Professor De Vico. Professor Favreau was involved in many things across the world. My...our job, was to look specifically at protein traces in test results to diagnose cancer at an earlier stage and so to provide early diagnosis. If we could diagnose earlier then we could treat earlier before the tumours grew or mastisised and so prolong life. I can't see how that can lead to someone being killed?" The Professor's eyes narrowed as Jeanne talked about the protein traces.

"Your work is pioneering and you are clearly very bright." If Jeanne picked up any hint of condescension, she didn't show it. De Vico was in full flow now.

"The area you are exploring is something that has been mentioned in dark corridors, but never properly explored. The medical community is slow to respond to new advances. Yes, we have started to look at neuro-immunology in connection with cancer, but that was first talked about twenty years ago. A friend of mine has been using a particular plaster for broken legs called Patella, Tendon Bearing. He has been using it for twenty five years after noticing how well the leg adapted to a lower limb prosthetic - we have the Middle East wars to thank for a rapid expansion in willing patients to experiment with prosthetic shapes and technology. For years he attended congress. That is what we call the gatherings of our groups. He talked to many of his colleagues, gave lectures, approached many leading thinkers in this area, but no one took on board what he said. Then slowly some people in the UK started to try his methods and found that they could not only build a more effective structure around the fracture, but that it was allowing a quicker recovery rate because the patient was able to add load to the fracture, increasing bone density and so strength. However, none of this mattered until he did a cost benefit analysis and showed how much money it could save the hospital over the course of a year. Since they were using fewer materials for less time and the patient was spending less time in physiotherapy, the cost benefit was huge.

As managers in the NHS in England got wind of this they decided to pursue it. Only in the last few years has it been seen as the way to treat fractures to the lower limbs. So you see my friends, it is not easy to get change within this profession unless there is money involved. It strikes me that your protein research may in some way have threatened some organisation's ability to make money. That is all I can think of."

I could not believe what I was hearing, that much of what happened in this profession came down to money and not patient care. I then began to think back to some news reports that I had read in the UK where they described patient care as a 'post code lottery.' If you lived in a certain area then the budget was sufficient to pay for expensive treatments. In other areas it was not and your health suffered. In some cases people were moving from one country to another, Wales to England, so that they could receive life saving treatments. The same was happening in America on the back of the Obama healthcare plan. Money was not available in many poor areas and people were dying. My mind came back to how the drug companies were playing a part in this.

"Professor, how do the pharmaceutical companies make a drug?" The way that he chuckled made me realise that my question was naive.

"That is a very interesting process. If a scientist synthesises a molecule, there is a good chance that he will become a, how do you say it, millionaire?"

We nodded in unison. "The pharma company will take this molecule and patent it. The patent lasts for twenty-five years and in that time they must spend vast amounts of money on clinical trials. The patent prevents anyone from copying the molecule, so it is in their interest to make the drug work in order for them to retrieve all the money they spend on clinical trials. Clinical trials will take about twelve years to complete and so for the next thirteen years the drug company must recoup all of the millions they have spent on getting the drug to market. They must do this before the drug goes generic and others are permitted to copy the molecule.

Copying the molecule is one thing, but like a cake recipe, if you do not use the flour from a certain region and put all the ingredients in at the right time and in order, the results will be very different and this can affect the patient's reaction to the drug - side effects. It is in the interest of the pharmaceutical company to get many people used to the side effects so that they demand the drug, even when there is a cheaper alternative, but one that their body is not used to and causes them to have unfamiliar side effects. They become dependent for life. This prolongs the life cycle of the drug: more money. The other question for the drug company to consider is the price they should set for the drug. If it for something like the influenza virus, then many people will use it and they can charge a low rate. However, if it is for a rare form of cancer, then they can charge a premium price as it will not be used as often, but will gain big headlines as it prolongs the life of very ill people. Therefore it will be used in many high profile cases and gain iconic status. The drug company will profit from having a very high profile to the general public.

This trial process does not always go to plan. There have been a number of cases where people have been adversely affected for life on the back of a trial drug, causing severe reactions and permanent disfigurement. In the 1960s Thalidomide was the big case but there have been more since then. As I indicated earlier, these companies are not charities. They have shareholders to keep happy and the title of 'Number One pharma company in the world' is very highly sought after."

Questions were going off in my head like popcorn in a pot. "How do they advertise their drugs?" I measured my sentence carefully.

"That is a very good question, young man. It depends on the country they operate in. In many of the old Eastern bloc countries they need to find middle men to arrange the distribution. It may mean paying off government officials who will sanction its use. They remain far enough away from this 'fixer' to be legally un-responsible. I think my lawyer friends call it Plausible Deniability. In most European countries with the exception of Switzerland, where you can say almost anything, they cannot compare their drug to other medicines. They must only show their results against a placebo in what is called a double blind test – those administering the test do not know if they are dispensing placebo or medicine. The trial results are shown to doctors in congress by leading doctors in their respective field."

"How do they recruit these leading doctors?" I tried to sound authoritative.

"Aha! Now that is where the Med Ed companies come in. A Medical Education company, which really is a licence to print money, will organise development workshops where the doctors will be given some interesting input on dealing with tough situations or presentation skills or perhaps some business planning. Woven into these workshops are presentations by these leading thinkers showing the results they have gained by using the drugs in certain ways: we call it efficacy.

For instance, one cancer drug cannot be administered in its usual doses to people of Asian origin. Their kidneys will fail. That is a genetic thing and could be catastrophic if not done properly, but is a procedure not known by many people. Good things come from these gatherings. However, other forces are at work. During these sessions, people are being observed for their willingness to engage with the ethos of the pharmaceutical company and its drugs. Recommendations for new, how do you say it, 'disciples,' are sought and these people are then asked to contribute more. They are then paid for their inputs and so the cycle goes on. Before too long they are heavily involved with the pharma company and delivering talks on how they use their drugs. Most of these doctors are at Consultant level or are very eminent - Professors indeed."

"So it is in these doctors' interest to promote the drugs and so perpetuate their income?"

"Exactly." A single word answer; unusual for this loquacious academic.

"But they can't just say anything because of restrictions in certain countries?"

"Correct. In fact the drug companies have enormous legal departments that vet every piece of information that goes out so that they do not contravene any of these regulations."

"This is mind blowing. In effect, these pharma organisations are manipulating the use of their medicines. They are encouraging doctors to prescribe their drug before a potentially more suitable and perhaps, cheaper alternative, and then they are encouraging addiction in the patient whilst at the same time charging a premium based solely on making lots of money and not on providing something that can help people live longer?" My passion fizzed as I spoke.

"That, if I may say, is a very pious view. There are many drugs in development that would not be brought to market if these enormous organisations could not afford to test and trial them. HIV would still be a killer illness were it not for the millions invested in finding drugs that could allow people to live through the disease. Sometimes you have to take the rough with the smooth. And can I just add, many are doing it; so if the patient is not prescribed a drug by one company, it will be the medicine of another that they are prescribed and these companies have got the market tied up in almost all areas."

"Can you tell me anything about Interzamabol?"

De Vico's eyes flinched imperceptibly behind his glasses before he replied. "A drug used for expectant mothers to reduce blood pressure. The trials were remarkably good; showing better than normal efficacy. There were some suspicions concerning this as no drug has ever been as impactful, other than the blue triangle, at achieving results in a very sensitive area. Pregnant women cannot really be exposed to many agents as they transfer over the amnion layer and are absorbed by the foetus. However there were other concerns with this drug too. The clinical trials never quite highlighted some of the alleged side effects."

"How do you mean Professor?" I sensed some unease.

"There were some results that did not remain in the public domain for very long. There was a suggestion of carcogen production associated in some cases with this drug."

"And these were widely known?"

"Not widely. You see, you only have to publish the results. On some occasions results have been manipulated to show better efficacy. Side effects just need to be listed on the leaflet and many of them are generic, dryness of mouth, sleepiness, etc. The longer term issues are not really focused on unless there are many public cases. When this does happen, the drug companies will do their best to sweep them under the... rug? Is that how you term it?"

"Your English is very good, Professor."

"Thank you. I spent many years in London working."

I hadn't asked our biggest question, but Jeanne was determined to do so.
"You have told us a great deal Professor, but I am not sure any of it really helps us. Were you aware of any fatalities linked with the trialling of any of the drugs that you and Professor Favreau were researching?"

The question seemed to unsettle him. He tossed his head back as he finished the last of his Espresso, his demeanour and tone darkened as he answered. "I was not, but I would think that the research done by Professor Favreau is the avenue to explore. I am not familiar with the main body of his work, and only spoke to him occasionally on it. Sorry I cannot be of more assistance to you. I must take my leave now as I have a flight to catch."

Jeanne looked at me, lips tightly compressed in obvious frustration. She spoke, with asperity. "Professor, are you saying that you know nothing about any trials that led to fatalities? I have evidence of multiple deaths, linked to some of the work that you and Professor Favreau were involved in. I believe he was killed because he was about to expose what was happening!"

De Vico stood up, buttoning his jacket. "Really? That is a controversial statement Mslle. Why would he expose something he was part of?"

Jeanne also stood up, looking directly at the obviously, discomfited academic. "Because he knew it was wrong, and wanted to stop it – wouldn't you?"

De Vico's brown eyes lingered on Jeanne's trembling lips. "Hmm, a very altruistic and noble thing, but I am a scientist, and find it hard to deal with rhetorical questions. Now I really must go!"

I interjected, "Somewhere nice?" Whilst slightly suspicious, I had kind of enjoyed listening to this avant-garde academic's extravagant and florid musings, and hoped to prolong the conversation for a few minutes more.

"We Professors are always being invited to talk about drugs in some part of the world. Today I am heading to Germany, Berlin, in fact, where I have to be very careful about what I can and can't say. I wish you luck in your quest: both of you."

We bade him farewell, watching him blend into the pulses of tourists who were now filling the square. I looked at Jeanne. She was deflated and frustrated." That was a waste of our time Bailey. We got nothing from him."

I slid an arm around her shoulders, and whispered, "No time I spend with you is wasted Jeanne. Please don't get upset. Now how about a real coffee?"

CHAPTER 24

As we walked along via dei Pastini, approaching Piazza della Rotunda, we could see an artist selling self-scrawled pictures of Rome. As we got closer, I realised it was the same guy with the big coat. Clearly the Trevi fountain crowds were too much for him. My brother Easton adored Vespa scooters and it felt only right that I got him a little souvenir from Rome. In the end I plumped for the red one; his and his mother's favourite colour. We got the picture in a small brown paper bag and walked towards one of my favourite restaurants in the world, Neapolitano's. I had great memories of the owners, Antonio and Philippe, who always looked after you when you popped in and never let you leave without trying some Pizza Genovese. It had Wi-Fi too which was always good for checking up on e-mail and up to date news stories. We ordered from a spotless waiter, and I was amazed to hear the memorable tones of Antonio and Philippe having a typical Italian sing-song spat; still here after all those years and still crazy, by the sound of it!

Jeanne looked at me. "What now?"

"De Vico talked for a long time without saying anything. Did he give us anything at all we could go on?" The bread and coffees arrived, along with a complimentary Lemoncello. Nice! I continued. "Don't know what to do now, but, really, we don't have time to think too much. I am just going over his conversation in my head. I can't believe that the drug companies can actually put things on the market and not consider the long term effects of their medicines."

Jeanne was looking at me in a vacant way. This was her vocation. She had been involved in pharma research for much of her adult life. The last conversation had blown away any moral-high-ground arguments that she may have been willing to put up. This whole experience had been tough on her, from losing the Professor to witnessing the shooting in the park right through to the fight on the train. She was beginning to crumble and I could see it now in her eyes. They suddenly filled with tears.

"I don't know if I can make any sense of this!" she blurted out. I moved my seat around the table and sat beside her, putting my arm around her shoulders.

"I am beginning to feel the same way." My thoughts began to drift off to the newspaper article. Was it really only a few days ago that I had heard the ping of that message in my in box? Was I on some wild goose chase across Europe for no good reason other than some misguided quest? Why should I continue with this, what was the point? And what about my brothers, in Berlin, with a complete stranger who may or may not have known Dad? I looked back at Jeanne. She had pulled the Vespa painting we had just purchased out of the brown bag, fanning herself with it while she looked at the image. As she flapped the picture back and forward I could see that there was some writing on the back; not just writing to describe the picture, but a label with some characters on it. I went to take the picture from Jeanne.

"Can you show me that a minute?" She looked at me in a strange fashion, something that often happens to me around women. As I turned the picture over, both of us leant in simultaneously to read the message.

"Gemini168" 168, the address from the e-mail. I sat stock still, unable to rationalise what this might mean.

Jeanne was staring at me. I did not look at her, but could sense her eyes boring into the side of my head. I kept my gaze on the label positioned on the back of the picture. Who had put that there and how? It slowly dawned on me; the picture salesman. Why had he repositioned himself to the corner of the Rotunda square? What was it about him that I found familiar? The movement of the hands? The arch of his back? What was it? I looked at Jeanne; my arm was still around her shoulders. I leant back removing my arm and placing it on her seat back. She leant towards me as I did this and allowed my arm to touch her shoulders again. "Jeanne, Gemini168 - don't you remember? It's the address from the e-mail I got in New York."

She sat back, her eyes flickering as she looked me up and down. I persevered. "Three possibilities: absolute pure chance; the picture man is my guardian angel; or he is someone that I know and he is helping me...or maybe it's my Dad!"

Jeanne looked at me dubiously. "That is four, Bailey. What did they teach you at all these different schools you attended?" I flinched at her attempt at humour.

"I think that it is chance, luck...maybe it is a catalogue number." She flicked her hands dismissively as she spoke.

I was taken aback at Jeanne's apparent scepticism; fearing her ridicule. I hadn't told her about the man in Paris, the data stick, the device names on Bluetooth. Her patent lack of belief was almost demoralising. I had to focus. I swallowed my disappointment and spoke matter of fact-ly.

"Let's reflect on Professor De Vico's conversation with us. He said that the pharma organisations will release a drug and don't need to send out all of the information about side effects. He said that they can sometimes manipulate clinical trial data to show better, what did he call it?"

"Efficacy - It is how effective the drug is in tackling the symptoms. He said that legal teams ensure that they say the right thing in the right places."

"'Tru-dat' Jeanne."

"Sorry?"

"No, I am sorry. He said there was some place where it was not so big a deal regarding the messages you put out about the medicine."

"Switzerland."

"That was it. So basically he said that you can say anything you like in Switzerland about the drug you are putting on the market."

Jeanne pursed her lips thoughtfully - she spoke slowly, thinking each word through. "Professor Favreau was in touch with colleagues in Switzerland, but I had no need to know who they were. We had many different work streams. Why don't we Google pharmaceutical doctors in Switzerland and see if anything is there that we can follow?"

I nodded. "Okay, simple, but anything is worth trying now."

The Wi-Fi in Neapolitano's was busy but still served its purpose. The Genovese bread was going cold, however, we had managed to inhale the Lemoncellos. Worryingly, mine didn't seem to touch the sides as I swallowed it. Alcoholism was just around the corner at this rate. "You look up Professors and doctors, I am looking up Interzamabol. Maybe we will get lucky on one of them."

I had recovered my confidence somewhat, but maybe now was not the time to try and tell Jeanne about the other Gemini168 stuff - I didn't want to distract her from what we were doing.

Jeanne had a habit of mumbling what she was reading, slightly off putting, but done with her French accent it was really quite endearing. She had stopped crying now and her eyes were narrowed in concentration.

I kept sneaking almost furtive looks at her; her long, dark brown hair, her perfect hands swiping the screen of her phone. God, she was beautiful! Poetry before me. What was happening to me? Was I really falling for this French scientist? My mind went back to the job in hand: Interzamabol. The first site I found talked about the success of the drug and then on to the company behind it – Zenden. I had never heard of them. Perhaps they had gone bust, but then, before the events of the last few days, I knew very little about anything to do with medicines. I read on and found very little more information other than the name of the scientist who had discovered the molecule. If Professor De Vico was right, then this guy, a Dr. Wengen, would be a millionaire by now. I ploughed on through a few more links and got very little else in the way of new information.

I needed another Espresso and cocked an eyebrow at Philippe, who was hovering near-by. He read my mind and flashed up the victory sign to me to indicate two cups. A quick nod and smile from me and he was on it like a car bonnet. Jeanne was still doing the mumbling and finger moving thing. "I am not getting anywhere fast," she mumbled. I almost missed what she said, thinking she was reading a piece from a web-site.

"We seem to be looking for a needle in a hay-stack made of needles" As I said it she turned to me.

"You have the funniest of sayings."

"I try hard, but I am not that funny."

"I find you funny," she breathed, almost sensually. I reddened self-consciously - be still my beating heart.

"Let's try something else. Could you look up Dr Wengen? I am going to look up Zenden."

The coffees arrived, along with two more Lemoncellos. All I remember was the heat in my throat. Once again, I had necked the lemon liqueur and had no recollection of doing it. Binge drinking with an Italian liqueur - not quite the same as burning out on whisky and vodka!

Trying not to listen to the background noise of Jeanne mumbling away, I immersed myself in researching background stuff on the company name of Zenden. They had survived for three years and did very little until they discovered a molecule called Exotropotine. This had become a moderately successful drug in alleviating Irritable Bowel Syndrome. However, it had become very successful when it was used in the reduction of high blood pressure during pregnancy and it had been named commercially as Interzamabol. It turns out that most drugs have two names: one the chemical name and then one the brand name. Zenden was then bought over by none other than the biggest pharmaceutical Company on the planet, Castralten.

"Bailey, I have got a Professor Wengen, who is on the board of Castralten. Do you think it is the same person?" What were the chances of it not being?

"How many can there be? Where is he and how do we get to him?"

"Let me look him up and see what he does. He has given his name to a great deal of research into high blood pressure. He seems like a good man. He is everywhere: there are mentions of him talking all over the world. Hold on..."

My heart was beginning to beat a little faster. "He is in Geneva talking tomorrow at congress. He is the key-note speaker on Interzamabol, its efficacy and its side effects." I almost could not control my heart, nor my speech.

"We've got to get a hold of my brothers and Mitch. We need to get to Geneva and we need to be there by tomorrow. We have a doctor to meet."

"Call your brothers and let's get to the train station. We can get part of the way at least tonight."

Philippe had brought two more Lemoncellos. I decided not to gulp mine down and left it sitting on the table. I left way too much money for the bill and started moving. "Arrivederci!" Called Philippe.

"Ciao, ciao, ciao!" I shouted back

We suddenly heard a commotion boiling up behind us. I looked around to see a smartly dressed man on the ground, surrounded by a crowd of concerned looking, babbling pedestrians. His attempts to get up were being hampered by a stocky, bearded man, who looked like he was trying to force him to lie down again. The prone man's pants were torn and bloodied at the knees.

Jeanne was pulling on my am. "Come on Bailey, we will miss the train!" I pulled back, drawn to what was going on. The two men were now grappling furiously, and the injured one became increasingly, almost uncontrollably irate, screaming invective at his older, heavier attacker. I could see two black-clad Carabinieri pushing through the throng. The injured man looked towards them, and then straight at me, and redoubled his efforts to get up and away from his assailant.

The crowd gasped and suddenly shrank back; a black pistol fell from the coat of the injured man to the sidewalk. "Attenzione, pistole, pistole!" someone cried out. The bearded man fixed me with a long stare, and then knocked his opponent flat with a looping punch. I felt a shiver - those eyes; what the Fuck!? The Carabinieri burst through the crowd and pinned the by-now apoplectic gunman to the ground, whilst the other man leapt onto a Vespa scooter and roared away in a cloud of acrid fumes. I squinted at the disappearing cycle; a heavy coat was draped over the pillion, just like that worn by the street artist we had seen earlier. Then he was gone; pursued half-heartedly by one of the sweating Carabinieri.

Jeanne pulled again, urgently now. "Come on Bailey, he was after us. There may be others, come on!" We were off and running to the train station. I took out the phone that Mitch had given me. I needed to call Anderson: no time for secrecy now!

Mitch looked up and saw the sign A10 - POTSDAM-FRANKFURT (ODER) - BERLIN-ZENTRUM. He yawned surreptitiously. He was weary, but there was only about an hour to go. His mind was thirty, but his body was fifty. How many times had he wished that the ratios had been reversed! They would pull up at a hotel, and freshen up before taking on the hunt for the Englishman. Holiday Inn at the Alexanderplatz would be just fine, and the food was okay too. He glanced at the sleeping brothers in the mirror. If only their Dad could see them now. He fleetingly wondered if David was alive - how could he be? The plane must have gone down smack in the middle of the lake. Mitch was imbued with the dark side of his business, and he knew that it was absolutely possible for things to be faked, covered up, whatever. David had been as close to a real friend as Mitch ever had, or allowed, and finding him alive would make him feel, well... good. His logical mind defaulted back to the present, he was tired and hungry!

They checked in at the Holiday inn just before midnight. Mitch turned to the raddled brothers as they loitered listlessly in the foyer. "Okay guys, we'll get some shut-eye, and meet down here at seven for breakfast. We need some planning for what we are about to do."

Easton scrunched his face up, ruffling his blond pelt as he emitted his signature raspberry "7.30? Do we get Reveille first?"

Mitch smiled. "You're a funny guy, and someday people other than yourself will realise that. See you both tomorrow."

Easton made a half-hearted attempt at a mock salute, before pulling his hand down, crestfallen, as Mitch's icy stare fixed on him. What a half-assed thing to do. He dipped his head apologetically.

Anderson snapped at his sullen brother. "What is it with you? Stop screwing around with this guy - he's on our side, and all you seem to do is tug his chain; enough already!"

Easton frowned dismissively. "Yeah, ok, whatever. Now let's get some sleep before Officers call."

Mitch was pacing the foyer like a two-legged big cat as the brothers tumbled out of the lift the next morning. The pugnacious jaw was freshly shaved, and he was dressed in a suit that looked as though the creases would cut paper. He looked at his watch, nodding. "Hey, good job, right on the nail. Okay, let's go eat!"

Easton muttered, "Ok Gunny, we're on it."

Anderson squashed the rising laughter in his throat. It was kind of like Heartbreak Ridge. Breakfast was a perfunctory affair and came to an end as Mitch shot out of his chair and loped off into the seating area in the foyer. Anderson wiped his face with a napkin as he rose, prodding the somnolent Easton, who let his mouth-bound spoonful of cereal drop uselessly back into the bowl before angrily scraping his chair back and striding after his brother. Mitch gestured them to a small couch in a secluded part of the lounge area.

He spoke, unchallengeable authority oozing from every word. "Okay, I'm going to outline how we go after this. I need you to listen until I'm finished, and then we'll talk about any of it that you want to go over again - Yeah?" Communal nodding from the brothers. "Okay, we are here because the Englishman recruits his resource here, and although *he* won't be here, we can get to someone who can tell us where he is, and what he is doing. You two will go to the Crescent club in Potsdamer Platz posing as doormen looking for work - I've got fake resumes pulled together, you'll be two ex-grunts looking for a little excitement in life. You'll have some stuff to remember, and you'll have to act like soldiers - should be less of a problem for you Anderson, so you lead it, try and keep Easton protected."

Anderson shot a glance at an equally disbelieving Easton.

Mitch came back "I see the doubt guys, but these are low-level operators. They don't normally take Americans."

"We're British!" interrupted Easton.

Mitch's look pinned Easton to the wall. "They don't normally take Americans, so maybe you'll get some slack being Brits. They usually talk to people while they check the resumes. They might be rough-assed amateurs, but they have state of the art information systems. If the information checks out, they hire you to keep the door, and if they like you enough, they offer other stuff: beatings, back up for extortion, small time jobs, and from that they lead you into the serious shit. You'll have maybe an hour before they make you. Your resumes won't check out, and they'll then kick your asses out of there. In that hour I need you to make this guy, and if he's there let me know."

Mitch slid a photograph onto the table in front of the brothers. A pock-marked, sallow face topped by thinning strands of coarse dark hair stared back at them. "Not a male model then?"

Easton's comment wafted unnoticed into the ether as Mitch started talking again. "Florian Balint, the Englishman's recruitment specialist, will know where he is."

Anderson waited until Mitch had finished. "Why can't you go in, Mitch?"

"Because I'll be made in seconds, they know who I am."

Another question. "What if he's not there?"

"He should be, He's certainly in town, but if he's not, it's an abort."

Easton asked the next question. "If he's there how do we get him to you?"

"I'll take care of that," he said flatly.

Anderson spoke again. "He's not going to just tell you all you need to know, is he? How will you get it out of him?"

Mitch replied curtly "I'll take care of that as well. Now you two need to learn your lines - we're going tonight."

The brothers gasped in sync. "Tonight?" croaked Anderson. Mitch nodded slowly and purposefully.

Easton sat back, putting his hands behind his head. "Okay, we need to get ready. How about some Jar-head coaching Mitch? I won't need any help with the doorman stuff, that's in my DNA now." Mitch chuckled; he was getting to like this boy.

CHAPTER 25

The night was warm and wet, and the streets glistened under the garish lights that proliferated in the city. Mitch and the brothers took the S-Bahn to Potsdamer Platz, mingling with the evening crowds on their way to whatever entertainment they chose in that reconstructed city. Easton looked Mitch up and down as the imposing American sat across from him. Put him in a suit, chinos, a wet suit or a fricking Coco Chanel dress and he'd still be a Marine, he mused - even the hairs on his hands seemed to stand to attention. Easton liked to cultivate his own reputation as a maverick, loose cannon, psycho, even, but this guy made him feel like John Boy Walton. Easton wasn't afraid of any human being, but he reckoned Mitch was maybe not part of that species. Easton turned to Anderson, who was sitting engrossed in the role he was about to play; mumbling lines and phrases to himself as he sat, eyes fixed on the myriad adverts plastered above the seats. The train emptied gradually, and the three men were eventually the only occupants of the carriage.

Mitch spoke. "Next stop, guys. Walk up the street and the Sony centre is on the left. Go right in, I'll be outside - remember, you'll have about an hour before they figure things out. Look around as much as you can. They are never going to tell you if Balint is there, so don't ask! Now I've got some shopping to do."

The two brothers walked across the Leibziger Platz past the graffiti adorned remnants of the old Wall to what was locally known as the Sony Centre. The entrance to the bar was straight ahead. "Nothing like where I work, is it!?" he whispered to Anderson as he scanned the immaculate paintwork and pristine facade. Two Neanderthals wearing impossibly tight black T-shirts and baggy black combat pants stared vacantly at them. Anderson approached them, talking as he walked. "Hey guys, we're looking for some work here. We were told that you might be hiring?"

The nearest Neanderthal spoke first. "American?"

"No, British" said Anderson, with conviction.

"Wait here." The man disappeared into the club, returning within minutes. "Come in, you got papers?"
Anderson was thrown temporarily. "Papers...I, er..."

Easton stepped in. "Think he means our resumes. Yeah, we've got them."

The Neanderthal smiled, a melange of yellow stumps, accentuated by periodic black spaces. "Blondie, clever boy. Yeah, we need resumes."

The brothers followed the doorman into the club, complying with his gesture to wait at the bar. The clientele was a mix of goths, moshers and incongruously suited and booted businessmen-types congregated in the numerous booths around a tiny dance floor. Mid seventies German synthesizer music pumped out of an elderly PA system. Tangerine Dream, or maybe Kraftwerk, mused Anderson. He and Easton scanned around the room, trying to cover every corner. A thin, Middle-Eastern looking man came out from behind the bar, trailing a plume of cigarette smoke.

He looked the brothers over scornfully. "Resumes?" he barked. Anderson handed the fabricated papers over. The smoker took them, and handed them to a plump girl, probably Turkish, who was working behind the bar, snarling some instructions as he did. She disappeared, and the smoker proceeded to ask the brothers a series of random, un-co-ordinated questions about their work history. The brothers fielded them comfortably, still trying to look around as they did.

Apparently satisfied with their answers, the smoker beckoned them to the bar. He called to a burly man working the tables.

"Tadeus, give these guys something to drink."

The man swaggered over to the bar. Easton looked at him distastefully; shaven-headed, pot-bellied, and wearing skinny stone wash jeans - not a good look. A jolt of electricity rippled up Easton's spine. He had seen this guy before. Jesus Christ, it was one of the Estonian pit-bulls from Paris! He turned to look for Anderson. He was over speaking to a customer. Easton called, as quietly as he could, to get his attention.

Anderson waved, calling back, "Hey man, I'm just going to the john. Back in a minute." "Fuck! This guy will recognise me," Easton screamed to himself.

The pit-bull was inches away from his face. What you want to drink, friend?" He was looking right at Easton, who lowered his eyes.

"Two Cokes will be fine, sir, just the bottles." The pit bull grunted, and reached into a drinks fridge, flipping the tops off of the bottles and planting them on the bar-top. Easton muttered thanks, looking out of the corner of his eye as the pit-bull resumed his table work.

Anderson reappeared. "Sorry bro, must be nerves. You okay?"

Easton pulled him close. "That guy clearing the tables; he was one of the mob who tried to take us down in Paris." Anderson's face froze, and he turned his head slowly to look where Easton's eyes were taking him.

He looked back, white-faced. "You're right, it's him, the one Bailey dropped outside the clothes store. He must recognise us, we were in his face! This should be fun. We've got to leave. I haven't seen this Balint dude, but we won't get out alive if we're made."

Easton made the move. "Let's go bro, we're leaving: go for the door now!"

The brothers had covered about half the distance when a loud voice called out, "Hey Blondie, nice shirt you are wearing, I remember you no like mine!" The pit-bull walked between them and the door, clutching a butterfly knife in his left hand. Five other men were gravitating to the centre of the small dance floor, where the brothers stood - rigid with adrenalin.

Anderson spoke quietly, "You ready for this, Easton?"

His brother nodded with a way too enthusiastic movement; he was going to enjoy this. "You got your side worked out? No waiting or coming back if one of us goes down. Get to Mitch. Let's hope none of them have a gun..."

The knife-toting pit-bull suddenly roared and flew at Easton. His looping swipe with the knife was easily avoided, and Easton, pumped and focused, crashed a right foot into his exposed armpit, clipping the hapless thug's head with a left foot as he fell. Two black-clad apes lunged at Anderson, arms flailing. He side-stepped the first, smashing an elbow into the back of his large head as he did. The other attacker planted a pudgy fist into Anderson's unprotected back. The blow stung and winded him, and a sudden weakness buckled his legs. He swung his arm back with all his strength and smashed it into the bridge of his attacker's nose. The bar had erupted into a welter of screaming, fleeing patrons, scattering like sheep, as black-shirted thugs fought to get at the brothers.

A few hundred metres away, Mitch picked up the faint noises of chaos emanating from the bar. "What the fuck!?" He cursed again, and started walking across the square towards the club, knowing exactly what to expect. Easton must have blown it.

Inside the bar, the brothers were using all of their considerable martial arts skills to fight for their lives. None of their attackers could individually match what they had, but sheer weight of numbers was beginning to tell. Easton felled an enormous assailant with a lightning combination of punches, at the same time taking the force of a baseball bat on his left collar bone. He had just moved in time and it did not hit him full on. The waves of pain made him dizzy, but nothing was broken.

Anderson moved over to him and, with one blow dealt with the baseball bat thug. "We're gonna get creamed here bro. Start thinking about exit plans!"

Easton saw the lights of the square through the pristine windows. One of the doormen was coming up behind Anderson, wielding some kind of club. Easton grabbed his brother's coat at the shoulders. "Hold tight bro, this might hurt!" The two brothers hurtled towards the disbelieving doorman, who dropped his weapon as the human snowball rolled him up in its momentum and smashed him though the front window of the bar and out into the square. Anderson sprang up immediately. "Some fucking exit plan! You could have killed us!" Easton prised himself away from the stunned doorman, shaking glass from his hair as he did.

"You had a better way out? We were in trouble...and still are!" as he pointed to the gaggle of heavies erupting from the club doors. Easton looked at Anderson, barking one word "Run!"

The brothers sprinted towards the Leipzig Strasse exit, pursued by the shouting thugs. They were younger and fitter than any of the posse chasing them, but had to move quickly. Anderson suddenly howled in pain as a thrown baton caught him around the legs, bringing him down on the ornate cobbles. Easton cursed, turning back to face the nearest of his assailants. The first one swiped wildly with a beer bottle, sailing over Easton's right shoulder. The next move was easy for him. Use the assailant momentum and throw him along the same line. He did and the thug crashed into a refuse bin head-first; his night was over. The other stopped, hands raised.

Easton was in a fury. "Come on you prick, make your move!" The thug stepped back, his nerve gone, and Easton smashed a foot into his face. He fell, his face a bloody ruin. Anderson was still down, and Easton knew he was on his own. A third attacker leapt at him, all swinging legs and eldritch yells. Easton blocked a leg with a raised knee, then swept the other away, causing the man to crack his head first on the ground. Jesus, it had been a while and he had forgotten how good he was at this! Adrenalin flooded his system. He readied to face whatever came next, but the remaining thugs had formed a rough semi-circle round him and his fallen brother, standing, unmoving, with extreme intent.

A balding olive-skinned man dressed in a suit moved to the front of the group. He was pointing a Walther pistol at Anderson's prone body. He spoke, in accented English "Enough of this shit. Now I can see why seven of my men did not deal with you in Paris, but you messed up coming here. Your time is over."

Anderson spoke, his voice thick with pain. "Easton, he's the guy, the Balint guy..."

Balint's eyes narrowed. "How do you know my name?" The brothers tensed, waiting for the inevitable bullet. There was a soft 'pop,' instantaneously followed by a red hole appearing just above Balint's left knee. He roared, fell back and dropped his gun to the cobbles. Clutching both hands over his wrecked limb, he rolled on the polished floor of the centre.

The rest of his men moved menacingly forward, until a familiar, clipped voice rang out from the muzzy shadows at the edge of the square. "Get back, or I'll put holes in all of you sons-of-bitches." Mitch stepped into the light, his Glock pistol held in both hands, combat style, in front of him. He pressed the silencer barrel into the pudgy forehead of the nearest heavy, denting the shaven flesh. "You stand here, lard-ass, while your buddies disappear. Go on, get going!" The remaining men scattered to all corners of the centre. Mitch fixed the quivering man on the end of his gun with a fearsome stare.

"You've been working too hard. Take an early finish tonight, on me!" he snapped, drawing back the pistol and bringing it down hard on the petrified man's skull. He dropped wordlessly to the ground.

Easton pulled Anderson up, glowering angrily at Mitch. "Well Mitch, how'd you think we did?" The American shot him a look that stifled any further comments, as he grabbed the still-moaning Balint's arm and hauled him to his feet.

The Romanian screamed in pain as he put weight on his shattered leg. He snapped at the brothers as he moved.

Mitch spoke sharply. "Come on boys, we're gonna do some water sports. Help me get this fucker out of here!" The brothers looked at each other incongruously but started to propel the moaning man along behind the tall American as they left the square, watched curiously by tipsy passers-by and perplexed performance artists.

Easton called out, "This guy needs a hospital Mitch. He can't walk!"

The hobbling Romanian stuck his face into Easton's, saliva shooting from his lips. "You will all fucking die. You don't know what you have done. You are all going to fucking DIE!"

Easton smoothed the flecks of foam from his face. "And how you gonna do that, drown us in spit? You can't even walk asshole, and I am thinking the big Marine up ahead has got some real good games for you to play!"

Mitch turned and strode up to the sweating, groaning Romanian: "Know who I am? I think you do, Florian."

Balint's eyes locked open. "You are American guy... American guy. You work with my boss. You bastard, why you fucking shoot me?"

"Your boss is an outlaw, persona non-grata, and you are going to tell me where he is!"

Balint seemed to be stunned by this revelation, but soon recovered his venom. "Go fuck yourself, American. He will come for you when he hear of this. You are in shit!"

Blackwatch, it seemed, kept property in many cities, used for various purposes in the course of daily operations. The group took a short walk to a row of shop units, where Mitch produced a key and opened the door of the third unit, which was vacant. The brothers exchanged another quizzical look. Mitch sensed their concern, winked and said, "When you do what I do, you have places like this. Bring him in. It is time for the water sports boys?" Uncomprehending, the brothers pushed a paling Balint into the stale darkness of the unlit space.

A light went on, and Easton noticed three five-pint bottles of water and some hand towels lying on the floor. He glanced at Anderson, who shook his head in reply, equally nonplussed. Mitch forced the recalcitrant Romanian to his knees; he screamed as his shattered limb touched the floor. Then Mitch pulled him flat down. The irate Romanian spat invective as the front of his body hit the oil-stained floor. Mitch, oblivious, yanked his arms back and clipped them together with two brightly-coloured Tie-its, rolling him over on his back as he finished.

Balint screamed and barked non-stop as Mitch worked. "What you do, you fuck! I will kill you for this, you listen?" The boys watched with rising concern as Mitch took a hand towel and wadded it to half its length. He then opened one of the bottles of water and soaked the towel thoroughly. He turned to the boys, speaking softly, "You won't like this, but this piece of shit won't tell us what we need to know unless I loosen him up a little, so if you don't want to know the score...look away now." He then placed the towel in the open, still ranting, mouth of the Romanian.

The brothers, shocked, suddenly realised his purpose. Mitch took the open bottle and dribbled water onto the hand towel, bringing strange, wet gurgling noises from the prostrate gangster.

Easton could take no more. "Fucking water-boarding! Jesus Christ! This shit is illegal man! I am just a doorman from New York. This is torture! You are fucking gone man!"

Mitch glared at the stunned brothers, struggling to hold the head of the by now, apoplectic prisoner. "So what should I do, sonny? Take him for a beer and talk it over?"

Anderson stepped forward, needing to do something, but unsure of what that might be. Mitch's voice rang in the enclosed space. "Stand fast boy, you stay right there! Not another fucking step; you hear?"

The fury of the retort seemed to crush Anderson, and he slumped against the bare wall, head in hands. More water dripped onto the towel, running over Balint's contorted face in rivulets. Mitch peered at the man below him. "Where is the Englishman? Tell us now, and make it right or you'll drown like the Captain of the fucking Titanic!" The spluttering, gagging Romanian shook his head vigorously, bellowing damply, "Huck-yoooo!"

The grim-faced American slopped more water onto the sodden cloth, simultaneously pressing his knee against the still-bleeding gunshot wound. Balint's cries soared to a new pitch, tailing off despairingly as the American suddenly pulled away. Mitch removed the towel from his mouth,

"Alright, I tell you, I tell you, please no more, no more! He is going to Geneva, Geneva, he leaving tomorrow."

"To do what, shithead, to do WHAT?" More gurgling entreaties from the tormented Romanian. Mitch clamped his fingers round the man's nostrils, ready to pour water into his open mouth.

"To kill someone, okay? To kill some Professor guy. I am drowning, please enough..."

Mitch, stood back, chest relaxing, his grey trousers splotched with blood and dark water stains. "Outstanding, still got two full bottles. We could get a refund!"

Easton bit his lip deeply, arms tightly folded, while an appalled Anderson stared, mouth open at the now-bedraggled American. Anderson's phone rang; it's tinkling tone, the theme from Big Bang Theory, filling the compact space and breaking the spell. He snatched it from his pocket, squinting at the screen." It's Bailey, will I answer it?"

Mitch compressed his lips, and nodded once, his grim work finished. "Answer it boy, and then we're on our way."

CHAPTER 26

I had been about to hang up when the phone was answered. Anderson's voice, distant and echoing, but still HIS voice, came down the line.

"Anderson, listen up, we're on our way to Geneva. There's a conference there at seven tomorrow night. A Professor Wengen is speaking. We need to get to him, he could help us. We've got the venue details." I heard Mitch's stentorian voice. "We're on it Bailey, the Englishman is also on his way to Geneva. I'd guess to make sure your Professor gets his lines right, or worse."

My naivety struck again, I wasn't sure what Mitch meant. "What do you mean, to kill him?"

The strident American voice boomed out of the phone speaker. "Come on, Bailey. He won't be giving him media training, will he?"

Cursing my gullibility, I tried to match his tone. "Okay, so are you coming to us?"

I could almost visualise Mitch sticking out his jaw and nodding as he replied. "Alright, we'll meet up at Gare De Cornavin at 1800 hours. That's enough time before it starts. Get moving." Anderson killed the call. The phone screen darkened as the shop went silent. Easton looked at the inert Romanian. "What about him?"

Mitch spoke as he pulled on his coat. "Could kill him..." The racked expressions on the boys' faces seemed to amuse him. "We'll leave him here. I'll call a doctor friend of mine, Russian, very efficient, and can use a gun as well. Don't worry, he won't die...unless he wants to."

Balint, now sitting up, looked in anguish at the brothers. "I will die anyway. My boss will kill me." Mitch grinned. "Well we'll get you fit enough to be killed, don't want you dying in a bad way!"

Balint's answering stare was silent and full of hate. Mitch spoke briskly. "Right guys, we're off to Geneva. We're leaving now: be about eleven hours, and we don't have time for planes or trains - okay with you guys?"

"Awesome!" muttered Easton, "Eleven more hours in a car with you. Water-boarding doesn't seem so bad now." Mitch chuckled - he *liked* this guy!

CHAPTER 27

The journey from Rome took us up through Milan towards Il Lago Magiori and then on to France and Switzerland. We talked briefly and matter-of-factly about the man with the gun in Rome. Funny how being a prey animal for a time deadens your fear of death. You kind of raise your level of adrenalin and get used to it. Jeanne worried me slightly, but for a different reason than before. She hadn't seen all of what I had, and listened dubiously as I theorised that the street artist had tried to warn us about being followed, and then had stopped the gunman from getting on our train. No matter how hard I tried to join up the threads, she remained unconvinced. I decided to let it go. We had a long journey ahead.

Some of the views were breath-taking as we came past Crans Montana and on into Montreux. Too many houses, too much urbanisation to be truly wild, but it was still beautiful. Jeanne's breath misted on the window as she took in the scenery, oohing and aahing at each new vista. I parked my concerns for the meantime, sat back in my seat and enjoyed the views.

As we stepped off the train in Geneva I was immediately taken by the clock on the platform. Mondaine clocks and watches are famous for stopping for two seconds on the 12 mark. Despite this fact all trains ran to the second. This rail network was second only to Japan for on-time arrivals and departures. We were bang on time – it was good to be back in Switzerland. My hope was that it would be worthwhile.

I loved Geneva, although it was five years or so since I had been here. It was clean and safe and of course, grindingly expensive. The food was always well varied and the hotels looked after you like you were the biggest money spinner on the planet: for all they knew, you were. Appearances in this part of the world could be very deceptive and many people played down their net worth. They were probably, after-all, secreting their money in an un-named account, and they wouldn't want to be spotted visiting the very establishment they were hiding their "black" money in.

On exiting the Gare de Cornavin familiar faces could be seen across Place du Cornavin. On the far side, Easton and Anderson were standing with Mitch beside his BMW eating what looked like kebabs. What was it I said about food in Geneva? As we crossed the busy intersection Anderson looked over and caught our eye. He waved and then the other two joined in. Hugs were delivered all round.

I ruffled Eaton's mane playfully. "Yo bro, what's happening?"

He smiled lamely. "Nothing much, Bailey. Anderson and I spent the last eleven hours comparing sore asses, it was cool."

Mitch suppressed a grin, and started the conversation. "So what did Rome throw up?"

I filled him in on what Professor De Vico had told us and how it all led back to Wengen talking today at the conference. He listened quietly.

"Hotel: Swissotel Métropole, 34 Quai General-Guisan" I read this from my phone. "Five minutes' walk from here across the Pont du Mont-blanc, right next to the Jardin Anglais." Jeanne was visibly agitated.

"We must tell the authorities! We cannot do this ourselves. We must tell the Police!"

Mitch looked at her curiously. "Tell them what, exactly? We'd all spend hours in a cell being interrogated about some wacko plot to assassinate a Professor and it'd be over before anything could be done; not an option Mslle!" That was curt. Jeanne waved a hand submissively. Mitch spoke again. "We need a method of getting in there. I've got some formal clothes that you can put on. You all can't walk in there looking like vacationing designer clothes dummies."

Easton looked over the immaculately dressed American and said sniffily, "Why don't we do what they all do in my night club - turn up and pretend we are on the guest list?"

"How do we guess what the names will be?" asked Anderson.

"Easy. We do what all my patrons do and ask to see the list. They are real good at it. They run their finger down the list until they get a name that they like. Boom! They are in."

"Wait. There will probably be some sort of name badges on a table somewhere. Why not just grab five of them?" I interjected.

"Dangerous," said Mitch, "but we have no time for any other plan. We need to remember in Switzerland they speak five languages; maybe we should stick to English."

"We can all get by on western European languages Mitch, but English should be fine. Jeanne, you and I can do the French thing if it makes you feel easier?"

Jeanne was happy with that although I sensed a reticence from her at gate crashing a medical seminar attended by many of her professional peers. By now I was getting used to all this subterfuge and suspected that my two brothers were the same. Mitch? He was a pro, who had lived this life for many years.

"What is our plan when we get in there?" I asked.

"We find this Englishman and stop him from killing Wengen, if that's what he's here to do, or we take him and see what we can get out of him," said Mitch. "We don't know what we are going to find in there, but my guess is that it will be a large room and Wengen will be near the front. If it were me, I would find a vantage point and take him out with a rifle, but I suspect that won't be possible, so it will mean a close kill with a handgun or knife."

"Or crossbow," I said.

"A what?" asked Mitch.

"There is a shop on the next corner that sells crossbows for €25. You don't need a licence and they can be smuggled, dismantled inside a dinner jacket. It is what I would use. A head shot will kill anything from 30 yards – no noise."

Mitch seemed, for the first time since I had met him, to be on edge. "How the hell do we allow for that?" His hands rubbed his cropped temples furiously - not a good sign, I had come to realise.

"What does this 'Englishman' look like? I asked. It occurred to me that only Mitch would recognise him.

"That is part of the problem. We have no images of him. I have met him a few times. He is non-descript. He is average height, medium build, kinda fair-ish hair, and he has maybe one distinguishing feature, a gap between his front teeth. He carries himself like a real stiff ass aristo, complete with accent, but the chances of talking to him before he fires his gun, or does the William Tell thing," he glared at me, "...are zero."

A raspberry burst out of Easton's mouth. "Great. So if I have got this right, we are going into a venue that we don't know anything about, we are looking for an assassin we won't recognise, and we don't know what sort of weapon we are facing. Oh and it's a party that we are not invited to. I'm not real happy about being here. A couple of weeks ago I was living an ordinary life. How did we get to this suicide mission?" Easton was obviously not keen on Mitch's strategy.

"If you are running scared, just wait here Braveheart, but I've seen you in action. You can handle yourself and we'll need you." Mitch wasn't given to persuasive language, but Easton didn't miss the compliment.

Still, he persisted. "I will stand with my brothers, and you, but this guy could be carrying some heavy weaponry, and we're going in with what? Your gun and a mobile phone you gave us? Not exactly Delta Squad operating procedure, is it?"

Mitch looked at each of us in the eye, obviously a well-practised procedure he adopted before going into dangerous situations. My thoughts were that he had done this so many times that he was just on auto-pilot. "Anybody else having second thoughts? Say now or we are going in."

A combination of fear of Mitch, adrenaline and stupidity stopped me from answering. Anderson looked at me for a response. On getting nothing, he remained silent. Jeanne did not even blink. God knows what she was thinking.

"Then we are good to go." At that, Mitch moved towards the gardens and the hotel beyond them.

"Go Rambo!" said Easton.

"Are you coming?" I asked.

"Yep, but I am not happy and I want it noted," Easton grinned archly.

"Noted. Now let's get suited and booted, then we'll split up and go, and be careful." Easton rarely showed any fear, of anything. His bravado didn't mask his genuine anxiety. I understood where he was coming from. Not that long ago I opened an email and within days we had avoided several attempts on our lives, seen innocent people die, and now we faced a well-trained assassin with one thing on his mind. I had to get to Wengen, I wanted answers, I needed answers. This was for Mom, and Dad. My fear was frozen, blocked out by my desire for closure. I glanced at Mitch, who was assiduously scrutinising his watch. Whatever, I was still so glad he was with us...

CHAPTER 28

As Jeanne and I walked along through the Jardin Anglais, I cocked a thumb at the fountain out on the lake. It was pretty close and in full flow. We sidled up to the entrance of the hotel and looked for some event signage. The hotel event boards carried the information that we needed and we walked briskly along a corridor to the conference and banqueting area. The corridor was lined with posters showing the sponsor's logo, and the signature product, and was manned by smartly dressed men and women who I presumed to be sales people.

A desk was positioned to the left as we entered and the middle-aged attractive lady driving it was busy talking to a couple of male Italian doctors, or at least they looked and sounded like Italians. It occurred to me again at this stage that many of these doctors were well dressed and looked like your average city suit, and that only Mitch would be able to pick the Englishman out among this throng. No matter.

First we had to get over the name badge hurdle. As the woman was talking, I got the chance to look at rows of badges which were all attached to lanyards. I was looking for two French or Swiss French names, hopefully male and female!! Half way down the second column I found one for Jeanne. 'Francoise Heptoire.' A quick glance further down and I found the one for me: 'Pascal Beaufort.' The receptionist looked at me questioningly and spoke rapidly in French. Jesus, French was not my best language. I got very little of what she said. I was scrabbling frantically for an answer when Jeanne stepped in and directed a torrent of liquid and extravagant French at the curious receptionist. The woman suddenly smiled, laughed heartily and waved us on. We were in, lanyards around our necks and milling with the crowds.

We walked to a little corner. I had to ask Jeanne; "What did you tell her?" She smiled. "I told her that you could talk about proteins all day, but that you weren't good on normal conversation." I frowned, "As long as you didn't tell her I was stupid!" Jeanne touched my arm and nodded in the direction of the door. Easton was over-doing the doctor thing and had somehow got a hold of a stethoscope, which he had draped around his neck. Christ Almighty! My heart began to race. He could so easily blow things here and Mitch had not even made it in yet. I pushed off from the wall and led Jeanne a little closer to listen in to the conversation with Anderson, Easton and the lady on reception. Anderson looked down the rows of badges and said, "Doctor Thomson. Thank you." He had obviously caught a name as he waited in line. The lanyard was handed over without demur. He was in. Easton shuffled up in the line after him.

He pointed at a badge. "That is me there. Dr Patel." said Easton. My heart stopped dead. 'Easton, what the fuck are you playing at!?' I screamed noiselessly, moving closer to the desk.

"Dr Pa-tel," said the receptionist. Her eyebrows and her suspicions were raised. "Easton, you shit head!" another helpless ejaculation of frustration bounced around in my head. Time for an intervention. Jeanne beat me to it.

"Dr Patel, how nice to see you again, and Dr Thomson, it was Paris the last time we met, was it not so? Your paper on protein detection was a seminal piece of work. I couldn't put it down!" I watched open mouthed as the receptionist basically bought it - Jeanne was learning: best not to over-do things though, so it was time to usher the group away from prying eyes and ears.

We made our way over to a quiet coffee station and helped ourselves. Easton self-consciously stuffed his stethoscope into his coat pocket. Three pairs of eyes bored into him. He coughed, and whispered croakily, "Sorry guys, almost blew the whole thing there." Anderson's teeth gritted as he spoke, slowly and clearly, "You fucking dumb ass!" There was no reply from my crestfallen brother. I scanned the scene looking for Mitch but he was nowhere to be seen. I was getting a little concerned.

At that the doors to the auditorium opened and everyone began to make their way inside. We looked inside and could see that there were two main blocks of seats with somewhere close to four hundred on each side. We decided to split, with Easton and Anderson working the left side of the room and Jeanne and myself working the far right. It was best to hang back a little to let everyone find seats and sit down. That way we could see who was in the room by standing off to the side. As everyone began to settle and go quiet, except some Italian people who were jabbering away about the quality of the espresso from the coffee station, some voices were being raised in the reception area. "Oh, oh! I thought," "Some of our stolen names had turned up." I caught a glimpse of Easton and Anderson on the far side of the hall. They were looking forward and it became apparent what had caught their eye. A glowering Mitch, complete with lanyard and stone face, stood about 40 feet in front of them and his eyes were looking sideways towards the centre row.

I tried to follow his line of sight, but it was difficult as we were at an obtuse angle from him and there were still some people unseated. Then it became obvious: a well-dressed man was making his way down the middle row, but he was not looking for a seat. His right hand was in his pocket and his eyes were fixed on a row of seats at the front of the auditorium. To the side of the stage was a row of black leather bar stools where a group of men and women were settling; the guest speakers. There in the middle of the group was an older man, of about sixty with grey hair and matching moustache. He was not very tall but his demeanour was visibly confident, almost arrogant. Wengen, it had to be. He matched the pictures that we had Googled. The group was clucking and fussing around him. Wengen looked very happy with himself amongst the group of experts that he was obviously presiding over. I nodded to Jeanne and she saw what I saw. We tried not to draw attention to ourselves but knew we had to act fast. As the lights dimmed I squinted over towards Mitch. The brothers were about thirty feet behind him, but he did not even notice. Events were about to begin in more ways than one.

I began to quicken my stride in the hope that I would get to Wengen before the potential assassin. The man in the middle row took his hand out of his pocket. In the gloom it was difficult to make out what he had but it was dark and rectangular. He quickened his pace and got to the front row, turning towards the bar chairs and as he did so he raised his right hand. I was about to shout out knowing that I had twenty rows of chairs still to cover. I looked for Mitch, but he seemed to be hanging back. The well- dressed man then waved his right hand and turned towards the stage. He climbed a set of steps and moved towards the lectern: a tablet computer in his right hand.

"My learned friends..." he began. Jesus, he was the event MC! I breathed a sigh of relief. Just as I did, three rows in front of me at the end of the aisle I was in, a man stood up and pulled a pistol from his coat, pointed it at the group of people on the stage and fired three times. Wengen's eyes bulged, and he slid soundlessly from his stool to a sitting position on the floor, blood pooling around him from the wounds in his torso.

Instinct took over I leapt on the shooter, but missed grabbing him properly and only succeeded in partially dislodging the gun from his grip. He threw a right elbow backwards at me, which I was ready for. The best way to deal with this attack is to step with the blow and use your right hand to deflect the arc of the elbow over your head. In doing this you give your assailant a chance to throw a left at you. I was ready for this too. I stepped inside the arc of his left and swung him round with me. The space was too tight and I stumbled back into the row of chairs. Jeanne was still two rows away and making her way towards me. Her progress was slow and it became apparent that utter panic had engulfed the room.

At the sound of the gunshots everyone had jumped up and a "sauve qui peut" melee ensued. Streams of people were heading for the exits. I guessed that this would prevent Mitch and the brothers getting to me quickly. As I fell back, the gunman threw a right towards my jaw. He had misjudged my fall and it merely glanced off my chin. He backed up and started his escape. I was trapped in a row of seats on my back and he was making his way out. Fearful that I would lose him in the panic, I scanned his features, stamping them on my memory. Short, sandy hair, classically side-parted, fresh, ruddy complexion, and an unmistakeable gap between his two... Shit - he was gone!

I heard Jeanne's voice and looked up to see her hand reaching down to help me up. As I rose, I looked for the Englishman and saw no sign of him, and then I heard a loud voice to my left. I looked over and there standing on a chair with a stethoscope dangling from his breast pocket, was Easton.

"Mitch! The fire exit to the left of the stage!" He was now climbing over the chairs row by row and pointing like a gun dog at the left hand side of the auditorium. Behind him was Anderson, I followed their eye-line and caught a glimpse of Mitch's head wading through the panic-stricken crowds. He was on it. My job now was to get to Wengen. I was still holding Jeanne's hand.

"Wengen! Let's find him." She nodded, but her eyes were wide with fear. We got to the row of bar chairs and there lying at the foot of the middle one was Wengen. In the chaos caused by the shooting, everyone had run for the exits leaving him on the floor. He was clearly dying. We did not have much time, but I felt no compunction about what I was about to do. I had waited too long for answers.

I knelt beside him, Jeanne on the other side of him. He had been shot high up in the chest to the right hand side and the blood was everywhere. I was kneeling in a pool of it. It was coming from his mouth too.

"Why did you hide the results of your clinical trials?" Wengen's pupils were dilated, his breath gurgling up through fluid-filled lungs.

"Who are you?" He asked. Blood oozed between his teeth.

"You knew that Interzamabol would cause cancer in patients and yet you hid the results."

"Who are you?" he asked again, straining his eyes to try and see me better.

"You did all of this for money, for greed. You killed thousands of people with your drug, because of your greed for money. Why did you never tell anyone that one of the side effects of your drug was that it caused cancer in patients?"

Jeanne cracked. "For God's sake Bailey, he is dying, leave him alone!" She grabbed his bloodied hands helplessly. Her touch seemed to rally the dying man, and after clearing the blood from his throat, he spoke quietly and clearly. "You would not understand. We are under a great deal of pressure from the pharmaceutical companies to produce something that can be sold. Profit depends on these trials. They do not take failure well." He was sinking. His words were coming out between splutters of blood. I looked at Jeanne. She shook her head.

Who are you?" he asked again.

"Who is behind all of this?" I pressed, uncaring of his impending demise.

Jeanne buffeted me with her bloody hands in an outburst of total despair. "Bailey, you have lost your mind. Enough!"

His voice bubbled and frothed again. "Who...ah, you cannot imagine. It is not just about corrupt pharmaceutical companies any more. This is about greed, corporate greed, and mine also. God help me." His Germanic accent thickened. It was becoming more difficult to understand him. "I am dying, say a prayer for me."

"Tell me who is behind all of this?" I pulled his blood spotted face towards me.

"Who are you? Why do you need to know? What is it to you?" he persisted.

"I am nobody, but I need to know who is behind all of this."

"I am dying. I could tell you anything. Why do you want to know?"

"Because you killed my mother. She was prescribed your drug whilst pregnant with my younger brother. She was diagnosed with cancer soon afterwards and died an agonising death. So you see I would like to know who is behind all of this, because it is only fair that they look me in the eye and explain why they think it is okay to kill thousands of people." His reply was now a whisper.

"You are American, yes?"

It's a long story. Too long for you, but go on." I said flatly.

"I was paid by the drug company, but your government knew about these trials as I and other scientists did." His whisper tailed off. I grabbed him by his coat lapels, all remorse or pity for this man gone.

"So you come up with a molecule, you push it in front of a pharmaceutical company, they like it and take it through clinical trials. The results are too good to be true, you make millions, cover up the fact that this drug kills people and you are telling me that this is all orchestrated by who? The CIA? The FDA? Who?"

"Money corrupts people. I am paying my price, yes? But others are... are beyond reach, and your government knows who they are. There are millions of Euros involved." His eyes suddenly lost focus.

I looked at Jeanne; her bloodied hands covered her face. I looked down at Wengen. His eyes were closed and he lay motionless. Jeanne leaned over, threw her arms around my neck and kissed me full on the lips.

I pulled back, stunned by what she had done. "Jeanne, don't be hard on me. I needed answers, my life has been leading up to this."

"It's alright Bailey," she whispered huskily, "I understand. I do."

I took her hand and pulled her to her feet, we had to go. We managed to catch the last of the crowd pouring out of the closest fire exit to the stage. I was covered in Wengen's blood and looked pretty conspicuous. I noticed that the floor was covered in discarded coats, bags and shoes left by the fleeing delegates. I grabbed a coat and wrapped it round my shoulders. I pulled Jeanne's lanyard off her neck, whilst ripping my own off simultaneously, and dumped them as we exited the building. We needed to get to somewhere and sort our heads out. We needed to track my brothers and Mitch. What was happening with them? I could hear distant sirens splitting the Geneva air. We would sit tight somewhere safe until Mitch or the brothers got back to us - we could do nothing else.

CHAPTER 29

Mitch was on the sidewalk outside the hotel. He did not know Geneva well, and cursed as he looked from side to side, trying to catch sight of his quarry. There was a park in front of him, a bridge to his left, and to his right the lake opened out from the mouth of the river Rhone. Little knots of scared people were milling around all over his line of sight, and he had lost sight of his man just after he had left the building. He stared hopelessly down the road to his left - a sign said 'Quai Gustav Ador.' "So what?" he intoned impotently, "This guy could have gone anywhere." Suddenly his eyes were drawn to a man in a dark suit who was walking along the road towards the lake: walking when everyone else was running. He narrowed his eyes, peering into the evening sun.

A voice came soaring over the general background noise, a loud voice, powered by well-conditioned lungs. "He's going for the boat Mitch, the boat at the Quay!"

Mitch spun around. It was Easton, about 100 metres away, perched on top of a red-faced Anderson's shoulders. The gruff American smiled to himself. "Outstanding, absolutely fucking outstanding!" Mitch fixed his gaze again on the walking man, and started to canter briskly after him.

The killer had obviously heard the shout, and after glancing round, picked up pace as he moved away. 'About 300 metres away,' reckoned Mitch, moving purposefully on. Whilst he had heard the noise of the shout, he had not heard the content, merely quickening his pace as a precaution. He was around 50 metres from the quay from where the little boats chugged to and fro across the lake mouth and beyond. He glanced at his watch; just in time, his getaway was on schedule. He looked around quickly at the crowds moving away from him and then lobbed his gun into the lake. The splash went unheard above the maelstrom of traffic, shouting people and wailing sirens; so far so good, now to the boat.

Mitch was pushing his way through the crowds when he became aware of thumping footsteps coming up fast behind him. He tensed, turned quickly and prepared to deal with whatever was there. Two panting, red-faced brothers pulled up as he faced them. He growled belligerently at them. "Appreciate the heads-up guys, but you are drawing fire here running round like that. Hold up!"

Easton replied, between gulps of air. "He's going for the boat. He's probably heading for Quai Mont Blanc on the other side of the Lake."

Mitch frowned. "Probably? Where else could he go?"

Anderson was more composed. "He could go to a few places Mitch, but unless he kidnaps the crew that boat only goes to one place."

Mitch's face twitched. "So how do we get across? Do you know a way?"

Anderson nodded, pointing at the bridge. "The way we came; the boat takes a few minutes. We could make it in time."

Mitch set his lips, eyes darting between the two brothers. "Okay, lead on, and don't wait for me!"

The Englishman was sitting on the boat gazing back guardedly at the chaotic scenes at the hotel. Four other passengers were with him, holding desultory conversations, obviously speculating about the events across the water. The boat man spoke to the distracted assassin in French. He was asking if he knew what was happening at the hotel. The Englishman spoke excellent French, but replied icily, "I don't speak Swiss."

The boatman glared at him. 'Bloody tourists, don't they know anything? Don't speak Swiss; always the bloody English.' His smile masked the unspoken venom in his thoughts. Not that his taciturn passenger cared.

His three pursuers were now on the bridge, almost parallel with the adjacent Ile Rousseau. The spectacle of these suited men running flat out across a busy bridge was beginning to attract unwelcome attention. Several anxious looking pedestrians were chattering into glowing cell phones, obviously picking up on the news of what had happened at the hotel.

Mitch burst to the front of the group, barking as he did. "Come on boys, we're looking too conspicuous here. We need to get off this bridge!" Easton, arms pumping, glanced sideways in affirmation, while Anderson lowered his head and pushed his legs harder.

Out on the lake, the Englishman's concentration was broken by the sudden lack of forward motion- they had stopped. "What's the problem?" he demanded curtly.

The boatman looked contemptuously at him, and replied slowly. "Pardon, don' speak English."

His irritated passenger got up and shoved his face into that of the now startled boatman. "Listen. If you don't get this tub moving again, I'll dangle you over the side until water comes out of your arse. Understand that!?"

The outraged Swiss wordlessly pointed over his abuser's left shoulder. A large, very expensive yacht was cruising across their course. The Englishman rubbed his chin, returning to his seat as he spoke.

"Okay, but get moving when you can, you understand?"

The mollified ferryman dipped his head once, mentally cursing. "Bloody English."

The boat docked at the Mont Blanc Quay a few minutes later, and the Englishman disembarked, watched by the sullen boatman. He turned left, strolling up the Rue de Mont Blanc, past the Casanova restaurant. He checked his watch again. On time. Well, he was in Switzerland and he was walking past a Swatch store. If he couldn't be on time here; he laughed at his little joke. He gazed for a few seconds in the window of the Swatch outlet, and then walked on, still guffawing to himself.

A broad, dark-haired man in his mid-twenties stood in front of him. He was wearing a just too-large suit, and, the Englishman noticed, scuffed and mud-caked shoes. The man spoke, in a strange accent. "Excuse me, have you got the time?"

The Englishman stared at the red-faced, seemingly out of breath apparition. Time? Are you fucking mad? Look around you. There's clocks everywhere, you half-wit. We're in Switzerland!"

The man did not flinch in the face of the ridicule, asking again: "Have you got the time?"

Angry now, the assassin grabbed the unkempt man by the lapels. "Not to waste it with a moron like you, now piss off before I..."

A taller, older man walked out from a doorway. "Before you what? Mr Fenwick, you're being a mite impolite to my young friend here."

Fenwick blinked in disbelief. Mitch McKenzie! A heavily built blond man stepped out of the same doorway.

"Impolite? I would say he's being downright rude to my bro. Get your hands off, Mister, before I pull them off and stick 'em up your stiff, bony ass." Easton's killer line brought a damped down grin to Mitch's face.

Fenwick tried to pull away, but Anderson grabbed his hands in a thumb lock. "I don't care for rude people much, and even less for murderers!" he hissed.

Fenwick was stunned, and stood, mouth working, staring at his captors.

Mitch spoke icily. "Don't think about trying anything, these guys will rip your head off before you get your moves going, and my gun is pointed straight at your crotch. Now walk with us, we're going to get a room. The Bristol here gets good reviews!"

Mitch nodded to the brothers. "Check all his pockets guys. He may have still have the weapon." Easton patted the recalcitrant Englishman down, removing his mobile phone, and then taking over the thumb lock on his left hand as they walked to the hotel.

As they entered the foyer, Easton gave Fenwick a few words of wisdom "I would love to snap you in two. I just need a reason. Please give me one, or maybe shut your mouth until we get you into a room." The brothers and their captive sat awkwardly on a red Chesterfield as Mitch spoke to a sceptical-looking concierge. After some minutes, Mitch walked over, holding a key card. "Let's go, I've booked a conference room: late night meeting time. Follow me. "The room had a long table, red velour chairs, some faded wall tapestries, and an arched bay window looking onto some green space, which mysteriously was three floors below the level of the entrance they had come in. Easton thumped Fenwick down on one of the chairs, as a watchful Mitch pulled up another and rested his arms on its back.

Anderson yanked out the room phone cable and used it to bind their captive's hands." Saw Jack Bauer do this once. Tie them in front, so you can see what they are doing."

Mitch rolled his eyes, pulled his gun from his coat, pointed it directly at Fenwick and sat on the table.

The Englishman spoke "Well, are you going to kill me, marine? Or are we going to have one of your lectures on morality in the free world?"

Mitch smirked. "Aren't you the feisty little limey? You just whacked someone in front of four hundred people. He might well have just been a bug; and you have absolutely no remorse."

Fenwick sighed. "Why do all you Yanks have to try and be Abraham Lincoln? I'm a soldier, a professional; same as you are. We kill people Marine; that's what we do."

Mitch's face tightened. "I don't get off on it the way you do. You would do it just for the rush, the power of life and death. Don't compare yourself to me!"

Fenwick put his arms behind his head and laughed. "I could never compare to you, Major McKenzie. I could certainly never be as big a hypocrite as you. I almost wish you would shoot me to spare any more of your fake mom's-blueberry-pie-outrage." The brothers both looked at Mitch. This guy was getting to him.

The American stood up, visibly angered. He pointed the gun at the haughty Englishman's head. "Okay, we'll pass on the anger management stuff, and get right to it. You are going to tell us what we want to know, or I'm going to blow you another hole in your head to sip your god-damn tea through, Capice? American enough for you?"

Fenwick nodded, replying in a low voice. "Capice indeed, now you're Joe Soprano. I love it!"

"Don't know who that is." said Mitch. "Some TV guy, by any chance?"

Easton spoke softly, his eyes burning into Fenwick's. "What do you know about my father?"

The Englishman smiled bleakly, and replied just as quietly. "Well, he'll probably be very wet, very cold and very dead. He is at the bottom of Lake Ontario, after all..."

Anderson moved across the room, with intent, leaning down into the smirking, arrogant face of their captive. "You brought his plane down, didn't you? You killed him."

Easton's knuckles had gone white as he clutched the back of his chair, his features working as he struggled to control the anger rising within him.

Fenwick was less arrogant now, he sensed the danger he was in. "Well, no, I can't claim credit for that; a really good operation carried out by one of my best men, Georgi Munteanu, He doesn't like Mitch very much, because Mitch killed his brother in Paris."

"And I'll kill that motherfucker as well!" exploded Mitch.

Fenwick swallowed hard, but tried not to show it. "Really Mitch? You know what these Romany families are like, they will come after you, and all that office air and rich food you've had in the last few years might have lost you your edge."

Easton suddenly threw the chair away and grabbed the Englishman's lapels, lifting him to his feet at the same time as Anderson grabbed his throat. "Who is behind all of this? Who's paying you? Who wanted my father killed?"

Fenwick gasped for breath, but spat back defiantly. "Piss off, ask your American buddy here how long I spent in the company of our mutual Iraqi friends, eating my own shit, and having two toes cut off with bolt cutters. Do you really think this will frighten me? Fuck off!"

Anderson's eyes flared wide open, pupils dilated as he grabbed Fenwick's legs. "Easton, let's put this shit to sleep! Come on!"

Easton roared incoherently and lifted the shocked Englishman onto his broad shoulders at the same time as Anderson raised the frantically kicking legs. "You're going out of the window, you murdering fucker!" The two brothers propelled the struggling man towards the bay window in the room.

Fenwick turned, wild-eyed, to Mitch, almost pleading. "Mitch, they've lost their minds. Fucking do something!"

Mitch stepped across to the window and flung it open. "They lost their father as well Captain Fenwick, Hope you remember your basic fall training."

Anderson pounded across the room, screaming at the top of his voice, followed by his enraged sibling. A keening cry of fear slipped from the helpless Englishman's throat as he tensed all his muscles for what was to come.

Anderson suddenly dropped his shoulder and let Easton's momentum smash Fenwick's body into the wall to the side of the gaping window. His choked gasp was followed by another shriller noise as Easton's 225 pounds of muscle crashed into him.

Fenwick let out a primordial scream as the sound of bones breaking echoed around the room. His arm was at a strange angle and he bent over sideways trying to sooth his broken ribs.

"You-fucking- shits!" Fenwick dragged himself up to a sitting position.

Easton, on his hands and knees, watched as Anderson smoothed his hair and sat down on one of the red velour chairs, anger apparently gone. "What the FUCK was that bro!?"

Anderson crossed his legs and looked levelly at his brother. "I was acting. I am an actor, Easton."

Mitch clapped his hands vigorously. "Outstanding! You had me son, and your brother. How 'bout you Cap? You sure as hell weren't acting!?" The Englishman glowered at his captors and tried to nurse his limp right arm, which was still tied to his left one, but said nothing.

There was a knock at the door. It suddenly opened before Mitch could get to it.

A concerned-looking hotel suit stood with an equally anxious waiter clutching a tray of coffee and Danish. The suit took in the scene before him, eyes flicking from side to side, with dubious energy.

"Er, we thought that you might need some refreshments. Is everything in order?" His English was clipped and precise.

Mitch smiled, reaching for the tray as he spoke. "Thanks, things were getting a bit heated there, you know how these strategy meetings can go. We were doing a little 'role play.' You familiar with that term?"

The suit eyed Fenwick's bound hands curiously. Mitch caught his look. "That's role play; all part of our training."

The suit spoke again. "Perhaps I can get Monsieur a softer chair? We have some in the foyer."

The Englishman shook his head. "Thank you, but the floor is part of what we are doing."

The suit gazed at the obviously-injured and dishevelled man and coughed. "Of course, and a mention that we are having a fire drill later today, so there will be no need to leave the room. Now, if there is anything else we can do...?"

Mitch put his arm around the men's shoulders and gently ushered them out of the room. "We'll let you know. Now if you don't mind, we have some important things to thrash out." He closed the doors and listened to check that the visitors had moved away. "They're gone. We need to get to Bailey and Jeanne, boys, so I'll call them. You two can tie up with them. I'll look after our limey and join you later."

Anderson looked quizzically at Mitch. "What are you going to do with him, Mitch? We're not going to kill him, are we?"

Easton tagged along. "Well Mitch, what *are* we going to do with him? We're not killers."

"No," Fenwick interjected, "but he is. He's killed women and children before, haven't you, marine?"

Mitch looked at an unseen point through the open window, folded his arms, and said simply, "Yes, I have. Collateral damage. Part of the risk that we take in this job."

Anderson became agitated. "No more killing Mitch, we won't be a part of it."

"Would you have killed to save your father, or your mother? There are choices in life and death."

Mitch's voice was thick, almost quivering, with emotion.

Easton shook his head as he spoke. "No more killing, Mitch. We won't allow it."

Fenwick spoke again before Mitch could react. "You boys are sweet, aren't you? But Major Mitch would have no compunction in ending my life, He would think no more of it than squashing one of his little bugs he is so fond of alluding to. So I am going to tell you whatever you want. I am no coward, but I am not ready for the endless sleep yet. A nice Swiss jail for me, for a few months at most, until Mitch's government gets me out, and tries to explain why it has pissed on yet another of its valued allies. Bit of a bastard coming so soon after all that renditions shit, eh Mitch?"

Mitch was saturnine, his gaze remaining fixed to the distance. Anderson jumped in. "Okay, so who is behind all these killings, and why!?"

Fenwick drew his legs painfully up to his chest and replied matter-of-factly. "The good old USA of course, as Mitch well knows. He's made his pension out of state-sponsored killing, haven't you Major?" No reply was made by the stone-face American.

Anderson spoke again. "Why was my Dad killed? Why would his own employers kill him?"

Fenwick dabbed at his brow with a spotless kerchief as he spoke. "Different thing, your father was working on something very big with the FDA. Someone felt he was getting too warm, and he was sanctioned."

Mitch suddenly snapped out of his icy calm. "We know that, but David was a trusted and valued man. Why would his own organisation take him out?"

Fenwick screwed up his face in exaggerated pain as he replied. "Not the organisation, but someone who works for that organisation with a vested interest in keeping things under wraps. Not all your countrymen are honest injuns Major."

Mitch leaned down and stared into the back of Fenwick's eyes. "Who then, who's gone rogue?"

Fenwick returned Mitch's unblinking stare with one of his own. He almost whispered his reply. "Herb Johnson. He's skimming; creaming off cash flow from PMC contracts, and he was on that project with David Marks, who obviously suspected something. Herb had us take him out.

"Fenwick's eyes darted across to the brothers. "It was a business transaction boys. Nothing personal."

Mitch grabbed the startled Englishman's chin and growled venomously in his face. "Herb Johnson wouldn't risk taking down David Marks for that kind of money. He's a fucking Xerox commando, losing a few grand a year wouldn't make him mad enough to sanction the murder of a US government official."

Fenwick angrily pushed away Mitch's gnarled hand. "What about two eminent Professors, or a journalist, or maybe three high profile socialite brothers? We're talking in millions here Major, not a few thousand grafted dollars. We're looking at global extortion and blackmail. Someone has built an empire here, and they're protecting it. Something's very rotten down on the Farm Major!"

Mitch rubbed his cropped temples robotically, not taking his eyes off of the Englishman for a second.

"That's it Mitch, we need to go to the authorities. If this guy is crooked, they need to know. We've done enough." said Anderson.

The American seemed to be wrestling with multiple demons as he replied. "Negative Anderson. DC is a rumour mill. Someone would get word to Herb Johnson before we got to him. We need to close this down ourselves, and then see who we can trust, assuming this prick is telling the truth."

"I have no reason to lie, Major."

Easton was incredulous. "What? This guy is asking us to trust him and not trust our own government. How do we know? What he is suggesting isn't about taxes and Obama care, it's about national security!"

Mitch's face softened, mollified by the younger man's obvious integrity and patriotism. "Easton, I've told you before, look at Contra-gate, Iran, Ollie North. So much goes on that is not officially sanctioned. Herb Johnson's whole department is a shadow op. No, we go after this without any help. It makes sense, because someone is paying this prick and it is big money - who can afford that? It all falls into place now. That is what your Dad was working on when he disappeared. Someone wanted to hide things, who else would it be?"

A rasping laugh leapt out from Fenwick's injured chest. "You'll all get creamed; a fucked-up Gulf vet and three spornosexual dabblers: you haven't got a prayer!"

Easton grabbed the sniggering Englishman's hair and hissed a sibilant threat. "That window is still open, you public-school prick, and you might still get launched through it!"

Fenwick's face froze into a look of pure bile: "You'll get yours, poster boy, don't you worry. You're dicking about with a fucking hand grenade here!"

"Enough, stow it Easton!" Mitch's voice cut through the tension. "You and Anderson go to the Rue Cornavin and bring my car back here. We'll drop this piece of shit off to the Swiss-Chocolate Police and pick up Jeanne and Bailey." The brothers exchanged a look, and moved towards the door.

Easton turned and grinned at Mitch. "No offence Major, but it'll be good to get this suit off and back into something a little more contemporary." Mitch's face creased into a wide smile. "Well, you looked good for a spell anyways, now get going!"

The door closed, and the American was alone with Fenwick. "You like that boy, don't you Mitch. You were almost paternal there."

Mitch ignored any darker meaning in the remark. "A stone-cold killer like you might not grasp the concept of human interaction. Talking to people can be more rewarding than putting a bullet in them."

Fenwick guffawed. "Bonding? Fatal flaw, marine. Not good for business. Bit like a meat-eater turning vegan, isn't it?"

Mitch looked down at his captive contemptuously. "I have no fucking idea what you are talking about. You Brits have a real talent for the abstract. How the fuck did you ever get an Empire?

"Fenwick grunted." Ha. We were born to conquer. Manifest Destiny and all that." The Englishman paused, and then spoke again. "Come on marine, one killer to another. We shared the same experience, fought for the same values, we're not that different."

The American cut him off brusquely. "You were a soldier before you became a killer, and maybe we did swallow the same dirt in the Gulf, Captain, but that's where it ends. You got greedy and lost your lines. You're an outlaw, and I might still kill you. You'd deserve nothing more."

Fenwick knew that the man facing him was as far from redemption as he was, and would snuff him out in a heartbeat. He decided that silence would be the best way to continue this particular conversation, and leaned back against the wall. Mitch pulled out his phone and hit the speed dial, his eyes never wavering from his captive.

CHAPTER 30

I jumped when the call came through, and fumbled clumsily around my coat pocket trying to find the phone. Finally I pressed the green icon. "Bailey, where did you have the fucking phone? You need to answer quicker. There's only one person who could call you!"

I squirmed with embarrassment as I answered. "Sorry Mitch, I wasn't ready. What's happening? Are my brothers' okay? Did you get the Englishman? What'll we do now?"

A deep sigh came down the line. "Still way too many questions, but your brothers are okay and we've got our man. We're going to hand him over to the Police. They'll deal with him. We need to get back to the States. That's where our end game is."

I had listened intently, but couldn't contain myself anymore. "Did you ask him about my Dad? Was it him who brought the plane down? What does he know about it? Christ Mitch, I need to talk to this guy before you hand him over!" I sensed the frustration at the other end of the line.

"Bailey, your Dad's dead. His death was ordered. Fenwick was contracted to kill him, and the contract came from another government agency. He was onto something big, and he had to be taken out. Talking to Fenwick won't get you any further towards the truth, he was just the tradesman here. That's why we need to get back to D.C." Mitch's tone had been measured and reasoned, but my head still swam with the implications of what he had told me.

I grasped the cell phone tightly, unable to articulate what I needed to say.

Mitch cut in. "Bailey, are you still there? Listen up. Meet us at the Gare du Cornavin, where we got you before. We'll be about twenty minutes. Got that?" "Yes, okay we'll be there. I..." The phone went dead before I could speak.

Jeanne had listened quietly to our conversation. She looked at me with huge, liquid eyes. Her hand crept into mine and gripped my fingers tightly. "I'm sorry Bailey, I know that you wanted your father to be alive, I 'm so sorry."

I looked at her silently for some seconds, realising that she was hopelessly in love with me, and was only concerned for my well- being. A sudden rage shattered my thoughts, and I pulled my hand away. "No, he's not dead, Jeanne and I don't need pity. Just someone to believe me when I say that! He's not dead. What about the street artist in Rome? Not to mention the other guy in Paris. Someone's been looking out for us, don't you see!?"

Jeanne sat motionless, her features frozen in shock, her hands clasped under her chin. Her words were almost inaudible. "Bailey, what happened in Rome was probably just a coincidence. Just some numbers on a painting - a passer-by, and the memory stick in Paris? Do you still have it?"

Her words lanced into my confused mind like hot needles; she genuinely didn't believe me. I felt a sickening wave of nausea welling up from my gut. Strange colours pulsed across my field of vision, saliva began to wash around my mouth. I was going to be sick. Jeanne jumped back as I stood up woozily, asking questions that I couldn't hear, as I tried to focus on her through the flashing lights that now blurred my sight. Events of the last week had caught up with me.

Somehow, we made it outside, Jeanne holding me as I tottered along the pavement. The nausea and lights abated somewhat, as wary pedestrians opened a path for us along the sidewalk. We eventually stopped and leaned against a wall about fifty metres from the hotel. Jeanne's anxious face gradually became clear as my vision returned to normal. She dabbed my forehead with a wet wipe, murmuring inaudibly as she did so. I realised then, as my senses returned, that whatever feeling had been building up inside of me for her, had gone, irrevocably. "Sorry Jeanne, maybe it was that bump on the head I got in New York finally getting to me. I don't know, but I'm okay now."

Her eyes lowered, her hands pushing her hair behind her ears as she talked. "I have upset you talking about your father. I am a scientist Bailey. I cannot deal in pure belief with no logic. I didn't mean to hurt you, but you must accept things. These obsessions will ruin you."

My eyes looked above her head as I spoke. "I don't put much stock in science, Jeanne. It killed my mother, and it's why my father is not here. Until I find out the truth, I'll follow my obsessions - on my own, if need be."

Jeanne jerked her head away, trying to conceal the tears oozing from the corners of her eyes. She too knew that the fragile bond between us had been splintered. She spoke tonelessly. "Come on, we have lost some time, we need to get to the station." I nodded, and we set off in silence to walk the kilometre or so to the station.

CHAPTER 31

Mitch stood, arms akimbo, looking disdainfully at his prisoner. Fenwick continued to nurse his injured right arm, supporting himself with his left on his lap as he sat. He had said nothing since their last acrimonious exchange, staring sullenly at his shoes as Mitch paced up and down, impatiently awaiting the return of the brothers. The clicking of the door latch signalled their arrival, and Mitch relaxed visibly as they stepped in the room.

Easton tossed the keys at Mitch. "Car's outside, we're ready to move." Anderson squeezed in behind his brother, standing alert and poised at the open door.

Mitch stood over the openly seething Englishman. "Move out Captain. Ready to do some Swiss time?"

Fenwick stood up shakily, nursing his broken arm. "Please, no humour Major, my ribs are sore enough. Lead on."

The brothers turned and went through the door as Mitch shepherded Fenwick after them. Easton looked back at the Englishman's twitching sardonic face. They looked deep into each other's eyes; the Englishman's face was expressionless, chilling. Easton felt a spontaneous shiver of apprehension. Bells clanged in his head; his stomach muscles suddenly went rigid. What came next played out in apparent slow motion, and Easton's limbs seemed to solidify as events unfolded. Fenwick's uninjured left arm shot back like a catapult into the left side of Mitch's face, catching him on the cheek and nose, followed by a kick so fast it was a blur.

The American crumpled like an empty overcoat and sank to the floor. Fenwick scrabbled for his gun. Easton caught the look of astonishment as the American's nose exploded from the blow, jerking his whole body back in a violent arc. As Anderson turned to look at his enraged brother, Fenwick's foot flew up, catching Easton's midriff, forcing his head back and into the face of his onrushing brother. The impetus of the resulting collision sent them both sprawling in the lobby. Fenwick moved like a cat, springing to his feet and pointed the gun at the prostrate American and the shocked brothers.

Mitch, dazed, could not react, and could only vaguely feel the firearm being pressed into his forehead. "Up. Get up, Major fucking Mitch. I told you, you were soft. Nothing like being out in the field, eh!?"

Easton peered painfully through the slick of blood oozing over his eyes, blood from a gash in Anderson's forehead. His brother lay prostrate on the thick carpet, mouth open, chest barely moving; clearly unconscious.

A voice pierced his veil of pain. "Come on Blondie, get your brother back into the room and help your uncle Mitch up. We're going to have a chat, and then... I'm going to kill you all. Not often I get so much work done in one day!"

Easton lifted Anderson's body under the armpits and dragged him back into the room. He then pulled the barely conscious American up into a chair at the window. Fenwick motioned to the adjacent chair. "Sit down. Untie my hands:" He thrust his hands in front of Easton's face with the gun pointing at his mouth. Easton untied him. "This won't take long. Wiping out a whole family will be a first for me. Well, first that I know of! Getting your brother and that French bitch he's with will be easy. He won't outlive you by much. For amateurs you have done a lot of damage. Captain America here has taken out some of my best operatives and you boys wrecked my resourcing department! Shame Mitch wasn't sharper, he might have saved you. Him first; then you Blondie. Your brother won't feel a thing at the moment, will he? So he can wait. Ha ha!"

Fenwick pulled Mitch towards him by his necktie and yanked it off, rapidly binding the American's arms behind his back. He then placed a chair cushion against his head to keep the noise of the gun down. "Got to improvise Major - something you fucking Yanks aren't good at!"

Fenwick placed the gun against the cushion, looking at Easton as he did. "Say ta ta poster boy and get in line."

Easton felt waves of despair and pain pulse through his body: he was helpless. A sudden shrill noise startled him, the fire alarm! The Englishman paused for a split second, eyes looking to the ceiling. Easton took his chance, and with all of his strength speared his leg across the Englishman's body, thudding it into the lower part of the arm holding the gun. The limb crumpled and the firearm went off. The crashing report filling the room, the bullet shattering the ornate coving around the mirror. Fenwick howled in pain, his broken arm flailing wildly as he pirouetted in agony.

Mitch recovered his wits enough to shout at Easton. "The gun, Easton. Get the gun!" Easton leapt on the Englishman's gun hand, putting both hands around the wrist and twisting it desperately. Fenwick grunted in pain. He wasn't finished yet, and smacked his head into Easton's face, sending him sprawling across Mitch's legs.

The American's voice, tremulous, but still strident, cut through the grunting and scuffling. "Easton, take this fucker out. He'll kill us all. Finish him." A clubbing blow from Fenwick's knee jolted Mitch's bloody head back, smashing it off of the wooden chair frame. His tongue slipped down his throat, and his eyes rolled and whitened as they closed, Easton was on his own. Even though Fenwick's gun arm was hurting, he could still use it. Easton reached for the weapon, clasping the hand that held it. Fenwick growled malevolently.

Strength drained from Easton's raddled body, he felt his resolve ebbing away, he was losing, and when it was finished his brothers would die too. Blackness was creeping across his field of vision, the contorted face of his assailant hovered inches away from his own. He felt the hot breath and flecks of saliva on his cheek. This was it; the end. They were all going to die. He saw the hazy outline of the gun above his head as Fenwick's hand forced it down to point at his face. He had to make a move. His dormant Kali training, from the pit of his memory, took hold. He shifted his hand to the barrel of the gun, and jerked it back with all his strength. Fenwick's trigger finger snapped back, broken cleanly in two by the leverage of the trigger guard. He roared in pain, dropping the gun to the wooden floor.

Easton moved rapidly, pushing Fenwick down onto the rug, he grabbed the weapon by the barrel and swung it down on the stricken Englishman again and again. Blood flecked the cuffs of his shirt, his hand and his forehead as the heavy butt split flesh and shattered bone. The Englishman's cries of pain stopped suddenly, and the only sound was the crump of metal hitting flesh.

A hand grabbed Easton's arm, and he heard a familiar voice. "Stop, Easton, for Christ's sake, he's dead. Stop!" Anderson, white-faced, stood over him, blood slowly running down his features.

The gun fell from his hands as he pulled himself up from the floor. He pushed Anderson's arms away and stumbled into a corner of the room. Mitch was slowly sitting up. Anderson untied his hands and he fingered his ruined nose. No one spoke for some minutes, with Anderson watching his brother intently as Mitch stared into a mirror, studiously wiping crusted blood from his craggy features. Fenwick's blood had pooled on the thick rug, and its warm, cloying odour filled the room.

Mitch looked to where Easton stood, head bowed, arms drooping by his side. "Thanks, son. It had to be done. It was him or us. That simple." No reply came.

Anderson walked over to his trembling brother and wrapped two strong arms around him. "Come on bro, sit down for a spell." Easton slumped into a leather chair, clamping his bloodied hands over his face as if to shut out any further contact.

Mitch looked back to the mirror, talking as he pushed his misshapen nose back into an approximation of its former shape. "We'll leave Fenwick here. The room's booked till midnight, so we'll be gone by the time they find him. I'll call my contact with the local Police when we're in transit. They'll have made Fenwick by now from the CCTV in the hotel, so they'll have their man. We haven't got the time right now to explain our part in all this. It'll be a risk, but we have to leave him."

"Leave him behind the curtains. No one ever looks there, do they?" Easton almost whispered it. The two other men exchanged a quick glance.

Easton stood up and spoke quietly. "Close the curtains. Dump him on the window sill. No-one will look there until they open them in the morning, will they?"

Mitch nodded; "Okay, good call. Let's wrap him in the rug he has bled into. Lend a hand." Easton helped slide the dead man wrapped in the rug onto the broad wooden sill, ensuring everything was tucked away before pulling the thick drapes shut.

The rest room was conveniently positioned opposite the room they had booked. A quick clean- up of some of the blood and they were ready to go. Mitch looked the two brothers over, trying not to catch Easton's bloodshot, unblinking eyes as he did. "Let's go, I'll drive to the station.

The three men filed silently from the room, glancing anxiously at the reception desk as they walked along the corridor.

The male desk clerk looked up, smiling innocently. "Ah gentlemen: taking a break? Perhaps dinner here before you go back? There are four of you, yes?"

Mitch pursed his lips. Way too many questions. "We're coming back in a half hour or so. One of the guys needs some thinking time. Can you see he's not disturbed?"

The desk man gestured affirmatively with a sweeping hand gesture. "Of course, he will call us if he needs us, yes?"

Mitch smiled: "I'm sure he will. See you soon." They were just about to step outside into the street when Easton turned back inside, walking to the door of the room they had just left. Anderson caught his breath; well aware of his brother's regular mental aberrations. His mercurial sibling reached up and flicked the little status sign on the door to 'Occupe' – 'Busy.' Anderson took a huge gulp of air, grabbed his brother by the arm, and hurried him past a simmering Mitch out into the night.

CHAPTER 32

Jeanne and I had stood in awkward silence as we waited for Mitch and my brothers to appear at the station. The mild evening breeze wafted her dark hair across her moist eyes, and she flicked it away with increasing irritation as time passed. I felt detached; distant from her, and had felt like that ever since our last conversation, rebutting any attempt she made to initiate anything. She had given up after a time, and had settled for gazing at the crowds beginning to clog the approaches to the station, occasionally stepping on to the road to squint at the line of brightly-lit cars crawling past.

She saw the car before I did, and pointedly made to sit in the front next to Mitch as I squeezed into the back alongside my brothers. I peered at them in the harsh light. "Jesus! What happened?" Mitch turned, revealing a crimson nose framed by two incipient black eyes. "The Englishman's gone, but it got a mite lively. Your boy here probably saved us all, Anderson and I were out of it. I'll let him explain it all to you."

I looked wonderingly at my brother. "You killed him? Christ, I'm sorry Easton, are you okay? How do you feel?"

His eyes hardened to a glassy blue. He fixed me in a long stare. "Like a killer, I suppose." His voice faltered.

Mitch boomed in. "Listen up, we need to get to the States. We'll get flights to London out of Lyon. From there, I'll go to Newark, you guys can go through Boston - just in case someone trails us. We'll arrange a meet time in DC; and we'll talk through how we go at it then. This is our final play, and we have no idea what's waiting for us. We need to be ready.

"To kill?" Easton's muted voice was barely audible over the noise of the idling car.

Mitch's eyes speared us with intent. "Yeah, if need be, "he drawled, "or to die." He turned brusquely and crashed the car into gear, screeching away from the kerb. I slid my arms around my brother's shoulders.

Anderson patted my hand comfortingly, but Easton sat motionless; wordless, eyes fixed on his boots. Best to leave him be for now, I resolved.

Half an hour later, having joined the A40 not far from the border of France, Mitch snapped the paddles through the gears and put his foot to the floor. We were going home.

CHAPTER 33

The journey was long and mostly silent. Easton slept, or maybe feigned sleep, and Anderson took his chance to tell me what had unfolded in the hotel. I listened sombrely, shaking my head occasionally in disbelief as the story was told.

Anderson noticed that Jeanne was also sleeping. He couldn't resist, "What is it with you two? You haven't spoken at all since we set off - problem?"

I sighed, knowing that sibling intuition would find me out eventually. "No problem. We're all good."

Anderson sat silently for a few seconds and then held up his hands, apparently baffled "What? What do you mean?" Time to feign a little sleep of my own, but Anderson was persistent. "What happened Bailey? I thought you two were getting something going."

"Well we weren't, aren't, whatever." I growled testily.

Anderson sat back, chastened. Emotion flooded into my voice. "Look, I'm just glad you guys are okay. It must have been rough back there. I'm sorry I wasn't around to help out."

Before Anderson could reply, Easton's eyes opened slightly. His voice was flat. "Don't worry bro, I managed to beat him to death all on my own." His face turned to the window, eyes glistening with unshed tears.

Anderson drew his hand across his lips; seemed like a good idea. We sat in silence again. I tapped Mitch on the shoulder. "Want me to drive for a spell?"

A perfunctory "no" was fired back. He didn't even turn his head. I sank back in the seat and closed my eyes: car journeys weren't my thing. We checked in at the Ibis, a couple of kilometres from Lyon airport, filing down to the lobby after dumping our scanty luggage in our rooms. Jeanne was already there, waiting, looking tense and drawn. She waited until the four of us sat down and then spoke clearly and precisely. "Gentlemen, I must go back to Paris. I am not coming to America with you."

Mitch clasped his hands and looked at her intently. Anderson blurted out first. "On your own? Not a wise move Mslle. There may still be some of Fenwick's people out there. Surely you're safer with us?"

Jeanne seemed to be disconcerted that Anderson, and not I, had spoken up. She talked to the group, while still looking at me. "I need to get answers from De Vico. Professor Favreau and Wengen have both worked with this man, and they are now dead. Why is he still alive? He knew much more than he told us in Rome. Do you agree Bailey?"

I shrugged non- committally, unwilling to join the conversation. She looked away quickly, obviously hurt. I felt a brief stab of angst, but my face betrayed nothing.

She composed herself and carried on. "I want to put what I have to the authorities. De Vico knows I have records of some of the clinical trials that were carried out on Interzamabol, but has no idea of what the specifics are. I will, how do you say, bluff him. He might think that I have much more than I actually have. I am certain that I can persuade the Police to at least question him. I believe he duped Dr Favreau into believing that he would support his work on the drug trials, pulling him into the open, causing his death. "Jeanne's eyes lowered as she spoke.

Mitch leaned forward. "I think Fenwick's whole structure has collapsed, and I don't think Jeanne will be in any danger from that angle, but if this De Vico is in this, we have no way of knowing what his connections are. Do you know where he is Jeanne?"

She nodded. "He is in Paris now. My secretary tells me he will speak at a product launch. I will go to him there. He may believe that I was taken care of in Rome. He will not expect to see me." Mitch nodded." You may be right. There's no one left free-or alive- to tell him any different."

Anderson looked over, waiting for me to speak. My continued silence obviously infuriated him and he pointed his finger as he spoke. "Bailey, talk to Jeanne. She should come with us. She'll be on her own here."

I, at last, replied. "She is a very capable lady, and can think for and look after herself as she has already shown.

She's not part of what we need to do in the States and it gives us the best part of a week to finish things off. Let her go."

Jeanne, her emotions tightly in check, inclined her head, whispered "Thank you" and stood up.

Mitch rose with her. "I will give you my number, Jeanne. If you need help of any kind, call me, and some of my people will be there. You understand? Don't put yourself at risk."

"Thank you Major. If I need to, I will call you. Now I must go, my train is leaving in forty minutes."

Anderson moved forward and hugged her, while Mitch shook her hand firmly. She walked over to Easton and drew her hand lightly across his cheek. His eyes looked upward and eventually his hand caught hers as it left his face, but he still didn't speak. She then walked hesitantly towards me. My heart raced as I extended my hand to her.

She looked at me, crestfallen, squeezing my hand lightly with one hand whilst the other covered her mouth. "Goodbye Bailey, I hope you find your truth, or your peace."

My reply stuck in my throat as I struggled to articulate a response. "Thanks, Take care Jeanne," was all I could work up. I felt so stupid. I was letting her walk out on my life all because she didn't believe my fantasy that my Dad could be alive. Acid poured into my gut. I felt a complete fool, but I still pulled my hand away and watched unmoving as she left the lobby and walked outside.

Mitch broke the spell of silence that had enveloped the room. "Don't really know why you did that Bailey. That girl would have walked over hot coals for you."

"No, Mitch," I sighed. "She couldn't have gone to somewhere that she didn't think existed, even if she wanted to. She doesn't think that way."

Mitch rubbed his temples ruefully. "Hmmm, maybe you need to take reality when it's there, Bailey, That reality is that your Dad is dead. He was murdered, and he won't be coming back."

Shaking my head vehemently, I strode up to the tall American, spitting my words out in a rage. "I know what happened in Paris and Rome, Mitch, and nothing can change that. Someone is trying to keep me, us, on the right track, and out of harm's way; and I think that person is my Dad!"

I was aware of Anderson mumbling curses to himself and shaking his head. "Fuck you, Anderson. I know what I saw. Don't you *want* him to be alive? He's your father too!" He quailed visibly at my sudden eruption of rage.

Easton interjected quietly. "Come on bro, that's a low shot. You believe. Ando doesn't and neither do I. There's no proof, Do you really think Dad would leave us alone to face what we have been through if he was alive? He's gone Bailey. We need to look after each other until this is finished. We don't think any less of you man."

I looked at my brother. Any lingering vestiges of boyishness and youthful glow had disappeared since Geneva, his voice had been flat, his words pragmatic.

Mitch laid a hand on my trembling shoulder. "Come on Bailey, he's right. Maybe we'll find some answers in DC, but we need to be tight on it, No distractions."

My eyes strayed to the car park, catching sight of a mournful-looking Jeanne boarding a shuttle bus. She turned and glanced back at the hotel, and for a moment I considered sprinting out to the bus and dragging her off. I knew Mitch was talking to me, but his voice became an unintelligible monotone as I followed the bus round the car park and out on to the road. 'Shit,' I breathed. Would I ever see her again?

Easton gently pulled me away from the window. "Come on bro, Mitch is trying to tell us some stuff." He had our attention. "Okay guys, as discussed, we know our routes into the States. You can get the AMTRAK from Boston, We'll meet up on Monday in DC.

"That's a seven hour train ride, Mitch. Do we have to?" Anderson looked at us for our approval.

The jutting jaw pointed right at us. "Yes, we don't know if we're being tracked. We need to be careful. I'll make sure my Ops manager, Dan De Marco, has a contingency plan for you guys if anything happens to me. He'll contact you through the cell phone I gave you."

"And if we go down?" Easton asked, almost wryly.

"I'll be on my own; hope it doesn't come to that. Been kinda nice having company on this one. Now, we got things to do. Let's get on it," breezed Mitch, peremptorily finishing the conversation.

So much had happened since we had left the States, our return promised to be no less eventful.

CHAPTER 34

Herb Johnson was a tormented man; his carefully built up world of protocol and procedure was collapsing. He knew someone had uncovered his scam, and he could do nothing but wait helplessly for the next blow to come. His plans for a quiet, sumptuous life in Long Island were shredded, and fear of finishing his days in a penitentiary crushed his very being. How could he get out of this? His job, his pension; everything would go. Dark dreams of tortured prison days clung to his psyche, draining his energy and appetite. He had lost twenty pounds in two weeks. Every phone call to the office brought on spasms of terror, of discovery, of consequence. Red had been surly and uncommunicative since Wes had gone, barely covering the basics of his job, but Kyle, as usual had betrayed not one jot of any angst or curiosity about anything; working through in that automatic, almost inhuman way that was his trademark. New leads had dried up as the team got distracted. Herb avoided contact with anyone who called or came into the office, leaving any decisions by proxy to Kyle.

It was Monday. Herb sat behind his desk, drinking his fourth coffee of the morning; the caffeine heightening his already rampant jitteriness. He had half-heartedly scanned through some flights to Mexico on his cell phone, daring himself to make the move, but he couldn't. How could he explain things to his family? How could he make it through border controls? Fuck! Why had he gotten up to his neck in his shit? His pension and pay-off would have been enough. He reached for the coffee percolator again, splashing a fresh refill into his stained cup. Kyle walked soundlessly into Herb's office, quietly closing the door behind him.

His raddled, sweating boss, started convulsively as he looked up. "Kyle; what do you want? Knock for Chris-sakes." Without invitation he sat down facing his boss. Something in Kyle's demeanour made Herb's hackles rise. "Well?" he snapped. "What is it? What do you want? I'm busy here." He picked up his cell phone as if to make a call.

The younger man's unnerving eyes speared across the desk, unblinking. "No, you're not. In fact the only time you are busy is when you are filling your belly, or checking out your retirement condo on line." Herb crashed out of the fog of anxiety that had been clinging to him. "What? What did you say? You watch your words, boy, or I'll kick your ass out of here!" Kyle was unfazed. "Well, go on. Fire me and every bit of shit you've pulled in this office will go viral in five minutes. I know what you've been doing, and how much you've got creamed off, but let's cool it down Herb. I'm here to help you."

Sweat beads pearled on Herb's florid face as he grappled with what had been said. No point in denying things now; he had to buy some time. He laid his cell phone carefully down on the desk. "Help me? How? I'm finished if this gets out, I'll lose everything. I'll go to prison: I'm royally fucked!"

Kyle leaned back, his glasses reflecting the office's garish lighting. "No need for that to happen, Herb. I can make everything disappear, take the pain away, but first we need to lose Red. He's out of control. He could blow the lid off this whole thing any time."

"Lose him? What the fuck does that mean, lose him?"

Kyle grinned frostily. "Well, we lost Wes before he spilled on you. Didn't know that he had gone to Internal Affairs, did you? We cancelled his appointment. He was going to out you to boost his resume."

Herb's pudgy fingers scraped the filming sweat away from his brow. "You had Wes killed? Taken out? Who the fuck are you?"

The grin straightened into a belligerent gash. "I saved your ass, and I think you owe me. I need all your passwords. I need to go through Wes' stuff to flush out any dirt and I also need to clear down all your files. There are a few people I need to fix."

Herb's brief show of resistance was snuffed out as realisation hit him. "You've been using my codes to authorise and fund marks; the killings in New York, Paris..."

Kyle interrupted, matter-of-factly. "And Geneva. Oh, and that Marks dude you were working with. We took his plane down."

"You what? Jesus Christ! You've killed Americans?"

Kyle smiled malevolently at Herb's outburst. "We're an inclusive organisation, nationality, religion, ethnicity, gender orientation. All are welcome. We don't discriminate. It's a global business, Herb. Evolve or die! Now, I need those permissions."

A tall, dark-haired man swept into the office as Kyle finished speaking. "Ah," he announced. "Herb, this is Georgi. He's going to take care of you." Herb regarded the newcomer nervously. He wore an expensive suit, and his thick black hair was cut in European style. Kyle leaned forward. "Passwords, Herb, and I need you to call Red. Call him in."

The agitated government employee slipped the paper detailing his passwords across the desk to Kyle, in an agony of angst and uncertainty. "I'm not calling Red in. You're going to kill him. I won't do it. You're way out of your league here."

The dark-haired man casually sat on the desk, pointing to the phone as he did. "Call him now – hands-free!" His accent was Eastern European, but his English was undoubtedly good. "Do it now, Mr Johnson. Remember, we are helping you now!"

Herb took the phone in his trembling right hand and pressed the hands-free setting, tapping a number in with his equally shaky left. Kyle glanced at his associate, nodding. The phone rang. Red's voice boomed tinnily around the office.

"Herb, what's up? You never call me on my day off." Kyle's ice drop eyes clamped on Herb like a tractor beam, unblinking, unrelenting. "You have to come in. We got some work in today that needs to be thoroughly checked and it's big. You can get the day back another time."

A snort of disgust leapt from the speaker. "Hell Herb, can't Kyle pick it up? He's in today, right?"

"He's here, but it's too big for Kyle to do alone and it is a priority phone tap we need analysed. Come on, the sooner you're here, the sooner you'll be done." Conviction had drained from Herb's voice.

Red cleared his throat, a rasping, angry sound. "This is shit, Herb. We sit idle all week and now suddenly there is something major. I just want it known that I am pissed."

"Noted. See you in twenty."

The line went dead. Herb placed his head on the desk top as he mumbled inaudibly. Kyle stood up, speaking in a brisk, business like tone. "Okay, I'll get on these passwords. You got the entrance covered Georgi? Don't want anyone walking in at this sensitive, important time."

"Covered. There will be no problems." His answer was clipped; confident.

Kyle persisted. "The only person due in today is the afternoon janitor. She'll be here around one." Another robust retort. "We will take care of her, don't worry."

"Hell Georgi. Mrs Bosely's been here for years. Don't be riling her, wouldn't be right!"

Georgi laughed chillingly. "Do not worry. We have a substitute cleaner, the work will get done!" They both laughed, not even looking at the crestfallen man who sat silently on the other side of the desk.

"What do you mean substitute? What's wrong with Mrs Bosely?" Herb was suddenly roused.

Georgi slid off the desk and barked into the hall. "Elena!" A slim, dark, well-dressed woman glided into the doorway. "Meet Elena, Mr Johnson; my sister, and she needs a job!" Georgi kissed the woman on the cheek, speaking quietly in Romanian as he guided her back out into the corridor. Mrs Bosely is old. She needs some help. Elena is very good." Kyle exchanged another look with Georgi, who laughed chillingly. "Yes, she will leave not one trace...of dirt."

Red bumped the kerb as he parked, having driven all the way to the office in a petulant rage, screaming at other drivers and hapless pedestrians who dared to get in his way.

He uncoiled himself from the car and slammed the door shut. He stood for a moment, trying to compose himself before he went in. Herb was pissed with him as it was. Better to calm down before he met him again. He swiped his card over the door sensor, listening for the click as the lock disengaged. Pushing in, his ears were assailed by rhythmic skeins of music. Kyle! Jesus; how could any work get done with that shit going on? He barrelled belligerently up the hall, vaguely aware that something wasn't right. No rent-a-cop on the door. Strange: he spotted a familiar figure further up the corridor, clinging grimly to a buffing machine as it hovered over the shiny floor. Mrs Bosely. Well, things must be okay if she's here, he reasoned. He called to her, straining over the too-loud music crackling out of the tiny speakers fixed to the walls.

"Chandra! How you doin'? Hey, Chandra." She was wearing earphones. "Jesus, what is wrong with people in here?" He gave up and continued on his way. The office door was ajar, spilling light into the darker corridor. 'Okay, let's see what all the panic is about. Better be good!' Red took a moment; breathed deeply, and went in to face his boss.

CHAPTER 35

The driver's manic voice burst over the PA again as we pulled into L'Enfant Plaza. "L'Enfant Plaza, L'Enfant Plaza; doors open on the leeeeft hand saaaide." He almost sung it.

A still jet-lagged and dyspeptic Anderson sitting opposite me groaned wearily. "That guy is on steroids, I swear. How can anybody be so cheerful and so loud for so long?"

Easton, sitting by my side on the other side of the carriage, closed his dark-circled eyes in agreement. Our journey had been long and tiring, accompanied by the usual shit that we always endured at passport control due to our dual nationality, but we had arrived. We stepped carefully onto the platform. A brief frisson of fear touched me as I looked at a subway track for the first time since I had been pitched onto one all those days ago. Anderson picked up my angst and gripped my arm as we walked to the station exit. An immaculately dressed Mitch loomed large at the top of the steps. His bruises had deepened in hue, making him look for all-the-world like a giant, malevolent panda. A heavily set, slightly shorter man with an improbably wild mop of hair stood slightly behind Mitch, who beckoned him forward. He then lowered his blackened eyes, looking fractiously at his watch.

Easton sighed: "We're twenty seconds late boys. Saturday morning detention for us!" Anderson and I laughed. It'd seemed like a long time since Easton had made us laugh.

"This is my Ops man, Dan De Marco. He'll be coming with us. Now let's go."

Dan uttered a brief "Hi" and turned to walk away. He was also dressed in a suit, but unlike his boss, somehow looked like he'd spent the night in a dumper; obviously not a great conversationalist either.

We followed as Mitch and De Marco strode towards a red Chrysler 300 parked a few metres down the road. The weather had turned unseasonably cold, and although we had picked up some warmer clothing en route, the biting wind still set our teeth on edge. We clambered into the car, glad that Mitch had put the heating on.

He spoke, as usual, clearly and with authority. "Here it is boys. Herb's office is on Seventh Street. He has probably two people on his team. There might be another and maybe some cleaning staff on top of that. Dan has had it under surveillance. One of Herb's guys was recently killed in what looked like a botched mugging, and basically nothing came out of the office for a few days after that. All activity seems to have been put on hold, but the team still go into work each day so they will be there now. We need Herb alive, and we need him to spill whatever he knows. I still don't believe he is capable of doing what Fenwick told us he is up to, but even if he's only running numbers, he's finished, and he will go down: not quietly. You boys can all shoot. I have guns."

"No guns." said Easton firmly. Anderson looked at me for affirmation.

"No guns." I repeated.

Mitch growled irritably, turned and started the car, roaring away from the station and cutting up several startled motorists as we sped through the intersection. The journey took less than five minutes through the sparse traffic, with neither Mitch nor Dan uttering another word as we travelled. We drew up on Seventh across the street from a flat-topped, unprepossessing building that stood on its own in middle of the street. Faded wooden window frames and water-stained concrete blocks added to the general air of decrepitude. A weathered front door, barely fitting the peeling frame, provided approximate security.

Easton spoke wonderingly. "My God, it looks like a homeless centre. This is a government office?"
"Yeah," drawled Mitch. "Should really have a neon sign up there, shouldn't they? Let everyone know it's not the Pentagon!"

Easton scowled. "Not what I meant dude. Just saying it doesn't look…official."

Mitch laughed, a short, sharp yip. "That's because it's an under-cover operation buddy. Urban camouflage. Now listen up, Dan?"

De Marco spoke flatly, economically. "Six people are on site; two women, including the cleaner. They always have door security, but he apparently went away about half an hour ago - kinda strange, but we'll have no issues with access. I got you an entry card. I have no idea who the other two people are, but I'll have the door and the roof covered. I'll be in constant touch with Mitch." At that Dan walked away, entering the building behind us. We crossed the street and moved up to the door, and through as it swung open. We were in, but we had been seen, and unblinking eyes followed our progress.

CHAPTER 36

Kyle looked over Herb's drooping head at the CCTV monitors lining the wall. He watched the four figures disappear through the door. "Shit, Georgi, we got company!" The Romanian, gun pointed at Herb and a quaking Red, cocked his head at the screens. He nodded once at Kyle, who fixed Red in that unnerving stare. "Red, we're gonna have to move things along here, we're being squeezed for time. We're letting you go. Don't take it personally, but we just haven't got the work anymore."

The sweating, palpitating redhead looked pleadingly at the somnolent Herb and then back to his emotionless workmate. "What? What is this? I knew something was going on. Why are you calling this, you little prairie-dog fuck? You're not in charge here. Herb, tell him."

Kyle laughed "Prairie-dog fuck? Way to go shit-kicker. Now we got no time for a proper exit interview. Report us to the Social Security. "He gestured to Georgi. "Do It!"

Red's shout of defiance died in his throat as the bullet smacked into the middle of his forehead. His head lolled back, a thin trickle of blood from the small hole looking incongruous against the violent gout of scarlet on the wall behind him. Herb did not move, beads of sweat dripping from his nose to the desk the only sign that he was alive.

Kyle pulled a gun from his coat. "Ready to take these people down?"

Georgi nodded grimly." Yes, I want the American."

"Well, he might not make it past Mrs Bosely." Georgi smirked.

Kyle's jaw tensed, his manic eyes burning into the top of Herb's head. "Get ready. I'll just need to wind things up with my boss here."

We were inching along the entry hall, the brothers screwing their eyes up in annoyance as raucous music continued to pour out of the PA system.

Anderson tapped me on the arm. "What's this all about, bro?" I shook my head. I had no answer. All of this was new to us. Mitch was the professional. I started to speak, but he pressed a long finger to his lips and gestured us on. The music swirled around us, making normal conversation impossible. Easton caught my attention, and pointed up the hall.

A woman, a cleaner apparently, was busy with a buffing machine she had just unplugged. She was oblivious to our approach, and continued to wrap the electrical cord around the appliance as we moved nearer. Mitch waved us back, and walked, silent as a cat, towards her. I pulled the brothers to my side and we stood, alert and poised for whatever was to come. Mitch had paused next to a cupboard. What was he doing? The song on the PA ended abruptly, and Mitch's head was cocked like a bird dog's. He opened the cupboard door slightly and peered in. Easton looked at me hopelessly. What was going on? Mitch's posture suddenly loosened, and he walked briskly towards the unsuspecting woman, his gun concealed behind his back. We watched, frozen by our fascination at what was unfolding. What happened next shocked us and left us reeling. The tall American moved stealthily to the middle of the corridor and stood stock still. At the same time the woman clapped her hand to her ear and seemingly galvanised, spun round.

"She's got a gun!" That erupted out of Anderson, as the sallow-skinned woman's features became visible for the first time.

"Mitch!" My shout floated up to the ceiling, but Mitch needed no warning. His gun hand had swivelled round and squeezed off two shots, their thunderous reports ringing back along the cavernous passage. The woman pirouetted crazily in the half light, momentarily regaining her balance before crumpling, stricken and shapeless to the floor. She did not move again. A dark splotch of blood oozed onto the polished floor. As one, we stood up and sprinted towards Mitch. He had gone back to the cupboard and fully opened the door. There was a quiet over the corridor.

We pulled up next to him and saw what he was looking at. A black, middle aged woman in her underwear was propped up against a tool stand. A smear of blood seeped out of her hair behind her left ear. Her mouth had been taped shut, her hands bound with tie-its. Her nostrils were bloody and contused. I felt for a pulse: nothing.

"Dead?" Mitch knew the answer to his own question. He leaned on the door frame, breathing slowing down; features working.

"This must have been the cleaner. She suffocated. Fucking animals. Probably took her last breath as I walked past. She was gone when I opened the door. They'll be tracking us on CCTV; that camera further up the hall."

Easton had gone over to the shot woman, turning her limp body over with his foot. She was smartly dressed under the ill-fitting overall she had taken from the murdered cleaner; with elegantly manicured and polished nails. He looked at me with narrowed, hate-filled eyes. I struggled to make myself heard. "She had an earphone, someone else was talking to her, keeping tabs on us; one of the Englishman's crew?"

I was still in shock, but Mitch answered vehemently. "Probably, and..." The corridor lights suddenly went out, leaving only an eerie yellow generated by emergency lights. Seconds later, ear-splitting music spewed out of the PA again; Gimme Shelter, by The Rolling Stones, I noted vaguely.

We looked to Mitch. He gestured us to follow, indicating some stronger, flashing light, emanating from an office about fifty metres along the corridor. We crept along behind him in the weird half- light, our ears pounded by the pulsing rock song that seemed to get louder as we moved towards the office door.

Mitch signalled to Anderson and Easton to hold back, beckoning me forward at the same time. His gun pointed out in front of us. We inched into the office, our eyes adjusting to the intermittent light as we did. A scene straight from Hell greeted us. A man sat open mouthed behind the desk facing us, a neat hole punched in his forehead; the obvious cause of the explosion of gore on the wall behind. To his left, a heavier, older man lay face down on another desk, the top of his balding head blown completely off. He held a gun in his left hand and a shattered pair of gold rimmed glasses in his right. Almost faint with shock, I tried to make myself heard above the music, but it was hopeless. Mitch, wild eyed, scanned around the office and, finding what he was looking for, picked up a fire extinguisher and smashed it down on a CD deck in the corner of the room.

The music ceased, but the ringing in my ears continued. "Thank Fuck for that. I fucking hate the Stones." growled Mitch.

"Herb Johnson." He pointed at the portly figure sprawled over the desk. "That'll be Red Belkevitz," gesturing at the other dead man across the room. He shouted out to the corridor. "Come in boys, hurry up, but be ready for what you see!"

Easton and Anderson burst in, recoiling instantly when they saw the carnage within. "Christ! What happened? Suicide? Murder? Anderson almost gagged as he blurted his question out.

"Looks like a set up." Easton seemed less fazed than Anderson.

I spoke haltingly. "Well Mitch, what do you think?"

The grizzled ex-soldier propped the fire extinguisher on the desk and leaned on it, seemingly drained. "Yeah, it's a set up. Herb didn't kill Red and he didn't kill himself. Herb probably never fired a gun in his life. Now he's dead and we'll get nothing from him. According to Dan two other men were in the building today. We know where the cleaner is, we need to find them before they find us. "He pulled the gun from the Herb's lifeless fingers, and then cocked it. "Nine shells. One of you guys needs to take it. We'll go in twos, a gun each. These guys will be packing. No sense in being stupid."

Easton held out his hand. "I'll take it." He presented it to Anderson, noting that it was a Colt. "Take it Ando. You've shot one of these. I'll go with Mitch; you and Bailey can pair up." I looked aghast at my previously haphazard brother, stunned at the way he had taken the lead.

Mitch nodded approvingly. "Good, Dan has got the only egress/access covered, and unless there is another way out, these guys are in here somewhere. Time to close this out boys. These guys need to be stopped, any which way!"

I felt a rush of anger redden my face. "We can't kill them without finding out what was going on, Mitch. Herb's dead. They are our last hope of getting to the root of things; about Dad and the other people who have been killed. We need to find out why."

Mitch had been topping up the clip in his gun while I spoke, cocking it with some venom as he finished.

"That'll be a nice to have Bailey. They might kill us first."

Desperation seeped into my voice. "Look, at least let me go through the PCs. I might find something; files, e-mails: let me look."

The grizzled head bowed momentarily and then his eyes met mine. "Okay, you stay with Anderson. I'll go looking with Easton. Get us on the cell phone if you find anything. We'll get back to you, or you might hear shooting, but stay here. Come on buddy, let's go."

Easton fist pumped us both before leaving. "Don't worry guys I'll be okay. The old guy needs back up! Come on Ando, take the gun." He took it, looking distastefully at the smooth metal firearm.

"Take care Harpo, remember we're a triple act." he murmured. His sibling grinned, and followed Mitch out into the corridor. Anderson steadied himself against the door, holding the gun tentatively despite all his years of fire-arms training. Must have been the sight of the two bodies in the room that unnerved him. He watched me as I powered the office PCs up.

"What can you do Bailey? They'll all be locked out."

"I know, but sometimes people make mistakes, get careless. This one was in sleep mode so I'll get in here - maybe find something that'll help me with the others."

Anderson, frowned, and resumed his vigil at the door. I opened the icons one by one: accounts, numbers followed by numbers; shit! I realised some of the keys were slick with blood, or worse. Jesus! Herb Johnson's head lay, blown open a few centimetres from me. I wiped the keys with a Kleenex, and continued to delve. Anderson occasionally glanced over questioningly, but I blanked him. This was my medium, I was good at this, I just needed some time.

Mitch and Easton had navigated a few of the seemingly endless passages that striated the ancient office complex with no alarms or surprises. Their eyes had adjusted to the minimal light, so progress was steady and measured. The whirring of the air con and the odd creak of an aged building were the only noises they heard. Mitch glowered at CCTV cameras that dotted the walls and hoped that there was only one set of screens. Someone could be watching them right now; waiting, waiting. He glanced back at Easton, who bristled with a heightened alertness which made Mitch feel good; comfortable, even.

Easton caught his eye. "Got your six, Major," He whispered.

The ex-soldier flinched, squashing a grin. "Yeah, you better have. Now, where are these assholes?"

CHAPTER 37

I sat back, exasperated, as the screen filled yet again with screeds of numbers, codes, and sub codes. Every icon opened, and nothing that helped us. I leaned forward, propping my head on my clasped hands. Too close to Herb's ruined skull. I moved back, pulling the PC mat across the desk as I did. A bloodied piece of paper slipped out from beneath Herb's hand. What was that? Picking it up gingerly, I wiped some of the mess from it with a Kleenex. These were access codes, permissions, unlock codes for encrypted documents, but where were these files? I had no idea where to look; and then I saw the cell phone lying on the desk, a pin point of green light pulsing from it. I picked it up and touched the screen: not locked. It opened on the voice recording page. It had two files, each about five minutes long, recorded about an hour or so apart.

Anderson noticed that I had gone quiet. "What is it, bro? You got something?" I motioned him to be quiet, clicking the first file open.

Male voices filled the office, and after about a minute I realised that it must be Herb, talking to another man. Somehow, he had managed to set his phone up to record the conversation. We listened, appalled, as another, foreign voice joined them. They talked about Dad, us, Paris, Geneva. Jesus! We heard them call Red in to meet his death: the recording finished.

Ashen faced, I turned to Anderson. "You hear that?"

My brother nodded dumbly, mesmerised by what he had just heard, finding his voice with difficulty. "They called that poor guy in to kill him, and they talked about murdering the cleaner as if her life had no value. Christ Almighty! "What kind of people are they?" I clicked on the second file. More voices; we heard Red shouting defiance as he was killed. The brutality was terrifying, remote, oozing out of the speaker and seeping into our shocked psyches. The file finished abruptly.

"We've got to get these guys, Bailey. We can't let this go on." I stood up, still shaking from what we had just heard. "I figure Herb's been on the take somehow, and these other guys have made him. They've been using his name, his say so, to get people killed. Mitch was right. It doesn't look like Herb was in that. These other guys were up to something much bigger, I'd say."

Anderson stared at me set-faced. "Big enough to want Dad and a few others dead. I hope Mitch knows what he's doing. This is beyond belief."

I slipped Herb's cell phone into my pocket, at the same time looking down at the smeared piece of paper on the desk. "I'll mess around with these passwords and permissions. See what I can dig out. We'll need to wait here until Mitch gets back to us anyhow." I suddenly realised Anderson wasn't talking, his breathing shallow and forced. Someone else was breathing with him. My eyes moved up hesitantly, the rest of my body stock-still.

A fair haired man wearing clear eyeglasses stood beside my white-faced brother, pointing a gun directly at his temple. "Stay still buddy, just stay still; hands on the table now. I could pop your bro here and get you before you got near me." The pale blue eyes behind the lenses seemed almost inhuman. I did as I was told, trying to match the intensity of his gaze. "Don't eyeball me buddy, doesn't faze me at all. Can it, or I'll blow your eyes out of your head, got it?" My eyes lowered to the desk, limiting my view to his faded Versace jeans and blue Nike sports shoes.

"You're Kyle, aren't you?"

"Yeah, whatever. You boys have been real lucky. We just haven't been able to kill you, have we? Like trying to take the fucking Terminator down. Jeez, your Dad was much easier." His mid-western accent grew more pronounced the more he talked.

"Why did you kill him?" Anderson barely moved his lips.

· Kyle spoke without shifting his gaze from me. "He was one step away from busting us wide open. He had Herb to rights, and that got too close to us - well, me."

"Close to you, were you skimming as well?" Anderson persisted.

The other-worldly eyes narrowed contemptuously; "Skimming? Herb was chasing a pension booster. I'm gonna get the big prize, and Herb will take the rap for it all. He didn't know his ass from his removable disk, and I took my chance. He had no idea of what I was doing, no idea. I could've hacked into the fucking Pentagon and that lard ass would have had no clue until a fucking ICBM landed on his fucking condo in Long Island."

"Don't let us die without telling us about our Dad. We need to know why you killed him." Anderson had cut across Kyle's flow, disconcerting him, but after a few seconds, he shrugged and carried on speaking. "You're right, I need to work on my empathy; it was in my last review. You guys will be dead soon, same as your brother and the old guy who thinks he's Chuck Norris. Georgi is the best." He smiled, but the pale eyes were dead, devoid of feeling. This man was clearly a psychopath, an exhibitionist, and probably a sadist. We were going to die. Where the fuck was Mitch?

Kyle ushered Anderson over to my side of the desk, and started to talk breezily, like someone having a discussion with work colleagues on the previous night's football game.

"Your Dad was investigating a commercial drug corporation called Castralten. Herb was providing some admin support. I had Herb's codes, and read the files. Some major shit was going down around the testing of certain new drugs. People were dying - terrible, ain't it?" We were silent, aware that any show of defiance could set this psychotic killer off.

"Well, they had this molecule, and some high powered Professors thought it could be huge so they kept on with the trials. More people died, investigations were started, and things took off. You guys getting all this?"

We nodded submissively. Kyle continued, getting into his stride.

"Your Dad was good, very good apparently, and he had persuaded one of the Professors to talk to a journalist. Things were going nuclear. I looked at the amounts of dollars that were involved in the research, and the potential sales yields, and decided it was time to make my pitch. I contacted Castralten and told them I could help them; for a price. A fucking big price!"

I had to speak. "Are you saying that someone from a corporate drug company to pay you to kill people? American officials, journalists, prominent Professors?"

Kyle looked at me incredulously. "They're *already* killing people with their fucking drugs. I was offering them a service; a get out. I would remove the obstacles to them getting their little molecule shoved down all these sick folks' throats. They'd lose the cash in litigation anyway, and who's ever heard of any of their hierarchy getting their asses sued?

Feeling him relax a little, I risked another question. "Why kill Favreau and Wengen and not De Vico?"

He blinked - a first. "Hey, you got all those ducks in a pretty little row there. You boys are pretty good. Different reasons, Favreau had a conscience, the stupid shit. Wengen had huge debts, got greedy, made demands; he designed the original molecule, very intelligent guy. De Vico: very vain guy. He needs the fame almost as much as the money.

He's helped us smooth things with his eminent colleagues; calmed a lot of the noise down, and as long as he stays useful, he'll be okay."

At that, Kyle stepped back, raising the gun to eye level. "Now don't think our little conversation will make me any less willing to end you. You got in our way, wiped out my contractor's whole network and came close to fucking things up totally for us; so you will still see your Dad, boys. Say hi from me!"

We were going without a whimper, executed. I tried something. "Kill Anderson first. I don't want him to see me die."

Kyle laughed again, "Hey, you won't have time to blink, be over in a second. Double tap."

Anderson caught my purpose. "Please, kill me first, that's all we ask."

Kyle frowned, nonplussed. "Hey, this is all real brotherly, to be sure. Hell, what for?" He was not a professional killer, and every second we could gain might save us. I gazed upwards at the ceiling. In times like this, when you are close to death the most unusual things come into your thoughts; like why didn't they make the skylight I was looking at out of clear plastic? It would have let in more light. I tensed myself for a bullet, intoning again and again. "Mitch, where the fuck are you!?"

Anderson tried to speak again. Kyle shouted. "Enough already!" The gun fired its noise ear-splitting in the enclosed space. Waves of shock coursed through me. My eyes flicked open. He hadn't killed Anderson, who still stood, rigid with fear, at my side. Our tormentor stood with the smoking gun, his hateful, frozen face slowly morphing into a malevolent half grin. "Gotcha boys, eh?! You almost shit your pants! Thought I'd break the ice some before I off-ed you. I kinda enjoy this shit!"

Anderson trembled uncontrollably. "You sick fuck. Just do it, fucking shit-kicker. Get on with it!"

Kyle's sinister smile vanished. "Now don't you be calling me a shit-kicker, I'm a sensitive guy." He grabbed Anderson's shirt and ground the gun into his temple. "Shit-kicker - huh? I'll enjoy this." Anderson braced himself, eyes tightly closed.

CHAPTER 38

Dan De Marco ground his eyes into the lenses of his ancient Zenith binoculars. He had spent a couple of long days perched on this roof surveying all that happened in and around Herb's office. Tedious, repetitive work, but kid's stuff for a man who had routinely spent endless, sleepless, days buried in Iraqi sand sucking on a bottle of Benzedrine. He almost missed the black shape moving on the opposite building. "Motherfucker!" He pressed his throat mic.

"Mitch, got movement on the roof. One guy is all I can see. I can take him down right now." He pulled a C15 sniper rifle up to his shoulder.

Mitch froze as the voice crackled in his earphone. Motioning Easton to stop, he crouched down against the wall. "Sure it's only one Dan?"

"All I can see right now. Will I take the shot?"

Mitch tapped the bridge of his nose with his gun. "Negative Dan. We gotta get up there. Where's the nearest roof access?"

Seconds passed. Dan's voice crackled back. "About thirty yards to your left."

"Okay, we're going up. Look out for us, and keep the target in view." The two men covered the distance warily and reached a red, cast iron, enclosed ladder which reached up to a trellised platform. Easton quickly climbed up, and reached down to pull Mitch up as he followed. A blue door with a push bar stood in front of them. "Dan; we are behind the access door, where's our man?"

Dan peered through the glasses; a black shape lay behind a vent shaft. "He's concealed himself behind an air conditioning vent about twenty-five yards away at two o 'clock."

Mitch soundlessly pushed the door open, turning to Easton as he did. "You hold here. Keep the door open. I'm going after this guy. Come when I say, do not put yourself in harm's way."

Easton gave a thumbs-up, watching as the tall American slid out onto the roof and moved towards the vent. Hardly daring to exhale, Mitch came round the back of the vent, glimpsing the flapping coat of his quarry. Covering the last few yards in seconds, he leapt up behind the vent; his gun pointed straight at a dark overcoat hung on the vent: an empty overcoat positioned on the vent to make it look, from a distance, like person.

A sibilant, accented voice filled his ears. "Hello American. You fell for a very old trick. Put your gun down and lie on the ground."

Cursing his stupidity, Mitch did as he was asked. A pair of brown brogues crunched on the gravel in front of him. "I am Georgi. You killed my brother in Paris, and you killed my sister today." The voice was drenched in venom and menace."

Mitch screwed his eyes upwards, catching a good look at the tall, dark-haired man. "Is that so: your brother and sister? Looks like the family business is all yours then." A brown brogue crunched into Mitch's face, snapping his barely healing nose again. The pain was excruciating, but the American did not utter a sound.

"Now you will die." The muzzle of the gun was rammed viciously into the nape of the American's neck.

Mitch tensed, "What are you saying asshole? I can't hear you, you speaking English?"

Dan had watched anxiously through the rifle sight as his boss flattened to the ground, unsure of what was going on. His view was obscured by the vent. He could hear voices in his headphones, but he couldn't make them out. Fuck!

Georgi leaned forward, putting a foot on his victim's neck. "You hear me now! This will be last thing you hear!"

Dan suddenly glimpsed the curve of a head. It might be Mitch's. "Shit!" Dan moved the cross hairs to the curve. "Fuck it! Here goes everything." He pulled the trigger. Mitch heard a noise like pizza dough hitting a table, a heavy body fell across his head, blinding and smothering him simultaneously. His training took over; he wasn't dead; or even hit. 'Ha ha. Well done Dan. Must be the other guy!' He heaved himself clear of the dead weight that had covered him. Dead weight indeed, Georgi's head had been opened like a pumpkin by the high velocity bullet. Fumbling for his mic, Mitch spoke in halting, breathless bursts.

Dan was panicking, not knowing who he had shot. He had lined the curve of the figure up and went purely on intuition. Would his boss have been in that position if he was okay? It had to be the assailant.

"Dan, you got him. Outstanding, soldier. I'll never badmouth a Ranger again!"

Dan sighed, relieved. "We can talk about it on my next review. After all, haven't had a raise in two years."

His boss smiled ruefully. "Don't get carried away now, Dan," Mitch said, tongue very firmly in cheek. "Now we need to get the other guy. Can you see Easton? He was holding the door open."

"Em. Yip, I have a visual."

"Great. I am on my way to him."

"No need boss."

A voice made Mitch turn suddenly. It was Easton. "Um; I heard the noise and came to get to you I closed the... Well, the door kind of closed in back of me: thought it would stop anyone else getting up here." He caught sight of Georgi's body. "Jesus - Dan? Quite a shot."

Mitch nodded grimly. "Yep, it was: and all you had to do was keep a door open."

Easton squirmed self-consciously. "I was coming to you. I knew you were in trouble." A perfunctory hand gesture silenced him, and he stood seething, as the Major wrestled with their new problem.

"Dan; where is the main office from here."

The reply was not encouraging. "I am guessing it has a skylight, but I've counted twenty-four skylights boss, and I'm not sure where they lead. They're not marked on my plan."

Mitch cursed mutely as he digested the information. "Okay Dan, get in here. You might have to let us down, and be careful, the other guy could be anywhere. I'll try Bailey's mobile" He plucked his handset from his coat. Shit! It was smashed; must have happened when he hit the deck. There would be no point in Dan calling the offices, someone else might pick up on it and in any case, which office should he call? The boys were in real danger; time was of the essence.

In the background he dimly heard Easton repeating his name. "Mitch. Mitch. MITCH, listen up!
"What is it boy? I'm trying to think us out of this mess you got us in to!"

Easton shoved his crimson face into the older man's. "All the lights are out in the place, except for one office - right? ...and there it is!"

Mitch's eyes followed the pointing arm. About forty yards away, one skylight was emitting a weak, irregular flashing light. His eyes met the younger man's, and he winked which made Easton feel strangely proud. Olive branches were so not his thing. He puffed up his chest and nodded in the direction of the luminescent skylight as if to direct the hugely experienced Marine. Mitch gave him a wry smile and said, "Lead the way, soldier." They crunched quickly across the gravel to the prism of light on the roof. Bolts and strapping secured the thick, opaque, fibre-glass to the window frame. They peered at the blurred shapes below, hearing nothing. Mitch looked across at Easton. "How do we do this? It's solid." Suddenly bits of fibre glass erupted from the skylight, followed by the unmistakeable sound of a gunshot. They stared at a newly made large hole in the skylight, cracks emanating from it in all directions.

Easton roared in shock, and then grabbed Mitch's hand, startling him. "Come on Major, we're going in!"

Mitch had no time to protest as Easton grabbed his other hand and fell backwards into the skylight. He heard the crash as they went down; tried to throw his arms up to protect his head, but they were in Easton's vice-like grip. He felt a searing pain in his ankles as he came down on the floor of the office, He heard a scream, the sound of furniture being smashed, and then gave in to the red shroud of unconsciousness that smothered him.

CHAPTER 39

We had seen the shadows hovering around the skylight, but were totally unprepared for what ensued, as bodies crashed and grunted amid the shards of fibre glass and accumulated dust that cascaded down on us.

Mitch had landed squarely with both feet on the floor, smashing his ankles and barging Anderson over. Easton had touched down cat-like on the desk in front of me, perfectly positioned for his attack, facing an astonished, seemingly paralysed Kyle. The mesmeric eyes flinched infinitesimally, trying to take in what was happening. Easton reacted first. He lashed out at the immediate threat pointing at us, spiralling the gun out of Kyle's grip and off the far wall. Kyle had been very bold while holding a gun, but the slightest trace of fear showed in his face now. Easton jumped down off the desk in front of Kyle, deliberately, like a predator, never taking his eyes off him.

Kyle threw a straight left. Easton was well capable of dealing with this, tapping the fist past his own left ear with a slap from the back of his left hand, then striking Kyle's elbow with his right hand to turn him side on. I watched spellbound, knowing what was going through Easton's head.

Never fight a whole opponent, get him sideways. When he is sideways you have a choice of targets. The takedown shot is the ear or corner of the jaw, the sport shot is the kidney, the disabling shot is the ribs. Easton went low to the bottom rib with a great deal of force. He put everything into it and his opponent buckled to his left when the blow landed. Kyle was still upright, but coughing blood. My brother had broken the killer's rib and punctured his left lung. The by-now terrified Kyle then swung a wild right at Easton's left ear. My brother blocked it by raising his left hand to his left ear and using his bent elbow as a shield. As he did this he threw a right hand using the heel to hit his opponent square on the sternum, winding him and throwing him back two paces. Kyle was reeling, his bravado and chutzpah gone.

I knew what was coming next and had seen the positioning of Easton's body before when, as a teenager, he was fighting a competition in Germany; he almost killed a boy with a blow to his nose.

"Easton! No!" As I shouted to him I leapt up from the desk to come round and prevent him throwing what would be the 'coup de grace.'

"It's okay, bro, I got this covered. We have an uninvited guest at our party who has been annoying some of the regulars. I just need to make sure he doesn't do that again." Easton spoke robotically as he remained fixed on the by-now helpless Kyle. We needed him alive, I had to stop what was about to go down.

I didn't make it in time. Kyle threw what would be his last- ever punch. Easton stepped slightly left and tapped the right hand of his assailant with his own left, simultaneously launching his right hand up under Kyle's extended right arm. Easton knew exactly what he was doing. The heel of his right hand smashed into the bottom of Kyle's nose, spearing the splintered bone into his brain. His face collapsed like that of some cheap, foam-rubber doll. He staggered back, already dead, his limbs jerking convulsively. A final paroxysm stiffened his flailing arms, and his rigid body crashed to the floor.

Easton stood over him, almost daring him to get up. Then he shrugged, barking, "Not such a big player now are you? You got yours, shithead!" The sheer ferocity and speed of our sibling's attack had left Anderson and I breathless, wordless.

Easton turned, "You guys okay?" His question hung unanswered as we fought to regain our hold on reality. I shakily pressed numb fingers against the fallen man's throat - dead. Jesus!

Emotion exploded within me. I grabbed both my brothers, pressing my head against theirs. Tears flowed as the pent-up angst and sheer tension of the last week or so finally found an outlet. We gripped each other tightly. We were alive.

"C'mon bro, you're crushing my face man!" Easton broke the spell, and we pushed back, spent, exhausted, but laughing. We were alive.

A deep, gravelly voice, indignant, soaked in pain, rasped out of nowhere. "When you three pussies are done pulling each other's peckers, I could use some help here." Mitch had woken up, and was looking anxiously at two swollen, unsymmetrical ankles.

Footsteps pounded along the hall, galvanising us temporarily, but our panic subsided as the bulky shape of Dan De Marco squeezed into the office. "Are you guys okay? I had trouble getting in. They had messed with the lock. Where's Mitch?"

The gruff voice rumbled testily, "I'm down here. I dropped some fucking loose change." Dan looked at his boss' mangled ankles.

"I gotta call an ambulance, don't move Mitch!"

His suffering boss grimaced. "If I could, I'd kick your ass for being such a jerk," then a pained, thin smile, "Thanks Ranger. It could have been a lot worse. I only got these to worry about."

I leaned down to get closer to Mitch. "It's all over Mitch, at least this part. We know what Kyle was doing."

Anderson interrupted me, holding up two data sticks. "Found these in his pocket, bro.Could be important and might match those access codes you found."

Mitch nodded gingerly. "We can take our time now. The Feds, the CIA will be all over this. We'll have some talking to do, boys. It'll be tough."

Easton was leaning on my shoulder, his left arm draped around Anderson. We fist pumped; still elated by the realisation that we were safe. Talking would be easy - a catharsis, after all we had been through. Let them come.

Jeanne fluttered into my head, out of nowhere. She'd be so happy - maybe just as well she didn't know what had gone down here, or maybe I was flattering myself. She had something to do her end to tie things up, and I knew she wouldn't let go until she did.

CHAPTER 40

Professor De Vico was feeling good about himself. His talk on chemo-therapy had gone well. He had sped through over sixty slides in his twenty minute presentation, showing the delegates how people of Asian descent could not absorb initial high levels of treatment for Renal Cell Carcinoma due to a genetic mutation. They had to have reduced doses, which could then be increased slowly over time. He had looked out over the group and had enjoyed passing on his knowledge, and his power. Yes, he had power. With the demise of his friend Professor Favreau, he had become Europe's, if not the world's authority on Renal Oncology. Favreau had been a good man, but a weak one; he could have been part of what De Vico was about to exploit. His thoughts trailed off abruptly. No profit in retrospective pity, he needed to make the most of his position.

He took his plaudits from fawning clinicians who would report back to their Medical Directors that he had been pivotal in convincing everyone that the drug of choice to use was that of Castralten. With that distasteful chore completed, he made his excuses and sneaked out for a quick espresso. He knew this part of Paris well and there was a small cafe round the corner which did reasonable coffee.

Not anything that could match a Gaggia using pure aqua Roma, but it would do. In his haste, he failed to notice the attractive brunette who followed his journey from the other side of the street.

He entered the cafe, which was remarkably quiet, empty in fact. He ordered his double espresso and moved to the side bar so he could add some sugar, perhaps one lump of brown. He remonstrated with himself for taking sugar. It was probably time that he cut it out altogether and looked after himself a little more. Life was good and he was now unchallenged at the top of his field. He should take steps to ensure he stayed healthy to enjoy the fruits of his success. His coffee arrived. He winced slightly, If only the French would make their coffee like the Italians. It was simple; put some sugar in the cup, then add a little coffee and mix them. When you have made a thin paste, add the rest of the espresso and mix it up. That was the proper way to do an espresso coffee. No matter, to Italians, the French were cultural ingenus in any case.

As he was lifting the cup to his lips, he became aware of a presence in the doorway. He masked the tremor of doubt that thrummed through his body.

"Mslle Salas. How lovely to see you." Jeanne took a tentative step inside the cafe. De Vico walked towards her. Even although she now detested this man, she could not stop herself feeling attracted to him. He oozed charm, and his sense of style, his intellect, his professionalism and willingness to listen made him a potent, desirable person. She snapped herself out of her reverie and drew herself back from De Vico.

He stopped. "I assume it is not merely a coincidence that brings you to this cafe when I am here?" Jeanne gave a very slight nod by way of reply. "How long have you known?"

"Since we met you in Rome. Maybe you did not expect to see me again?"

The anxious academic frowned quizzically, his voice laden with false charm. "What do you mean? Why would I not want to see someone with your obvious gifts again?" Jeanne's eyes rolled in contempt at his insincerity. He dropped the pretence. "What alerted you?"

"It was when you suggested that my friend, Bailey Marks was being a little, how did you word it? Righteous..."

"Pious."
"That was it Professor, pious. You turned that situation round on him. He was speaking to a person who's sole purpose should be to keep people alive, yet when he challenged you about the integrity of the Pharma companies and how they may be putting people at risk with their manipulation of clinical trial results, you deflected the point away from saving people when treating them for Renal Cell Carcinoma and talked about the greater good that drug companies were doing. What could be greater than saving lives? I have not worked in this profession as long as you, but everyone I have met would sacrifice themselves before they sold their integrity to drugs companies. It is something that I learned soon after I started working with Professor Favreau. He would tell me to make every decision with the view of preserving life. That belief kept me safe and stopped

me from being overly influenced by any outside factors. He taught me well."

"Medicine is not as binary. No, what is the word? Polarised, as you are making out, mademoiselle. These companies do a lot of good and we would be in a very bad place if they were not around."

"Really, Professor! Do they do so much good that you are willing to let them kill people to prove that they can keep some alive? Is it okay to turn the other cheek when you know they are causing some people so much harm? Is this all about money Professor? Many people have died trying to discover what has been happening here, some innocent, one close to me and a so-called friend of yours. You tricked Dr Favreau into thinking that you wanted to help him expose the testing problems. You lured him out, and you are responsible for his death. Do you think that is an acceptable price to pay so that these companies can prosper?"

"Your emotions are taking over your judgement, Jeanne. You must look at the wider picture here. These companies do a lot more good than harm. There will always be a price for that."

"If this is how they do business when they are under close scrutiny, what would they be like if we all had your view? De Vico blinked rapidly, grappling for a retort.

"I notice you are alone. Where is Signor Marks?"

"He has gone back to America to look for answers there. I am here to pass on what I have to the authorities. It is obvious someone was orchestrating the cover-ups we spoke about, and the killings. I have passed papers to the Police Nationale."

De Vico's face puckered with sudden doubt. "I see Mslle, you already have told the authorities here? Jeanne nodded. The Professor smoothed a hand across his troubled features. "How long do I have?"

"You were not thinking of running away were you?" Jeanne's eyes met his uncompromisingly.

"Oh maybe; although it would be somewhat undignified at this point. I am not yet guilty of anything."

"Suicide perhaps? You seem to have some false sense of nobility in what you do, Professor."

"Mademoiselle Salas, there is too much living to do on this planet to consider suicide."

"Tell that to the families of those who were killed because of all of this. Tell that to Bailey and his brothers, who lost their mother because of people like you and Wengen, and who have to live knowing that those who are supposed to save lives are allowing others to take them for money. You have about one minute and I don't think you will be doing much living where you are going."

De Vico pointed a manicured finger at Jeanne as he spoke, his voice thickening; "You may think that Jeanne, but these pharmaceutical companies have very good lawyers and I am worth a great deal to them."

"Dead or alive, Professor? Has it never occurred to you that the safest place for you now may be in a prison? You are now a threat to your paymasters; worse, an inconvenience. You will be taken for questioning, investigated. It will take time, not good for your sponsors. Your coffee, Professor. You will have time for that."

De Vico gave Jeanne a withering look, blinked hard and then turned his eyes to note two figures in the doorway. The Police Nationale had arrived. He would have a long time to think about whether he should tell his side of the story. He quaffed his coffee in a single gulp, turned to Jeanne and bowed slightly. One of the Policeman gestured to Jeanne, who nodded affirmatively. He started to go through the protocol with De Vico, who quickly stopped him and said briefly, "Let's go. A bientot Mslle."

Jeanne replied immediately. "No Professor, it is adieu; as we say in France." The policemen lead the scowling clinician out of the door. Jeanne pulled out her cell phone and texted a quick message. Her work here was done.

CHAPTER 41

The Hard Rock Cafe in Washington sits at the corner of E Street N.W. and 10th Street N.W, opposite the back of the J. Edgar Hoover Building; the HQ of the FBI. We hung out in these places wherever we went. The food was consistent and fairly priced, and they always reminded us a little of home, but most importantly the music was great. The two guys, Isaac Tigrett and Peter Morton, who set the first Hard Rock Cafe up in London in 1971 had all this nailed when they embarked on the venture that turned into a worldwide phenomenon. We had convinced our server, Wayne, to play some tunes by the British band Razorlight and we sat bobbing our heads in time as they banged out 'Before I Fall to Pieces.' Johnny Borrell's vocals were humming away in my ears and I was relaxed, almost content, more so than I had been for weeks.

We had taken a table near the door just to the right as we came in. We were meeting Mitch, who was due any minute and we wanted to make it easy for him. As it was relatively quiet, we were able to settle and get served quickly. We had ordered some drinks and got ourselves into a feisty fraternal conversation about our favourite Marx Brothers movie. 'Duck Soup' did it for me, but Easton and Anderson preferred a 'Day at the Races.' My all-time favourite scene was when Groucho wise-cracks his way through Rufus T Firefly's introduction. You can tell there was a fair bit of ad-libbing in it as he hopped around the stage. Priceless. Anderson and Easton talked about Harpo in Animal Crackers, laughing heartily as they discussed how, at various steps, he had most of the female cast hold his right leg before depositing an entire canteen of cutlery on the floor whilst being grilled by the Police captain about being a thief. They don't make them like they used to.

From where we sat you could see most of the restaurant, something that prior to our recent adventures we would never have considered but we were different people now and wariness had ingrained itself within our consciousness. Over to our left as we entered there were about ten tables and around half of them were occupied. Everyone seated looked and sounded like Americans. Their nationality was in their speech, their clothes, and their demeanour. Further over to our right beyond the low partition another twenty or so tables sat, which were again about half full with American tourists, some deep in conversations, others deep in publications, some on their own and some kids blasting away on their tablets. For a mid-afternoon in May it was relatively quiet. The clientele looked normal, ordinary. No one in here looked like a threat to us. We had found it hard to drop our guard, but normality was slowly returning to our lives, and nothing was more normal than us having an energetic critique of Marx Brothers' films.

Our conversation was getting more involved in the scenes from the movies when the door to the restaurant burst open. Eerily it stayed open, although we could see no one. Clearly it was being held and the three of us began to rise from our seats, realising that lately events like this tended to end up with us in a whole heap of trouble. Just as we were about to move into action we heard a recognisable sound, the sound of a crutch bashing on the floor. A leg was the first thing to be seen. It was in a cast, then in came a crutch, then another crutch. Judging by the groans and muffled expletives, this person was clearly not happy with their plight and even less happy with how stiff and awkward this door was to manoeuvre. Then that all-too-familiar protuberance of a chin jutted beyond the frame of the door. The change in our demeanour was palpable and we began to ease ourselves back down in our seats. Major Mitch was coming in to meet us.

None of what we had just done was discussed nor had we made any eye contact to prompt it. A fraternal thing, I guess, almost telepathic, sharpened by weeks of tension and ever-present danger. Mitch's face screwed up in frustration as he lugged himself through the door. You could tell that even having broken both ankles, this man was never going to accept a wheelchair to improve his mobility. The surgeon who set his ankles probably had to endure Hell to get Mitch to agree to have his legs repaired. His face was a rictus of barely concealed pain and fury as he pushed his feet in front of him and got his crutches lined up to take his next step on his plastered, unstable legs.

He looked up for the first time to catch our eyes and simultaneously, as one, we each raised a finger to point at Mitch and all burst into laughter.

The retort was vintage Mitch through and through, "Assholes!" His belligerent bark only made us laugh more heartily. "Now one of you dumb asses get up and give me a seat." Easton, who was sitting opposite me on the outside of the table, with his back to the door, got up and came round to sit next to me facing the door. Mitch made his way towards the vacant seat on shaky legs. I rose to give him a hand and instantly realised it was the wrong thing to do. "Don't even fucking think about it, Groucho. I will do just fine on my own."

I waited for him to struggle in to the seat before I sat back down and looked at him. All told, it must have taken him two minutes to walk the ten paces from the door to the seat, during which time the three of us never uttered a word, but we did laugh a lot. Task completed, Mitch drew a long breath, and growled, "Good to see you boys again, and I'm fine. Your concern is touching!" Communal laughing again broke out, and handshakes were exchanged all round.

When all the joviality died down and the food arrived, we began to eat quietly; occasionally commenting on the quality of the dishes, and the enthusiasm of our server. Mitch pecked at his club sandwich, frowning now and again as he shifted his ankles to ease the obvious pain he was in. My mind drifted as I ate, as it often did since that day when we had, well, cheated death, basically. I watched Easton taking huge bites out of his burger, until his mouth was so stuffed he could hardly talk, showering Anderson in sesame seeds and flecks of mayo as he tried to argue him down, prompting Anderson to try and tuck his napkin around his neck. They looked so normal, but none of us would ever be the same again. The endless interviews and questioning we had been subjected to by various government agencies had forced us to confront what we had been involved in: what we had done. People had been hurt, some died. Our lives had been threatened, and my brother had killed to protect us. My irascible, loveable brother had dealt out cold, violent death to save us, but he wasn't a killer, was he? We were still alive, remarkably, and our relationship had moved to a new level, more non- verbal, intuitive, symbiotic. We knew how close we had come to oblivion.

We had uncovered a major fraud and public deception by some high ranking official in a quasi-legit Shadow Ops department. We had travelled all over Europe in our search for the truth, and we had at last some closure on Mum. Her death hadn't been useless, insignificant. We had helped stop the tests that had killed many people. She would have been proud of us, we were sure of that. What about Herb? He had started out siphoning some funds for his pension only to be set up as the fall guy for multiple murders and embezzlement. Kyle had been a psychopath, with the innate conviction held by his type that they would never get caught or held accountable. None of us had any problems justifying his death. Dad? I still had dreams, nightmares about him. Was he dead? Was it time for me to let go?

Mitch cut my reverie short. "Hey, eat! Your food will go cold!" Very parental.

I laughed. I was eating a salad. "Taking anything for your pain, Mitch?" I probed.

He smiled. "Why would I do that? Pain is good. Pain is pure!"

Easton shook his head, guffawing. "You really get off on it, Major. I like that quality in you. Glad to help!"

Mitch's smile broadened, showing his square, white teeth. He had grown to like Easton a lot. "And I'll return the favour someday -you bet!" More laughter.

I had one thing that I needed to get out. Now was the time.

"So guys, the email I got that started this whole thing rolling. Gemini168, have you figured it out yet?"
Easton was first to respond, "Yep, it is easy. Clearly this was a set up by Mitch."

Mitch swivelled his whole body; plastered legs at a forty-five degree angle to face Easton and uttered his response. "Negative Harpo, I had no reason to involve anyone else. I would have dealt with it myself, as I ended up having to do."

Easton fixed him with a stare, feeling somewhat more confident of taking Mitch in his incapacitated state. He would have a little sport while he could get away with it. "Of course we would never have managed anything without Captain, sorry, Major America here!"

"That's right. You would have been dead in a street in Paris or Berlin but for me." Mitch shot back with more than a hint of affection.

"True dat, but you would have been nailed by your buddy Fenwick in Switzerland but for me!"

"You've got me dead bang there Easton, but maybe my fucking legs would still be operating if you hadn't dragged me through a sky-light."

"We will put that down as an occupational hazard, Mitch." said Easton triumphantly.

"Yeah, if you are a stunt man," chimed in Anderson.

"Exactly! Thank you Anderson," said Mitch in a more emphatic way.

"What about you, Anderson?" asked Mitch. "Do you have a theory in all of this?"

Anderson looked at me and said, "I want to go along with Bailey's theory. He's told us often enough, but I don't want to build up my hopes. Our lives have been full of difficult situations and I just want to keep things on a level. That way my emotions are stable and I don't have to spend too much time worrying about something that might be, might not be."

I felt my gorge rise as he spoke, but stuck to my thread. "It's all clear to me guys, and I have figured out that last part of it all. The e-mail which set all of this off had to come from someone who knew I would pursue it and not give up. I had a guardian angel that showed up when I was in harm's way; outside the train station in Rome being a prime example of that, when he took care of the guy sent by De Vico. Surely you don't think that was just coincidence? The other clues that we were given along the way; the data on the memory stick, the number on the painting in Rome, the guy on the train who warned me to get back to Jeanne. These all add up to it being someone that was guiding us; someone who knew us."

Anderson testily shoved French fries around his plate as he answered. "I get you Bailey, but that does not just point towards Dad. It could have been another colleague of his that we don't know of, someone who wanted to take care of us."

"Yes Anderson, it could have been someone like that, but the chances are Mitch would have known who that could have been, or someone in the CIA would have triggered a reaction due to the chain of events. These guys keep across all the news stories and would have been on to us or Mitch when they read about the various killings in New York and Europe. This was someone on the inside who was mopping up that flow of information and was not too worried about anyone in the agency asking questions because he had them covered with answers. This was someone who was trusted in the CIA and who was steering us with the best intention. This was someone with a reputation for thoroughness. This was Dad."

"You believe Bailey. I want to believe," said Anderson.

"And me," said Mitch.

"You haven't got me yet, Groucho," said Easton. I knew he was having a little tickle at me by calling me that name and referring to the way that Groucho could always convince his brothers to believe him, but I also knew that he was serious in that he was not yet sure of my theory.

"Okay then. Try this one. Have you figured out the significance of this Gemini 168 moniker?"

"Not yet," said Easton, but I bet you have another one of those theories of yours that are logical but just beyond believable and you are about to lay it on us."

"Well let's try it with you guys. Star signs. Gemini, when is that?" The group exchanged perplexed looks.

"21st May to 21st of June." chimed Anderson, warming to my challenge. The thespian knew his star signs alright.

"Correct, and what about the 168 guys?" As I asked this question I looked into their eyes to see if any of them had twigged.

Mitch was fishing around for something significant and his eyes were darting between me and Easton to my left. Easton was looking at Anderson and giving him that questioning look of 'Where is Bailey going with this?' Anderson had a flicker in his eyes and then blurted out a statement that would change all of their thinking.

"Is this about the number of days in the year?

"Go on," I said.

"Is it the 168th day of the year?"

"Which is?" I said looking deeper into Anderson's eyes to encourage him.

"C'mon Bailey, you're talking in tongues here! Give me a minute while I get my abacus out." But he was almost there and he could sense it in my eyes. "June 15th. No, 17th. June 17th. The day after Mum died."

"Good man, Anderson. You have almost got it. Mum died on June 16th, but she died in a leap year. In a leap year the 168th day of the year is June 16th. Whoever sent this message knew that and was trying to point us in that direction. Get it guys? This was for us, and us alone. That is why I think it came from Dad. It is too much of a coincidence."

The company had fallen silent. It was Mitch that spoke first.

"That makes sense Bailey, but how come you never recognised him on the occasions that you saw this 'guardian angel' and why would he involve you guys when he could have got me, my company, my connections onto this?"

"I just have a feeling that all of this was inevitable. He could have disguised his appearance. The guy in Rome was Dad's size and build. Although he looked different, the way he moved and looked at me were too familiar. The guys in Paris and on the train had the same eyes -Dad's eyes, He might not have trusted the agencies he had relied on before, after all, you thought for a time someone in your place was involved. So Anderson, Easton, think about all the travelling across the world, finding different, less well known ways into countries and continents, the archery and shooting lessons, the martial arts classes, the ski trips. He was preparing us for something like this. We didn't have a normal kid's life, did we? And maybe this isn't the end of it all.

"Fuck off Bailey! I have just about had my head blown off in Geneva and the bruises from Berlin and Washington haven't even cleared up and you're telling me there is more to come?" Easton was funny when he got going.

"Get in line buddy," said Mitch. "I'll see your bruises and raise you two broken ankles." We all laughed, but I pressed on.

"Can you see my point guys?" I had laid it all out. If they didn't buy it now, I had no idea what to do.

Anderson was first on side. "I get it in spoons, Bailey. Those cold nights with the archery gear, the martial arts, the ski lessons, when we just wanted to hang with our buddies at a mall; and I remember those long conversations on trains about how to travel Europe, and just about anywhere without ever having to show identification or showing up on any systems that could track your credit card and whereabouts. At the time, I hated it more than you could know."

Easton chirped in. "Me too. With you there, bro."

Anderson acknowledged that with a flick of his hand. "But it kinda makes sense to me now that you have laid it out."

"It's good Bailey, "added Mitch." But you can't talk somebody back to life. Other agents were on his plane. Where might they be? I can't believe that your Dad wouldn't have come to you by now if he was alive."

Anderson, almost wearily, spoke again. "I want to believe you Bailey, but the Gemini thing could just be a coincidence. I understand all the other stuff you are saying, but are they not just down to the fact that Dad was an active person and wanted us to have active lives? And he wanted to keep us together, busy, without too much time to miss Mom."

Easton spoke again, quietly, with real conviction. "Yeah, I never got the time to miss her; none of us did." Wrappings were being torn from old family wounds, deep and painful reminders of a lonely, almost Spartan childhood. I couldn't let it go, and knew that my brothers hated talking about that time, and hearing me drag things out into the daylight again and again.

As we got into this further, the waitress appeared asking if she could take away our empty plates and if we wanted anything else. The guys all looked at me and I knew this meant it was time to think about moving on. "No, we are all good to go, thanks." As I was talking to the waitress a guy nudged past her on his way out, lightly brushing my shoulder and squeezing past the waitress around her back. There was plenty of room so it was an unusual manoeuvre. I could just see him from behind, his long tweed coat and dark baseball cap, about my height. He was gone out the door quickly and I reflected on how long it had taken Mitch to get in that same door.

"Can we have the cheque please?" I asked the waitress.

"No need. It's paid for already." I looked at her questioningly and then at the guys around me, drawing a blank from each of them, and in Easton's case an over exaggerated shrug.

"Who by?" I asked.

"This guy," she said, showing me the receipt. My eyes must have been on stalks, for as I looked at the slip of paper, I could see out the corner of my eye both Easton and Bailey rising out of their seats. Even Mitch made an effort. There, written on the bottom of the cheque, was the moniker Gemini168.

"Where is this guy?" I asked her. My heart was racing. This was it. He was here! I was about to see Dad again. We all were, now they'd believe me!

"He just left. That was him who squeezed past me a second ago."

The sound of chairs being thrust back and falling on the tiles was way too loud for this place, and anxious heads turned anticipating trouble. Easton was climbing over me to get to the door and Anderson had pushed Mitch, still sitting in his chair, aside to make it outside. We stood on the street squinting around us in the sun, panting. There, on the opposite side of the street, about 30 yards to our left in front of the J Edgar Hoover Building, was the guy in the long coat and dark hat. I made to run across the street but it was busy with a two way flow of heavy traffic. A tourist bus was pulling up on the other side in front of The Overcoat Guy. The three of us were all shouting instructions to each other on what direction to take to get over, but the speed and volume of traffic made any crossing impossible. The bus pulled in front of him. I looked through the windows to see him. It was dark in the shady interior of the bus and I could not make anything out clearly.

We found a gap in the traffic and split up to stop the bus, which was now pulling away from the kerb. I got in front waving my arms and trying to look round the side to see if he was still on the sidewalk. Easton had gone round the back. Anderson had run past me and was now banging on the door to be let on board. The driver had no choice but to open up and let us on. I did the talking while the other two searched, first the downstairs and then the upstairs. The middle aged, grey haired driver had a look of bewilderment on his face. "Sorry buddy, this won't take long, but the guy on the street you just stopped for, did he go upstairs?"

"Nope! What in Sam Hill is this all about? Some guy in a winter coat in the middle of spring stops a bus and then don't get on it? Then you guys come charging over the street and make me open up for you? Who are you guys and what is with the funny accents?"

"Wait! Did you just say he did not board the bus? Is that what you just said?" My heart was pounding in my chest and my palms were wet. Easton and Bailey had come down the stairs and were shaking their heads at me.

"That's what I just said. He walked away around that corner. Didn't even try to get on my bus, after me pulling up for him. He never even thanked me and nary a look back: some kinda nut!"

I could feel the tears welling up in my eyes. I muttered hopelessly to myself. "Jesus Christ, why are you doing this to us Dad? Where are you?" I glanced at Easton and Anderson, looking for all the world as if they had just been forced to witness me taking a beating. We stood, motionless on the bus in the middle of Washington and for the second time in a few weeks I felt the darkness come down.

EPILOGUE

Castralten Pharmaceuticals: Geneva
Two executives identically suited, in a bland magnolia-painted office are sitting on opposite sides of a non-descript desk.

"So DeVico has been arrested?"

"Yes. We have Hans Gestler from Legal sourcing a very good lawyer for him as we speak."

"Hmmm, that is good, but Europe has become a little too hot for us at the moment. It may lead to difficult questions if we cannot ensure that DeVico remains true to his word and says nothing."

"You're right. Let's concentrate on Russia for a while. Europe will settle soon and we can re-group when that time comes. If DeVico tells them anything we can have him ...silenced."

"Silenced? We no longer have our contractor."

"Whatever is the best option at the time, and I am sure there are other willing contractors who would help us. We will see."

THE END

Printed in the United States
By Bookmasters